The bronze giant, who with his five aides became world famous, whose name was as well known in the far regions of China and the jungles of Africa as in the skyscrapers of New York.

There were stories of Doc Savage's almost incredible strength; of his amazing scientific discoveries of strange weapons and dangerous exploits.

Doc had dedicated his life to aiding those faced by dangers with which they could not cope.

His name brought fear to those who sought to prey upon the unsuspecting. His name was praised by thousands he had saved.

DOC SAVAGE'S AMAZING CREW

"Ham," Brigadier General Theodore Marley Brooks, was never without his ominous, black sword cane.

"Monk," Lieutenant Colonel Andrew Blodgett Mayfair, just over five feet tall, yet over 260 pounds. His brutish exterior concealed the mind of a great scientist.

"Renny," Colonel John Renwick, his favorite sport was pounding his massive fists through heavy, paneled doors.

"Long Tom," Major Thomas J. Roberts, was the physical weakling of the crowd, but a genius at electricity.

"Johnny," William Harper Littlejohn, the scientist and greatest living expert on geology and archaeology.

**WITH THEIR LEADER, THEY WOULD
GO ANYWHERE, FIGHT ANYONE,
DARE EVERYTHING—SEEKING
EXCITEMENT AND PERILOUS
ADVENTURE!**

Bantam Books by Kenneth Robeson
Ask your bookseller for the books you have missed

Coming in June 1984 a double volume of
Laugh of Death and *King of Terror*

Two Complete Adventures in One Volume

THE GOLDEN MAN
and
PERIL IN THE NORTH

Kenneth Robeson

BANTAM BOOKS
TORONTO · NEW YORK · LONDON · SYDNEY

THE GOLDEN MAN
PERIL IN THE NORTH

*A Bantam Book / published by arrangement with
The Condé Nast Publications Inc.*

PRINTING HISTORY

The Golden Man *was originally published in* Doc Savage *magazine
March 1941. Copyright 1941 by Street & Smith Publications Inc.
Copyright © renewed 1968 by The Condé Nast Publications Inc.*

Peril in the North *was originally published in* Doc Savage *magazine
November 1941. Copyright 1941 by Street & Smith Publications Inc.
Copyright © renewed 1968 by The Condé Nast Publications Inc.*

Bantam edition / February 1984

ISBN 0-553-23851-5

Published simultaneously in the United States and Canada

PRINTED IN THE UNITED STATES OF AMERICA

O   0 9 8 7 6 5 4 3 2 1

Contents

THE GOLDEN MAN

Contents

Chapter 1
THE SUPERNATURAL

It began on the American passenger steamer, *Virginia Dare*, while the vessel was en route from Portugal to New York with a load of war refugees. It was at night.

Mr. Sam Gallehue, in spite of the full-bodied Irish of his name, his West Tulsa, Oklahoma, birthplace, his American passport, was really quite English. Quite.

Referring to the incidents of that night, "Disturbing," Sam Gallehue said. "Disturbing— Yes, definitely."

But *disturbing* was hardly a strong enough word.

Lieutenant Colonel Andrew Blodgett Monk Mayfair had a word—several words, in fact. But his words were not from Sunday school, or from any respectable dictionary, although expressive. Unfortunately, they were not printable.

Brigadier General Theodore Marley Ham Brooks had no word whatever—the thing left him speechless. Ham Brooks was a noted lawyer who could talk a jury out of its eyeteeth, and it took a lot to make him speechless. But, as everyone admitted, what happened that night was a lot.

First, there was the star.

It was a clear night and the usual number of ordinary stars were visible—the Encyclopedia Britannica states the unaided human eye can see about six thousand stars on a clear night—in the crystal dome of a tropical heavens. The sea, with no more waves than a mirror, was darkly royal-blue, except where now and then a porpoise or a shark broke surface and caused a momentary eruption of phosphorescence that was like spilling sparks.

As to who first saw the star, there was some question whether that honor fell to Ham Brooks or Monk Mayfair.

Both these men were standing on the starboard boat deck, where there was a nice breeze. It was a hot night; it had been hot since the *Virginia Dare* had left Portugal, and Monk and Ham— so had everyone else, too—had grumbled extensively about the heat, although there were scores of Americans on the ship who should have been overjoyed to be there instead of in Europe, dodging bombs, bullets and blitzkriegs.

1

The truth was: Monk and Ham were irked because they were leaving Europe by request. Not at the request of anybody in Europe; they would have ignored such urging. The request had come from Doc Savage, who was their chief, and who meant what he said.

The mess in Europe had looked enticing—Monk and Ham liked excitement the way bears like honey—and they had slipped off with the idea of getting their feet wet. Doc Savage had cabled them to come back—quick—before they got in trouble.

"Trouble!" Monk snorted. "Compared to the kind of things Doc gets mixed up in, Europe is peaceful. Hey, look!"

"Look at what?" Ham asked.

"Over there." Monk pointed out over the sea.

They could see the star plainly. It was not a star in the sense of being a planet or a heavenly body twinkling far off in outer space. This was an actual star; a five-cornered one.

The star was black. In the dark night—this fact was a little confusing to newspaper reporters later—the star could be readily distinguished in spite of its blackness. This black star could be seen in the black sky because, around its edges, and particularly at its five tips, it had a definitely reddish, luminous complexion. As Monk expressed it later—Monk's descriptions were inclined to be grisly—the star looked somewhat as if it had been dipped in red blood. The star was high and far away in the night sky.

"Hey, you on the bridge!" Monk yelled. "Hey, whoever's on watch!"

Monk's speaking voice was the small, ludicrous tone of a child, but when he turned loose a yell, the seagulls got scared a mile away. An officer put his head over the bridge railing.

"What the blankety-blank goes on?" the officer asked. "Don't you know people are trying to sleep on this boat? You'll wake up the whole ship."

"Look at that star!" Monk said. "What the dickens is it?"

The officer stared, finally said he would be damned if that wasn't a funny-looking thing, and pointed a pair of strong night glasses—the night glasses being binoculars with an extraordinary amount of luminosity—at the star. He handed the glasses to Monk, then Ham. The consensus was that they didn't know what the thing might be. Something strange, though.

The steamer, *Virginia Dare,* was commanded by Captain Harley Kirman, a seaman of the modern school, with looks, dress and manners of a man behind a desk in an insurance office, although he loved his ship, as much as any cussing, barnacle-coated bully of the old windjammer school.

Captain Kirman was summoned from a game of contract bridge. Another participant in the card game, a Mr. Sam Gallehue, accompanied the skipper when he reached the bridge.

The captain stared at the star. He unlimbered a telescope as large as a cannon—inherited from his seafaring grandfather, he explained—and peered through that. He took off his hat and scratched his bald spot. The bald spot was crossed from right front to left rear by a scar, that was a souvenir of a World War mine. Captain Kirman's bald-spot scar always itched when he got excited.

"Change course to west, quarter south," Captain Kirman ordered. "We'll have a look."

Monk propped elbows on the bridge rail and contemplated the five-pointed thing in the sky.

"What do you suppose it is?"

Ham shrugged. "Search me. Never saw anything like it before."

Monk Mayfair was a short man, and wide. His long arms—his hands dangled to his knees—were covered with a growth of what appeared to be rusty shingle nails. His mouth had startling size, the corners terminating against his tufted ears; his eyes were small and twinkling, and his nose was a mistreated ruin. The narrowness of his forehead conveyed the impression there was not room for a spoonful of brains, which was deceptive, since he was one of the world's leading industrial chemists. In general, his appearance was something to scare babies.

Ham Brooks has good shoulders, medium height, a wide, orator's mouth in a not unhandsome face. His clothing was sartorial perfection; in addition to being one of New York's best lawyers, he was its best-dressed man. He carried an innocent-looking dark cane which was a sword-cane, tipped with a chemical that could produce quick unconsciousness.

They watched the star.

"Blazes!" Monk said suddenly. "Look at the ocean. Right under that thing!"

Mr. Sam Gallehue hurried over to stand beside them. Gallehue was a lean man with some slight roundness in his shoulders that was either a habitual stoop or a sign of unusual muscular strength. His face was long, his jaw prominent, a combination which expressed sadness.

Mr. Sam Gallehue wore his usual ingratiating smile. He was a man who invariably agreed with anything and everything anyone said. If anyone should state the ship was sailing upside down, Mr. Gallehue would agree profusely in a phony English accent.

"That's puzzling," Monk said.

"Yes, puzzling, definitely," agreed Mr. Gallehue. "Very puzzling. You're right. Very puzzling."

They meant the sea. It had become—the phenomenon was confined to one spot directly beneath the luminous-rimmed black star—filled with a fiery brilliance that was astounding, because it could hardly be the natural phosphorescence of the sea. Phosphorescence like a multitude of sparks pouring through the water in momentary existence, was visible here and there, but this was different. It was not like sparks, but a steady luminance, quite bright.

"It covers," Ham decided aloud, "less than an acre."

"Yes, you're right," agreed Mr. Sam Gallehue. "Less than an acre. Exactly."

The steamer plowed through the dark sea, with the only sounds the faint steady rushing of water cut by the bows, and tendrils of music amidships that escaped from the first-class lounge where there was dancing. But on the bridge there was breathless quiet, expectancy, and eyes strained ahead. The luminous area was still on the sea, the black star steady in the sky.

The lookout in the crow's-nest gave a cry.

"Man swimming!" the lookout yelled. "Off the starboard bow. Middle of that glowing patch of water. Man swimming!"

Captain Kirman leveled his granddad of telescope and stared for a while. The he scratched his bald-spot scar.

"What's wrong?" Monk asked.

Wordlessly, Captain Kirman passed the big telescope. Monk discovered that the instrument was one of the most efficient he had ever used.

The crow's-nest lookout had been wrong on one point—the man in the sea was not swimming. The man lay perfectly still. On his back, with arms and legs outflung. He was a large, golden man. There was something unusual about him, a quality distinguishable even from that distance—something about him that was hard to define, yet definite. He was not unconscious, but merely floating there.

Monk lowered the telescope.

"Well?" demanded Ham impatiently.

"It's kind of indecent," Monk explained. "He ain't got on a darned stitch!"

The *Virginia Dare* lowered a lifeboat with speed which demonstrated the efficiency of modern davit machinery. Captain Kirman dashed into his cabin and came back with a blanket and a pair of trousers. "Put the pants on him before you bring him in," he said.

The modern steel lifeboat had a motor which, gobbling like a turkey, drove the craft across the sea into the luminous area, and, guided by searchlights that stuck straight white whiskers from the liner bridge, reached the floating golden man.

The bright area in the sea slowly gathered itself around the lifeboat. A phenomenon so startling that Monk and Ham stared at each other, blinked, then peered at the sea again. "D' you see what I do?" Monk demanded.

"The phosphorescence is gathering around the lifeboat," Ham said.

"Yeah. Only I don't think it's phosphorescence. The stuff glows too steadily, and the color ain't like phosphorescence."

They stared, dumfounded as the glowing patch in the sea followed the lifeboat to the steamer. When some fifty or sixty yards separated the lifeboat and ship, the luminous area rapidly left the smaller craft and surrounded the liner. The *Virginia Dare* was much larger, and the glowing mass spread out thinly to entirely surround the vessel.

Monk grunted suddenly. "Where's a bucket, a rope, and a jug?"

Ham said, "I know where there's a jug. I'll get it. You find the rope and the bucket."

The dapper lawyer secured from the bar a clear glass jug which had contained foundation sirup for a soft drink. He rinsed it hurriedly.

They hauled up a bucket of sea water, poured it into the jug, and inserted a cork.

"I swear I never saw water shine like that before," Monk declared. "I'm gonna analyze it."

Ham held the jug up to the light. He shook it briskly, and the water charged back and forth against the glass with bubbled-filled fury.

"Kinda spooky," Ham said in an awed voice.

Monk carried the jug to a darkened part of the deck, and held a hand close to it. His palm was bathed in reflected magenta radiance.

"What *is* that stuff?" Ham asked.

"I'll have to analyze it," Monk said. He sounded puzzled.

Ham rubbed his jaw, his expression thoughtful. "You ever hear of ectoplasm?" he asked.

"Eh?"

"Ectoplasm," Ham said. "The stuff spiritualists and mediums talk about. When they perform, or pretend to perform, the feat known as telekinisis, or locomotion of objects at a distance—such as making a table lift, or causing rappings on a table—they claim the phenomenon is the work of ectoplasm."

"Hey, wait a minute," Monk said. "What're you talking about?"

"Ectoplasm. E-c-t-o-p-l-a-s-m, like in a ghost. It is supposed to be a material of living or protoplasmic nature, drawn either from the medium or from some other presence, which is independently manipulated after being drawn."

Monk considered this.

"Nuts!" he said finally.

Ham shrugged. "Ectoplasmic material is supposed to be manipulated or controlled through an etheric connecting link, so that a tremor or vibration in the ether, such as a light wave which normally excites the retina of the eye, is detrimental to its activity."

"Where the hell'd you get that stuff?"

"Out of an encyclopedia one time."

Monk snorted. "Oh, be reasonable. This stuff is just something in the water that happens to glow."

"Then what made it follow the lifeboat?"

"I don't know."

"The golden man was in the lifeboat. It followed *him*."

"Huh?"

"And, when the golden man was taken aboard the steamer, why did it surround the bigger ship?"

Monk peered at the jug of luminous water with a mixture of emotion. "I got half a notion to throw this overboard and get rid of the whole mystery."

Ham strode out on the open deck and looked upward, craning his neck.

"That black star is gone," he announced.

Chapter 2
THINGS TO WONDER ABOUT

The rescued golden man had been taken to the ship's hospital. Monk and Ham accompanied Captain Kirman to the hospital, and the agreeable Mr. Sam Gallehue brought up the rear, being stickily polite whenever they gave him a chance.

Monk carried the jug of luminous water under his arm until he passed his cabin, where he paused to deposit the jug on the table. After he had left the jug, Monk hurried forward and touched Ham's elbow.

"Hey, what got you started on that talk about ectoplasm?" he wanted to know.

"It just occurred to me," Ham said.

"But that's spook stuff."

"Sure."

"There ain't no such animals as spooks."

"You'll find a lot of people," Ham said, "that will argue there is such a thing as spiritualism."

"Yeah," Monk agreed. "And you'll find in the United States about five hundred institutions for treating insane people."

The hospital was situated in the midships section of the liner, on B deck. They found the officer who had been in charge of the lifeboat standing outside the hospital door, which was closed.

Captain Kirman asked the officer, "Was he conscious when you picked him up?"

"Yes, indeed, sir."

"Was he injured in any way?"

"He did not appear to be."

"Who is he?"

The officer looked somewhat queer. "He said that he did not have a name."

Captain Kirman frowned. "That's a strange thing for him to say."

"I know, sir. And that wasn't the strangest thing he said, either. He said his name might be a problem, because parents usually named their children, but, since the sea was his mother and the night was his father, and neither parent could talk, getting him named might be a problem."

Captain Kirman scowled. "Are you drunk, mister?"

The officer smiled. "It did not make sense to me, either."

Captain Kirman rubbed his scar, chewed his lower lip in exasperation, and finally knocked on the hospital door, which was opened by a genial gentleman—he was looking bewildered just now—who was the ship's doctor.

"How is he, John?" Captain Kirman asked.

The doctor looked at Captain Kirman steadily for almost a minute. "What *is* this?" he asked finally. "A rib?"

"Eh?" Captain Kirman was surprised.

"This man your sailor just hauled out of the ocean." The doctor jerked a thumb over his shoulder at the hospital door.

"What about him?" Captain Kirman asked.

"He looked me in the eye," the doctor growled, "and he said, 'How are you, John Parson? I believe you will enjoy living in that little villa in Maderia. It is very peaceful there.'"

"Oh," said Captain Kirman. "An old friend of yours, is he?"

The surgeon swallowed.

"No."

Captain Kirman peered sharply at the doctor. "Hey, wait a minute! *You don't know him?*"

"Never saw him before in my life. So help me!"

"But you just said he called you by name."

"That's exactly what I did just say."

"But—"

"And that isn't the half of it," added the doctor. "You heard me say he mentioned that villa in Maderia."

"What about the villa?"

"Nobody on this green earth but myself and the man who owns the villa knows I have been dickering to buy it. And here is something else! *I don't know myself whether I have bought it yet.* The man had to talk to his daughter about selling, and she was going to visit him last week, and he was going to cable me in New York, and the cable would cinch the deal."

Captain Kirman's laugh was a humorless spurt of breath past his teeth. "And you never saw this man we rescued before?"

"Never."

"Somebody around here must be crazy."

Monk Mayfair had been taking in the conversation so earnestly that he had his head cocked to one side. Now he interrupted. "Dr. Parsons," he said. "I'm Mr. Mayfair—Monk Mayfair."

"Yes. I've heard of you." Dr. Parsons smiled. "But I'll confess

I've heard more about the man with whom you are associated—Clark Savage, Jr. Or Doc Savage, as he's better known. I've always hoped I would some day meet him. I've seen him demonstrate surgery.''

Monk said, "Let's try something, just for fun, doctor."

"What do you mean?" Dr. Parsons asked.

"Just for fun," Monk said, "let's send a radiogram to that man you were going to buy the villa from. Ask him if he really sold it to you."

The ship's physician gave Monk a queer look. "So you've sensed it, too."

"Sensed what?"

"That this man we rescued tonight may not be—well, may be different from other men, somehow."

Monk said, "I haven't even seen the guy, except through a telescope. What do you mean—different?"

The physician examined his fingernails for a moment.

"You know, I think I'll take you up. I'll send that radiogram about the villa," he said.

Captain Kirman snorted, shoved open the hospital door, and entered. Monk was about to follow the skipper when Ham tapped the homely chemist on the shoulder. Monk turned. Ham said, "Aren't you the guy who was sneering at spiritualism a while ago? Now you want radiograms sent."

"I just want to satisfy my curiosity," Monk explained sheepishly.

"You saw the golden man through the telescope," Ham said. "Have you ever seen him before?"

"I'm sure I haven't," Monk declared.

"What if he knows all about *us,* too?"

"Don't be silly," Monk said, somewhat uneasily.

They entered the hospital, a white room with square windows, modern fluorescent lighting, and neat equipment which included a nurse who was eye-filling.

The golden man lay on the white sheets on a chrome-and-white examination table. He was not as large as Monk had somehow expected him to be—he was very little above average size, in fact. His shoulders were good, but not enormous; the rest of his muscular development, while above average, was not spectacular. His body did give the impression of perfect health and magnetic energy.

Monk decided—he checked on this afterward with Ham, Mr.

Sam Gallehue, Captain Kirman and others, and they agreed with him—that the golden man's face was the most outstanding of his features. It was hard to explain why it should be outstanding. The face was not a spectacularly ugly one, nor a breathlessly handsome one; it was just a face, but there was kindliness about it, and strength, and power, in addition to something that could hardly be defined.

The golden man spoke in a voice which was the most completely pleasant sound Monk had ever heard.

"Good evening, Captain Kirman," he said.

Astonishment jerked Captain Kirman rigid. The golden man seemed not to notice. He turned to Monk and Ham.

"Good evening, Mr. Mayfair and Mr. Brooks," he said. He contemplated them and seemed to radiate approval. "It is too bad the human race does not produce more men like you two and like the man with whom you work, Doc Savage."

Monk became speechless. Ham, fighting down astonishment, asked, "Who are you?"

For a moment, the golden man seemed slightly disturbed; then he smiled. "I have no name, as yet."

"Where'd you come from? How did you get in the water?"

The golden man hesitated, and said finally, "The sea was my mother and the night was my father, but you will not believe that, so perhaps we should not discuss it."

Ham—he confessed later that his hair was nearer to standing on end than it had ever been—persisted. "There was a black star in the sky," he said, "and there is something that glows, a kind of radiance, that is following the ship. What are those things?"

The golden man sighed peacefully. "Do not be afraid of them," he said. "They will go away, now that I am safe, and you will not see them again."

He leaned back, closed his eyes, and, although Ham asked him more questions—Monk also tried his hand at inquiring—they got no results. The golden man simply lying, conscious and composed, seeming to care nothing about them or their questions. The nurse finally shooed them out of the hospital, saying, "After all, no telling how long he had been swimming in the sea before we found him."

In the corridor, Ham asked, "What do you think, Monk?"

Monk became indignant. "How the hell do I know what to think?" he growled.

The sea next morning was calm, so Monk and Ham breakfasted on the private sun deck—they had one of the high-priced suites, with a private inclosed sun deck adjoining—under a sky that was the deep, cloudless, blue color of steel. They could look out over a sea of navy corduroy to the horizon. Smoke from the funnels trailed back like a black tail astern, and there was a lean, mile-long wedge of wake.

Ham had orange juice, toast, delicate marmalade, a kipper. Monk had a steak, eggs, hot biscuits, four kinds of jam. The breakfast steward was pouring coffee when Dr. John Parsons, the ship physician, arrived.

Dr. Parsons grinned wryly. "Remember that radiogram we talked about last night?"

Monk nodded.

"Well, I sent it," the physician said. "And I got an answer a few minutes ago."

"What did the answer say?" Monk asked seriously.

"I had bought the villa."

Monk peered at his coffee cup as if it was a strange animal. "Now—how do you figure this man we found in the ocean knew that?"

The physician jerked at his coat lapels impatiently. "I wish *you* would figure that out," he said.

After Dr. Parsons had gone, Monk and Ham drank coffee in silence. There seemed to be no words. This verbal drought persisted while they fed their pets. The pets were a pig and a chimpanzee. The pig, named Habeas Corpus, was Monk's pet; the chimp, Chemistry, belonged to Ham. Both animals were freaks of their respective species, Habeas Corpus being mostly snout, ears, legs and an inquiring disposition. Chemistry did not look like chimp, ape, baboon, orang, or monkey—he was an anthropological freak. Chemistry did look remarkably like Monk, which was one of the reasons why Monk did not care for the animal.

Ham broke the silence. "How long did you hang your head out of the porthole after I went to bed last night?"

"Last night—you mean when I was looking at that glowing stuff in the water?" Monk asked.

"Yes. How long did the glow stay in the water around the ship?"

"Until about an hour before dawn," Monk confessed.

"It followed the ship all the time up until then?" Ham demanded.

"Yes."

"How did it disappear?"

"It just faded away."

"How fast was the ship going all that time?"

"Over twenty knots. Practically top speed."

"How do you explain that?"

"The top speed, you mean?"

"No, the luminous stuff following the ship."

Monk grimaced, and did not answer. He never liked things he could not understand.

It was ten-o'clock-beef-tea time that morning—the *Virginia Dare* was a Yankee ship, but Captain Kirman liked the English custom of serving beef tea at ten in the morning, and tea and crumpets about four in the afternoon, so he had instituted the practice on his vessel—when the golden man appeared.

The golden man joined Monk, Ham and Captain Kirman, who were on the promenade deck, sprawled in deck chairs, balancing napkins and cups.

The golden man approached them with a firm, purposeful stride. Monk noted that, although the suit the man wore was a spare from somebody's supply and did not fit him, yet the fellow had a kind of majestic dignity. Monk noted also that Mr. Sam Gallehue was trailing along behind the golden man, but that was not unusual. Mr. Sam Gallehue almost invariably trailed along behind people.

None of them ever forgot what the golden man said. It was a verbal bombshell.

"This ship is going to be destroyed at about eleven o'clock this morning," he said.

Then he turned and walked away, leaving his listeners to stare at each other. Monk started to get out of his chair and follow the man. But Captain Kirman dropped a hand on his arm and halted him.

"The poor devil is crazy," Captain Kirman said.

Monk, although he nodded his head, was not so sure.

Chapter 3
THE WEIRD

The ship did not sink at eleven.

It sank at seven minutes past eleven.

The explosion took about half the bottom out of Hold 2, ripped a little less of the bottom out of Hold 3, and tore approximately eleven by twenty-eight feet of steel plates off the side of the ship above the waterline. There was no panic. Alarm bells rang throughout the vessel for a moment, then became silent. Thereafter, they rang at intervals of two minutes, short warnings. There was very little excited dashing about. Unruffled officers appeared at strategic points and began steering passengers to their boat stations.

Ham Brooks was knocked down by the explosion. He was not hurt, and he was slightly indignant when Monk solicitously helped him to his feet. He had lost his sword-cane, however, and he spent some time hunting it. After he found the cane, he and Monk went to the bridge to offer their services, but it developed that these were not needed.

Captain Kirman and his crew were almost monotonously efficient in abandoning the ship. It was necessary to abandon the ship, of course. The *Virginia Dare* was sinking, and fast.

"What was it?" Monk asked. "A boiler let go?"

"Torpedo," Captain Kirman replied cryptically.

"What?" Monk ejaculated.

Ham put in, "But we're not yet at war!"

Captain Kirman shrugged. "I saw the torpedo wake. So did my officers. It was a torpedo, all right."

"But anybody could see this is an American vessel."

The liner, as was the custom for the last year or two, had huge American flags emblazoned, two on each side of the hull, and large stationary flags painted on the deck, fore and aft.

Monk said, "I can't think a sub would be crazy enough to torpedo an American ship."

Captain Kirman shrugged. "We got torpedoed, anyhow."

An officer walked up, saluted with smartness. "Submarine has appeared off the port quarter," he reported.

They crowded to the rail and strained their eyes, then used binoculars. The submarine was there, plain for anyone to see. There was no doubt about her identity. Numerals and letters were painted on the conning tower, and the design of the craft was itself distinctive enough to answer all questions of nationality.

The sub belonged to a country presumably friendly with America.

"I'll be damned!" said Captain Kirman fiercely. "This is going to cause plenty of complications."

The sub apparently satisfied itself that a mortal blow had been struck, then submerged and did not appear again. It had not offered help.

The *Virginia Dare* sank.

Captain Kirman was, in the tradition of the sea, the last man to leave his vessel. In the lifeboat with him were Monk, Ham, Sam Gallehue, and the strange golden man who had predicted this disaster. Captain Kirman cried a little when the blue-green sea swallowed his ship.

Monk and Ham—they had brought their pets—were not excited. Excitement was their business, in a manner of speaking. For a number of years they had been associated with Doc Savage in his strange career, and it was an existence that had accustomed them to trouble.

They were, however, puzzled. Puzzled by the golden man, who had such a strange personality. Circumstances under which the fellow had been found—the black star, the strange luminosity in the sea—had been startling, even weird. The fact that he had calmly predicted disaster to the ship, and the disaster had materialized, was something to wonder about. Monk stole a glance at the fellow.

The golden man lay relaxed on a thwart of the boat, his manner so completely calm that his presence seemed to have a soothing effect on those around him.

Monk moved back to the strange man.

"Mind answering a question?" Monk asked him.

The golden man smiled placidly and nodded.

"How did you know our ship was going to get torpedoed?" Monk asked bluntly.

The golden man's smile went away for a moment, then came back. "I suppose I was looking at my mother, and the knowledge came to me," he said. "I guess one would say that my mother told me."

"Your mother?"

"The sea."

This was too much for Monk; he gave it up. He went back, sat down beside Ham. "He's a goof," Monk whispered. "He says the sea told him the ship was going to be torpedoed!"

Ham absently scratched the back of his chimp, Chemistry. "I wish I had something to tell *me* such things," he said. "For instance, I could use some nice advance information about what the stock market is going to do."

Monk growled, "Listen, you overdressed shyster—you don't believe that guy can *really* foretell the future."

Ham shrugged. "If he didn't, what *did* he do?" he demanded.

Monk gave up, and lay back, eyelids half-closed against the noonday sun. He spent a long time furtively examining the golden man. There *was* something a little inhuman about the man's appearance, Monk decided.

The breeze dropped. By two o'clock, the sea was glassy, the heat was irritating. Future prospects were none too good, for the nearest land was some hundreds of miles away, and the lifeboats were hardly capable of making such a distance. To further darken the situation, the radio operator was not sure that his S O S signal had been received by anyone. The torpedo had damaged the current supply to such an extent that the radio had been able to put out only a weak signal.

Captain Kirman, his face showing a little of the strain, got out his navigational instruments, current tables, and charts, and began calculating.

The golden man looked at him. Then spoke quietly. He said, "You are preparing to plot a course to the nearest main land. It would be better not to do so. We should remain here."

"Remain here?" Captain Kirman lifted his head to stare at him.

"At six o'clock this evening," the golden man said, "a steamer will arrive at this spot. It will be the Brazilian freighter *Palomino*."

Captain Kirman bacame pale. He sat very still. Finally he put away his charts and instruments. "Pass word to the other boats to remain here, in a close cluster," he ordered.

The steamer *Palomino*—she gave the first impression of being mostly rust, but she floated, so she was welcome—arrived on the horizon a few minutes before six o'clock.

The effect the appearance of the *Palomino* had upon passengers and crew of the sunken *Virginia Dare*, adrift in lifeboats, was inspiring. There were cheers, shaking of hands, kissing.

Stronger than these emotions, however, was stark amazement. The story of the golden man's predictions had gone from boat to boat during the afternoon. Of course there had been profound skepticism. More than one passenger had voiced an opinion that Captain Kirman must be touched, or he wouldn't have taken the word of a half-stupefied castaway that rescue would turn up if they waited.

Most affected of all was Captain Kirman. He lost his temper, sprang to his feet, and collared the golden man. "How the hell did you know that ship was coming?" Captain Kirman yelled. "And if you say your mother, the sea, told you, damn me I'll throw you overboard for the sharks to eat!''

The golden man replied nothing whatever to this outburst. His face was placid; his smile, although slight, was unconcerned. The composed confidence of the fellow, and his strangeness, further enraged Captain Kirman. The captain whirled on the radio operator. "You sure no ship acknowledged your S O S?"

"Positive, sir," declared the radio operator.

"Was this"—Captain Kirman jerked his thumb at the golden man—"fellow hanging around the radio room at the time?"

"No, sir."

"Have you seen him near the radio room?"

"No, sir."

Captain Kirman gave up, red-faced, and bellowed greetings to the steamer *Palomino*. The sailors on the rusty hulk bellowed back in their native language, which was Portuguese, then rigged davit falls and hoisted the lifeboats of the *Virginia Dare* on deck. There were blankets for everybody, food and hot wine.

It was soon learned that the *Palomino* would put the rescued passengers and crew of the *Virginia Dare* ashore in Buenos Aires, South America, but first the vessel would have to go directly to another port, not so large, in another South American republic, to take on fuel and deliver cargo.

The captain of the *Palomino* made this very clear in a little speech he delivered through an interpreter.

Monk asked Ham, "Do you speak Portuguese?"

"Sure," Ham said.

"How much?"

"I used to know a Portuguese girl," Ham said, "and I learned enough that we got along."

"That'll probably be a big help," Monk muttered. "But come on over anyway. Let's brace this skipper." He hauled Ham across the room. "Ask him how his ship happened to show up where we had been torpedoed. He was off his course. How come?"

Ham put this query to the *Palomino* commander. Monk's conjecture about Ham's ability with the Portuguese must have been approximately correct, since the palaver went on for some time, with much grimacing and shaking of heads. Finally Ham turned to Monk.

"He ees say that she very fonny business," Ham said.

"You can skip the accent," Monk growled. "What does he mean—funny?"

"It seems," Ham elaborated, "that the captain of the *Palomino* got a radiogram today about noon that caused him to change his course and head for this spot. The radiogram was an S O S from the *Virginia Dare*.

"Oh, so they heard our S O S, after all. That's fine—" Monk's jaw fell until his mouth was roundly open. "When did you say that radiogram came?"

"About noon today."

"Noon!"

"Yes."

"But the *Virginia Dare* sank at eleven!"

"Uh-huh."

"Hell, the ship couldn't send an S O S after it sank."

"Sure," Ham said. "Sure it did. But that isn't all."

Monk got out a handkerchief and wiped his face. "If that radiogram was sent at noon—who sent it? There was no radio in any of our lifeboats. How in the dickens—" He fell silent, pondering.

"I said that wasn't all," Ham reminded.

"Huh?"

"They have just discovered in the last half hour that the radio operator of the *Palomino* never received such a message," Ham explained.

Monk gaped at him. "No?"

"The message never came over the radio."

"Say, what is this?" Monk growled. "The *Palomino* skipper says there was a message, then he says there wasn't! Is that it?"

Ham explained patiently, "Here is what happened. The message was handed to the captain of the *Palomino,* on the bridge, shortly after noon. The message was brought by a man who wore a radio operator's uniform, but at the time the captain was figuring out his midday position, and didn't pay too much attention to the man."

"When the skipper read an S O S message, he surely called the radio room to check on its authenticity," Monk said.

"Yes, he did. But there is a speaking tube that leads from the bridge to the radio room, and the skipper used that. He says a voice answered him, and it sounded like the regular radio operator. The operator—or this voice through the speaking tube—told the skipper that there was no doubt about the message being genuine, and to go ahead and steam full speed to help the ship. That satisfied the skipper. Incidentally, if it hadn't been for that radiogram, we would probably never been found. This is a mighty deserted stretch of ocean."

Bewildered, Monk asked, "Where was the radio operator when all this was going on?"

"In a trance."

"Eh?"

"The radio operator's story is queer. He says that, a little before twelve, he felt strangely drowsy. This drowsiness came on all of a sudden, and he dropped off to sleep. He claims now that it wasn't exactly like dropping off in a nap—he says it was different, kind of like a trance. And during this trance, he remembers just one thing, a black star."

Astonishment yanked at Monk's face. "Now wait a minute! What was that he remembered?"

"A black star."

"You kidding me?"

"I know it's crazy," Ham admitted. "A black star. The radio operator says it was on his mind when he came out of this so-called trance—he came out of it incidentally, about one o'clock—but he don't know whether he saw a black star, or had it impressed on his subconscious somehow, or what made him have it on his mind."

Without a word, Monk wheeled and walked out of the cabin. He strode on deck, where he leaned against the rusty rail and let the wind whip his face.

"When we found that guy swimming in the sea," he muttered, "I wonder *just what we did find.*"

There was one more incident. This occurred when the golden man unexpectedly approached Captain Kirman that afternoon. About the golden man was his typical impassive calm, dignity, and power of character that seemed to give him a hypnotic influence over those with whom he came in contact.

He said, "The submarine which torpedoed your vessel should be punished, Captain Kirman."

Captain Kirman swore until he ran out of breath, then sucked in air and said, with careful self-control, that he wished to all that was holy that he knew some way of seeing that the job got done.

The golden man stated quietly, "The submarine will be meeting a supply ship." He named a latitude and longitude. "You can radio the American navy to send a cruiser to the spot."

Captain Kirman blinked. "Why not a British boat? There may not be an American cruiser in this part of the ocean."

"One is now less than seventy miles to the west of the spot where the submarine will meet the supply ship," the strange golden man said peacefully. He started to move away, then paused to add, "The submarine is not actually the nationality which she pretended to be."

Captain Kirman could only gape at him. Later, Captain Kirman found Monk and Ham. The captain gave the scar on the top of his head a furious massaging with his palms as he told about the conversation.

"This thing's got my goat," he confessed. "I'm not a man who believes in spooks, but I'm beginning to wonder if we didn't find one swimming in the ocean."

Monk asked, "You going to notify the American navy?"

"Would you?"

"I believe I would," Monk said.

Captain Kirman grinned. "I guess you're getting as crazy as the rest of us."

The matter of the torpedoing of the American liner *Virginia Dare* became, in diplomatic parlance, what was termed an incident, which was another way of saying that it came within a shade of plunging the United States into a conflict.

The American cruiser, as a result of a radiogram which Captain Kirman sent, at sunset that evening came upon a freight steamer and a submarine holding a midsea rendezvous. The cruiser came up quietly in the dusk, and very fast. It put off a plane, and the plane dived upon the unsuspecting freighter and submarine without warning.

The observer of the plane used a good camera, getting enough pictures to tell a story—the photographs showed sailors at work with paint brushes, wrenches and welding torches, changing the appearance of the submarine back to normal. The pictures proved beyond a shadow of a doubt that the submarine belonged to one European power, but had been masquerading as belonging to another.

The sub made a frantic effort to submerge when discovered. This caused a disaster. Someone forgot to close the hatch, and the U-boat never came up again. There was, of course, no actual proof that the submersible accidentally destroyed itself, but there was never any doubt in the minds of pilot and observer of the U. S. navy plane.

As for the freighter, it got away. It was not the ponderous hulk it appeared to be, and it left the vicinity at a speed which almost equaled that of the navy cruiser. It managed to escape in the extremely black night.

Washington diplomats—largely because they did not have absolute proof—decided to soft-pedal the incident somewhat. There was never any doubt, however, that a European power had made an attempt to arouse American public sentiment against another nation by trying to make the public think one of that nation's submarines had torpedoed an American liner without warning.

Chapter 4
THE UPSET PITCHER

The steamer *Palomino* was a slow hooker. Days elapsed before she drew near the small South American seaport where she was to refuel before continuing to Buenos Aires. Eventually, the South American coastline did appear like a black string lying on the western horizon.

That night, Ham came upon Monk in the bow. Monk was pulling the large ears of his pet pig, Habeas Corpus, and staring at the deck.

"Ham, I been thinking," Monk muttered.

"What with?"

"Oh, cut out the sass," Monk grumbled. "You go around claiming I'm dumb, and personally, I'm convinced you're so stupid you think the eternal triangle is something babies wear. The point is, maybe we're both kind of dumb."

"How do you mean?"

"About this fellow they found in the ocean—this golden man," Monk said thoughtfully. "I've been studying him. And I can't make up my mind."

Ham nodded soberly. "I've been doing the same thing."

"Apparently," Monk said, "he has some kind of power. Apparently he knows about things that are going to happen before they happen. Apparently such things ain't possible."

Ham grimaced. "It's crazy, and we both know it," he said.

"Sure—it's impossible," Monk agreed. "But just the same, what are we going to do about the evidence that is in front of our eyes?"

Ham said abruptly, "I'll bet we've both thought of the same thing."

"Doc Savage?"

Ham nodded.

"Well, it's the smartest idea you've had recently, because it's the same as mine," Monk declared. "If Doc Savage could talk to this golden mystery guy, and examine him, we would know for sure whether he has some kind of supernatural power."

Ham said, "There's another angle to it, too."

"How do you mean?"

"This will sound crazy."

"Well, what is it?"

"If this fellow they found in the sea *does* have supernatural power, he ought to be protected. It would be too bad if he had a power like that, and crooks got hold of him."

Monk pulled at one of his tufted ears. "I thought of that, too."

"A bunch of crooks, if they got something like that," Ham said, "could cause a lot of trouble. Think of what you could accomplish if you *knew what was going to happen in the future.*"

Monk grinned. "That does sound crazy."

Ham scowled. "Well, we better take this man to Doc, anyway."

"He may not want to go."

"We can ask him."

"And if he don't say yes?"

Monk grinned. "Then," he said, "he can look into the future and see that we'll take him whether he wants to go or not."

The golden man had one particular trait which by now had been noticed by everyone. This was his preference for solitude. He never took part in conversation, and when spoken to about some trivial matter, did not trouble to answer. He had placed a deck chair on the top deck in a lonesome spot where the wind blew the strongest, and he spent long hours there, lying relaxed with his eyes half closed, as if in inner contemplation.

Monk and Ham found him there. They explained that they wished to converse privately.

"It's important," Monk said.

"If you wish," the golden man replied placidly.

They could not help being impressed by his calmness. Neither Monk nor Ham was easily awed, for they themselves were famous men in their professions, besides being additionally noted because of their association with Doc Savage. The feeling that the golden man was an extraordinary individual disturbed them.

For the conference, they selected deck chairs under their windows. It was rather hot to retire to a stateroom, and there was no one in view on deck.

Ham, who was more silver-tongued than Monk, took the burden of explanation. He did a good job of it, using a normal but earnest tone, speaking simple-worded sentences that were effective. As he talked, he watched the face of his listener, distinguishable in the glow from an electric deck light nearby. He got the idea his talk was doing no good, and after he finished, he was surprised to receive a lecture in return.

"Clark Savage," said the golden man, "is, as you have just told me, a great man, and a kind one. He follows a strange career, and in being fitted for this career, he was placed in the hands of scientists at childhood, and trained by those scientists until he came to the estate of man. Because of this, many people do not understand him, and accordingly regard him as a kind of inhuman combination of scientific wizardry, muscular marvel, and mental genius. Those who are close to him know differently—they know that he has strength of character and genuine goodness. They know that he would have been a great man without the training of those scientists." The golden man sat silent for a moment, as if musing. "It is unfortunate for humanity that the world does not have many such as Doc Savage," he continued. "If ever the world needed men who combine scientific ability and moral character, it is now."

Monk took in a deep breath. "How about going with us to talk to Doc Savage?" he asked.

"Of course."

"You'll go!" Monk exclaimed, delighted.

"Yes."

"That's swell!"

Apparently feeling the matter was satisfactorily settled, the golden man got to his feet and walked away. The placidity of his going kept his departure from seeming curt.

Monk and Ham were silent for a while. Then, "He knew all about Doc," Monk ventured.

"Yes, seemed to," Ham admitted. "But that's just another of the strange things about him. Incidentally, I sent Doc a radiogram, describing this fellow fully, and asking Doc if he had ever heard of him. Doc radioed back that he had no knowledge of such a man."

"Well, we got him to agree to see Doc," Monk remarked.

They still sat there when the noise came from behind them. A noise from their stateroom. The sound of something upsetting, breaking with a crunching shatter.

They exchanged stares.

"Stay here," Monk breathed.

The homely chemist whipped out of his deck chair, got up on tiptoes, ran to a door, veered through it, took a turn into a corridor, and reached their stateroom. The door was closed. He put an ear to it, heard no sound. He hesitated, then entered.

When he rejoined Ham a few minutes afterward, Monk was calm.

Ham was excited. "What was it?"

"The jug of water was on the floor," Monk said. "I guess it rolled off the table, or something. It broke."

"You mean that jug of glowing water?"

"Yes."

"Broke?"

"Yes."

"But the boat hasn't been rolling."

"I didn't think it had, either," Monk admitted.

They were both rather silent.

Chapter 5
THE FIFTH COLUMN

The name of the town was not *La Corneja*, but that was what Monk always called it. The name *la corneja* was Spanish for crow, and the place was a crow among towns, far the most drab and shabby seaport on that coast of South America, so the name Monk applied was not unappropriate. *La Corneja* was not the principal seaport of the republic; the republic itself was one of the smaller ones in South America. Certainly the town had none of the beauty and prosperity which marks—to the astonishment of American tourists—much of South America.

Monk and Ham went ashore as soon as the steamer *Palomino* tied up to a dock for coaling, to stretch their legs. Later they had a surprisingly good luncheon. Then they took a stroll.

The stroll accounted for two things. First, it enabled them by chance to see the thin man with the scar under his left eye. The man was talking to Captain Kirman of the *Virginia Dare*. The two men were conversing in a small bar. Monk and Ham placed no significance in the incidence then, although later they attached a great deal.

The second incident of the stroll was a street fight which they witnessed. This occurred later in the afternoon. The fight broke out suddenly in a market where they were standing.

One native hit another with a ripe and squashy fruit, at the same time calling the man a crawling dog, and adding colored information about his ancestors. The fight spread like flame after a match is dropped in a gasoline barrel. There was suddenly excitement all around Monk and Ham.

They were bumped into, jolted, shoved about, although no one swung any blows at them. After being jammed in a struggling group for a while, they extricated themselves. Once clear, they stood, well on the outskirts of the fight, and watched the melee. It was good entertainment.

Then someone yelled, "The police!" in Spanish. The fight ended more suddenly than it had started. Participants scattered in all directions. One moment, they were there; the next they were gone. Monk and Ham prudently took to their heels also.

"Wonder what they were fighting about?" Ham pondered. "Didn't seem to start over anything."

Ham shrugged. "Search me. They wanted the exercise, maybe. I've seen times when I just felt like starting a scrap."

They dismissed the fight as a welcome piece of entertainment they had witnessed, and wandered along the streets, examining the shop windows.

They were on a side street when the thin man with the scar below his left eye approached them. He had a bundle under his arm. He was excessively polite, and nervous.

His English was good enough. "Señors," he said, "I saw you back yonder, looking at that fight. It later occurred to me that you kind Americans might help a poor man who is in trouble. I was the cause of that fight. A man and his relatives hate me because of . . . er . . . a matter about a woman. I have married the woman, their sister, and they do not like that. I love Carlita, and she loves me, but if we stay here, there will be *much* trouble. We want to leave, to go to some other place, and be happy by ourselves. But we have no money. I have only some fine silken shawls which cost me much money, but which I will sell very cheap. Could you good Americans help out a poor man by buying my shawls?" He said all this in one rush of words, tinged with frantic haste.

Monk and Ham exchanged amused glances. This was an old gag. It was an old trick for selling shoddy merchandise. Gyp artists in New York often used it. The fellow must take them for suckers. The shawls would be shoddy.

But, to their astonishment, upon examining the man's shawls, they found them of exquisite workmanship and quality. The price named was a fraction of their real value.

"Bargain!" Monk whispered.

Ham agreed. He appreciated a bargain.

They bought the shawls.

The thin man with the scar under his eyes almost sobbed as he parted with the merchandise. Then he fled down an alley with his money.

Monk and Ham, feeling proud of themselves, walked along the street.

"You know, these are darn fine shawls," Monk said. "They must be worth a hundred bucks apiece."

"Much as I hate to agree with you," Ham said, "we did get a buy."

They were arrested on the town's main street.

Nearly a dozen neatly uniformed officers—it developed that they were Federal police—closed in. Monk and Ham were handcuffed, searched. Howling protests were ignored. They were dragged off to the city hall, which also contained the jail, and stood before an officer.

"What's the meaning of this?" Ham demanded indignantly.

The officer in charge spread the shawls out on a table. He examined them, then grunted angrily. He indicated the unusual design.

"These shawls," he said in a grim voice, "are actually maps of this country's fortified zones. In other words, you two men seem to be spies. Fifth columnists, I believe is the term."

Both prisoners protested a mistake.

The officer shrugged. "The commandant will arrive shortly. He will hear your stories."

Their jail cell turned out to have one window, size eight-by-ten inches, a wooden frame on the floor filled with straw for a bunk, and walls over two feet thick, of stone. There were other inhabitants in the form of bugs of assorted sizes.

"No wonder that guy sold the shawls so cheap!" Monk growled.

Ham nodded. "It was a frame-up. We took the bait clear up to the pole."

They moved to the window, tested the bars. These were as thick as their wrists, of steel, and solid.

Monk said, "Say, earlier in the afternoon, I remember seeing that thin guy with the scar under his eye talking to Captain Kirman."

"I saw him, too."

"You suppose there's any connection?"

Ham scowled. "There's sure something phony about this."

The door of the cell was unlocked shortly, flung open, and policemen entered with guns and grim expressions. The officers proceeded to strip all the clothing off Monk and Ham, and take the garments away. The two prisoners were left naked.

"A fine out!" Ham yelled, almost hysterical with rage. "There'll be international complications over this!"

"Oh, shut up!" Monk grumbled. "You don't really get mad until somebody steals your clothes."

Ham had an hour in which to fume. Then the police were back again, and with them, the commandant. The commandant was an athletic man of middle age, efficient, speaking English smoothly.

He had their clothing.

"You two men," he said, "became very careless."

"We're getting mad, too," Monk assured him. "Or at least one of us is."

The commandant indicated their clothing. "In the pockets of your garments, we found incriminating documents. In one was a forged passport. In another suit, there were letters which you had already decoded, that proves conclusively that you are spies of a European power."

An indignant protest from the two captives led the commandant to exhibit the evidence. It was exactly what he had said it was.

"How did your men come to arrest us?" Ham demanded, his voice ominously calm.

"We received a telephone tip."

Ham turned to Monk. "That fight we saw was part of the frame-up. Remember how they crowded against us, and shoved us around? The passport and these letters were planted on us then."

"Yes," Monk said. "And you remember last night, in our cabin—I bet somebody was eavesdropping."

The commandant smiled, but with no humor. "So you claim you were framed?"

Indignantly, Monk announced his identity, and added further that they were survivors of the torpedoed American liner, *Virginia Dare*.

The commandant was slightly impressed. "We will check that story," he said. "We wish to be perfectly fair."

The commandant then went away.

He was back before dark. His face was not pleasant.

"Captain Kirman," the commandant informed them grimly, "declares that he never heard of you."

Monk was stunned. "You're *sure* of that?"

"There is no doubt."

"You really saw Captain Kirman?"

"Yes."

"He has a scar on his head. Are you sure—"

"A scar that was the result of a mine fragment in the World War," the commandant said impatiently. "Yes, we discussed the captain's scar."

Monk and Ham had been reluctant to capitalize on the name of Doc Savage, and their association with him. But now the situation demanded that. With earnestness, they told the commandant that they were associated with Doc Savage, and that, if he would radio Doc, he would receive confirmation of the fact.

The commandant crisply agreed to send the radiogram.

The answer came the following afternoon. By that time, the *Palomino* finished fueling and had sailed for Buenos Aires.

The radiogram was to the point.

> TWO MEN YOU HAVE IN CUSTODY ARE IMPOSTERS. MY AIDS MONK MAYFAIR AND HAM BROOKS ARE IN MY NEW YORK HEADQUARTERS NOW.
> DOC SAVAGE.

Monk became pale.

They were court-martialed that afternoon. They were convicted. They received the traditional funny-paper sentence—but there was nothing funny about it.

They were sentenced to be stood against the stone prison wall at dawn and shot. The sentence prescribed the size of the firing squad which was to do the job—it was to contain eleven riflemen, and one rifle to be loaded with a blank, so that no member of the squad need be absolutely sure that his bullet was a deadly one.

Chapter 6
THE BROKEN FRAME

Fourteen weeks later, Monk and Ham were still in jail. Same jail. Same cell. Fourteen weeks was a long time, about as long as fourteen years, but that was about all they had learned. They had lost weight, had become prospective mental wrecks. They had even stopped quarreling.

It had been two weeks before they learned why they had not been shot immediately. The commandant was convinced they were Fifth Columnists and he was trying to break their nerve and get a confession that would involve associates. The commandant hoped to clean out the hotbed of foreign agents and saboteurs which had descended like a locust swarm upon South American republics with the advent of the European fracas. Since they had nothing to confess, Monk and Ham were under unearthly strain, expecting each dawn to stand in front of the firing squad.

The commandant had adopted their two pets, Habeas Corpus and Chemistry, but that was vague consolation.

They were held incommunicado, as far as the public was concerned. In fact, no word of print had appeared in the newspapers concerning their arrest.

Ham kept a calendar by scratching marks in the cell wall. "Three months and two weeks," he said one morning.

That was the day the commandant unlocked their cell, gave them their clothes, and a profuse apology.

Said the commandant, "There is something very strange about this matter. We now discover that you two men are actually the men you claimed you were—Ham Brooks and Monk Mayfair, aides of Doc Savage."

"A fine time to be finding that out!" Monk said.

The commandant was genuinely regretful, he said. He added, "Only because Doc Savage began an investigation to determine your whereabouts did we learn the truth." The commandant then exhibited a radiogram which had been exchanged between himself and Doc Savage in New York, and between himself and the American State Department.

Monk was convinced the commandant had really been fair. He controlled his rage and demanded, "But what about that radiogram you first sent to Doc? How come you got a faked answer?"

"I am sorry to say," the commandant explained, "that we have discovered an operator of the local commercial radio station was bribed to supply the fake message."

"Who did the bribing?"

"A man," said the commandant, "who told the radio operator his name was Captain Harley Kirman of the torpedoed ship, *Virginia Dare*."

"You met Captain Kirman," Monk said. "Was it the same man?"

"According to the description—yes."

"Then Captain Kirman got us in this mess?"

"Yes."

Monk gave his belt an angry hitch. "How soon," he asked, "can we charter a plane that will fly us to a place where we can catch a Pan-American plane north?"

"I will see that you are furnished with an army plane," the commandant volunteered.

The taxicab which took Monk and Ham to the airport was trailed. The hack Monk and Ham took was a secondhand yellow cab imported from the north, but it was called a *fotingo*. All cabs in the town were called *fotingos*, for some reason or other.

The man who did the trailing also rode a *fotingo*. The man had lived for the past fourteen weeks in an apartment across the street from the jail. He and a partner had managed to keep almost continuous watch on the jail. Always close at hand, they had kept a high-powered rifle equipped with a telescopic sight. Unfortunately—or fortunately, depending on the viewpoint—Monk and Ham had not come in range of window or rifle. And a few minutes ago, when the pair had left the jail, there had been too many police around.

The shadow watched Monk and Ham depart from the airport in an army pursuit ship. Then he lost no time getting to the telephone office and putting in a long-distance call.

He called a number in New York City.

"Pollo?" he asked.

"Yes," said the New York voice.

"Juan speaking."

"Yes, Juan."

"I have bad news," said Juan. "The truth was found out about them today. They have left the prison. They have also left the city—in an army plane."

"You fool!" said Pollo. "You stupid idiot! If you think you are going to get paid for failing to do the job, you're crazy."

Juan jammed his mouth close to the transmitter and said, "Perhaps you would prefer me to sell certain information to the police? Or to the man called Doc Savage."

"Now," Pollo said hastily. "We can settle this without unpleasantness, I am sure."

"Of course, we can settle it," Juan assured him. "You have my money cabled down here by tomorrow morning. That will settle it."

Pollo was silent for a while. "Yes, I guess that is the way to do it," he surrendered reluctantly.

At the New York end of the wire, Pollo put the telephone receiver on its hook. He was a thin man with a scar under his left eye. He took hold of his face with his left hand, and the enraged clenching grip of the fingers twisted that side of his face and made more unpleasant the scar below his eye. His thin body shook with rage. Great feeling was in the flow of profanity which he kept up for about a minute and a half.

The telephone rang, and the operator said, "The other party wishes to reverse charges on the call you just received from South America. Will you accept the charges? They are thirty-six dollars and eighty-seven cents, tax included."

"Yes," Pollo said through his teeth. "I'll pay it." The swearing he did afterward eclipsed the streak he had just finished. "Fall down on the job, will he!" he gritted. "And then it costs me thirty-six dollars and eighty-seven cents to find out about it." His face was purple.

When his rage had simmered to a point where it was only heat that whitened his face, he got up and went into another room. The place was an apartment, and large, located in the busy downtown section where comings and goings did not attract too much attention.

Four men were seated at a table, giving their attention to a bottle, a pack of cards and stacks of chips. They looked, in the tobacco smoke that was a hades-blue haze in the room, a little like four well-dressed devils. The police had fairly complete histories of three of them. The fourth had been lucky thus far.

Pollo growled at them, and they looked up.

"Things went wrong in South America," Pollo explained. "Those two men, Monk and Ham, got away in spite of that fool Juan I had hired to see that they remained there. Now Monk and

Ham are probably on their way up here. I imagine they will come by plane."

The four men looked at each other. One of them, who had been about to deal, laid down his cards.

"Which adds up to what?" he asked.

"When Monk and Ham get here, we will have to get rid of them." Pollo made a pistol shape with his right hand, and moved the thumb to indicate the imaginary gun was going off. "Like that."

Then the man who had put down the deck asked, "Do you know about this Doc Savage?"

"What has that to do with it?" snapped the thin man with the scarred face.

"For me personally, it has right considerable to do with it," the other man said dryly. "I have had certain parties who were friends of mine, and who went up against this Doc Savage, and I have not heard from them since. I know other parties who have had friends, and the same thing happened to the friends. Also I have heard rumors about Savage, and I have heard the rumors are not exaggerated."

"Who's afraid of this Doc Savage?"

"I am." The man got up from the table and put his hat on his head. He said, "Well, good-by. I may see you again, but I doubt it, particularly if you go up against Savage."

His three companions also got up and put on their hats. They walked to the door.

"What in the hell are you doing?" Pollo demanded angrily.

"Savage scares us, too," a man explained. "We think we'll leave with Jed, here."

"But damn you," Pollo yelled, "I'm paying you big money."

"They don't make money that big," Jed said.

He left, and the other three with him.

Pollo felt like swearing some more, but he had another feeling, a cold one in the pit of his stomach, that kept him silent. He went to a telephone, dialed, but got no answer. He sat before the telephone for something over an hour, dialing at intervals of fifteen minutes, until finally his party came in.

"Hello. Pollo speaking, chief. I thought Jed and those other three men you sent me were supposed to be tough."

A voice in the telephone assured him, "They do not come any tougher."

"When I mentioned Doc Savage, they got up and walked out. Quit cold."

There was a silence of some duration, and more meaning, at the other end of the line. "*Who* did you say you mentioned to them?"

"Doc Savage."

Over the wire came a sound that was not coherent.

"What did you say, chief?" Pollo asked.

"I said that I know how Jed and the other three felt," the voice responded uneasily. "Tell me, Pollo, just what has gone wrong?"

Because telephone lines are not the most private things in the world, Pollo told a story about a prize calf named Fair of May, and another one named Evening Brook, both of which escaped—so the story went—from the pasture where they were being kept down on the farm. The escape had been accomplished in spite of two keepers, one named Juan, who had been on hand. The calves when last seen were believed heading north.

"You understand?" Pollo finished.

"I do, and it does not make me happy," his boss said.

"What are we going to do about it?"

"I have some farmhands who are not scared of those calves or the bull that they run with. We will put them on the job. While these calves are heading north, we probably could not find them. So we will get them when they reach the north pasture. They will probably go straight to their home shed. Station the farmhands at the shed. We will have a barbecue. Do *you* understand?"

"Fully."

"Good. By the way, have you any qualms about the bull I mentioned?"

"Doc Savage?"

"Yes."

"Not a qualm."

"Have you ever seen him?"

"No."

"That would explain the lack of qualms," the leader said dryly.

Chapter 7
THE LAST MINUTE

Arriving in New York, Ham Brooks was neatly groomed, correct in afternoon coat and striped trousers, and far the best-dressed man who stepped from the plane at La Guardia field. He had wirelessed ahead to Miami, the stop, giving size, color, fabric, so that a tailor could furnish him with a complete outfit.

Monk wore the same suit which he had worn during the finding of the strange golden man in the sea, the torpedoing of the *Virginia Dare*, their long incarceration in jail. "If this suit was good enough for all that, it's good enough for New York," Monk insisted. Actually, he knew the scarecrow garment irritated Ham.

They strode through the airport terminal, and it was warming to be back. People stared at them, at their two unusual pets, Habeas Corpus and Chemistry.

But almost at once, Monk got a shock. He was passing the center of the terminal, where there was a circular dome and windows through which the afternoon sunlight slanted. The sunlight chanced to fall across a woman's right hand, particularly across a ring the woman was wearing. Monk's eyes protruded a little.

He touched Ham's elbow, whispered, "Turn around and walk back with me."

"What ails you now?"

"Take a good look at the ring on that dame's right hand. The one in the mink coat."

They strolled back, and casually examined the ring in question. "You notice it?" Monk whispered.

Ham nodded. He was startled.

There was no doubt but that the strange set in the ring the woman was wearing on the small finger of her right hand was a star. A black star. A star edged with red, which caught the light and sent it glittering.

Monk asked, "Does that star remind you of the one we saw in the sky the night the golden man got found in the sea?"

"Yes, it does," Ham whispered.

"I'm gonna brace her. Ask her about the ring."

Ham plucked at Monk's sleeve. "Better not. I happen to know who that woman is."

"Who?"

"Mrs. H. Courtney van Stigh."

"So what?"

"She has more social position than the King of England, and more dollars than Europe has soldiers."

"That's nice," Monk said. "We should get along great." He started toward the lady of social and dollar prominence.

"You'll get a coat of icicles," Ham warned. Ham had heard Mrs. van Stigh had a notable record for snobbery, so he was astonished when Monk approached the lady and said, "Beg pardon, but I'm interested in your black-star ring," and Mrs. van Stigh gave Monk a *friendly* smile. "Yes, that ring is my most precious possession," she said.

"Does the ring represent something?" Monk asked breezily.

"Oh, yes," she said. "The sea was his mother, and the night was his father. There was a black star edged by fire in the night, and an ectoplasmic light in the sea, and they were his guardians. The dark star is the symbol."

Then she glanced toward the clock on the wall, gasped something about missing her plane, and scampered off.

Monk was rooted to the floor.

"What the hell!" he muttered, finally. "She isn't crazy, is she?"

"Not," Ham told him, "that I ever heard of."

They took a taxicab. When the machine was moving, Monk said, "I remember somebody who said his mother was the sea and his father was the night."

"You and me both," Ham said.

"The man who was found in the ocean."

"Yes, I know."

"Suppose there's any connection?"

"How the heck *could* there be?"

Monk said thoughtfully, "Her voice got sort of strange when she started talking about the ring. She sounded kind of like a mother speaking of her new baby. And didn't you say it wasn't like the old heifer to condescend to even speak to a mere stranger."

Ham nodded. "Particularly a mere stranger who looks like a bum," he added.

"Bum? Meaning me?" Monk became indignant. "Listen, why should an old moneybags like that high-hat *me*? I've got plenty of culture."

"The only trouble with your culture," Ham told him, "it's all physical."

They fell to quarreling enthusiastically, and soon felt better. Their squabbling—it was so fierce that the taxi driver looked infinitely worried—served them, like it always did, as a tonic; it got rid of the rather eerie sensation which had resulted from seeing the dark star ring.

It was good to be back. The cab was now bright; the interior was clean, fawn-brown; the radio was clear. The new superhighway up and across the Triborough Bridge was smooth. The sun glowed.

They were filled with that fine getting-back-to-God's-country feeling.

In this mood of rejoicing, they came in sight of Doc Savage's headquarters, which occupied the top floor—the eighty-sixth story—of one of midtown Manhattan's most spectacular buildings. The skyscraper was like a spike of gray ice probing up at the placid cumulous clouds.

"I don't know when I've been more glad to get back," Monk said. And he added hopefully, "Now, if we can just have some excitement."

Monk said that last as he was getting out of the cab backward, so that the man who came up behind him and put the hardness of a gun muzzle where it was unmistakable against the homely chemist's back, answered by asking, "How is this for a start?"

Monk stood there—he was half in and half out of the cab—and asked, "What do you want me to do, pal?"

"Get back in the cab," the man said.

"Then what?"

"Just sit there." The man showed the gun to the cab driver. "Look, hacker," the man said. "I think the thing for you to do is take a walk."

The cab driver thought so, too. His walk was a run. He headed for the nearest corner.

The man with the gun said, "I am going to go away. You two fellows sit here. If one of you wants to make a move, he had better first consider whether he is bulletproof."

Then the man put his gun in his pocket—he had not displayed the weapon prominently enough for pedestrians moving on the sidewalk to notice it—and walked away.

Monk and Ham were puzzled by the performance. But only for a moment.

Up the street, a sedan, black and inconspicuous, moved from the curb. In the back seat of the sedan were two men and blued steel. The windows were down.

"Machine guns," Monk croaked.

He did not add that they were army caliber and could cut through the taxi as if it was paper. Ham would know that. Ham's mouth was open, his eyes stark, both hands gripping his sword-cane, which he had recovered in South America.

Ham said, "They tried to get rid of us in South America. Now they're trying the job again."

Monk's nod was hardly perceptible. "Think of something," he said hoarsely.

They could do two things. Stay in the cab, or get out. The only difference seemed to be one of getting shot while sitting, or while running. There was no protection; there was no time to reach, for instance, the entrance of the skyscraper. Monk and Ham watched the dark sedan.

There was—while they watched—suddenly blue-red flame under the front wheels of the approaching sedan. The flame came suddenly, was about ten feet across, approximately circular in shape, flat at first, but becoming tall, and with jagged petals like a monstrous red-blue rose that had blossomed. As the rose of flame grew tall, it lifted the front of the dark sedan until the car was practically standing erect on the rear wheels. Tires and tubes came off both the front wheels. One front fender detached and arose some forty feet in the air, twisting idly while it lifted, like a large black leaf.

There was a concussion that laid their ears back.

A second blast occurred sometime during the big one, but this one—it was not much more than good firecracker noise—was lost in the echoes that gobbled through the street following the greater blast. The smaller explosion took place on the sidewalk a few inches from the feet of the man with the long blue revolver. It caused smoke, about a tubful of smoke to begin, but this swelled to a roomful, and more, and more. It enveloped the man and his revolver.

In the smoke, the man screamed two or three times. His revolver popped loudly, adding blasting echoes to the discord. Then the man and his gun were silent inside the smoke, except for moaning.

In the taxi, Monk clamped both hands over his ears to muffle the uproar, and put on a grin.

"Sounds like Doc was around," he said.

The dark sedan, having balanced on its rear wheels for a moment or two, fell back with a crash to the street, and the frame bent, and all four doors flew open.

The three men in the sedan—only one of the pair in the back seat still retained his machine gun—piled onto the pavement. They put their chests out and ran. They headed north.

By running north, they got behind the cloud of black smoke—this had obviously come from a smoke grenade—which had enveloped the man with the gun.

One of the trio in the wildness of flight veered over so that he got into the edge of the smoke. There was tear gas in the smoke.

The man yelled. He rubbed at his eyes. Although suddenly blinded, he had the judgment to dash to one of his companions, so that he could be guided in his flight.

The three of them reached the end of the block. They had a second car—this was the machine the man with the long blue revolver had intended to use—parked there. Two of the three men—the one who did not have the machine gun, and the one who was tear-gassed—ran on to the car.

The man with the machine gun stopped. He waited. There was wind that had blown the smoke aside.

The victim of the tear gas had dropped his long blue revolver. He was down, squirming around on the sidewalk, distraught from blindness and from not knowing which way to flee.

It was obvious that he could be captured by anyone who cared to take the trouble.

The man with the machine gun made a fish mouth and braced the rapid-firer barrel against the corner of a building. His forefinger tightened. The gun poured staccato thunder into the street and made his body shake violently from head to foot.

The tear-gas victim on the sidewalk suddenly relaxed and a red lake spread around his body.

The machine gunner then ran to the car, which was already moving slowly. He climbed in. The car jumped ahead.

"You fix Ike?" the driver asked.

"I fixed Ike. He won't tell them anything!" Still wearing his fish-mouth expression, the man looked at his machine gun. "Smart thing is supposed to be to throw one of these guns away, ain't it?"

"Machine guns are hard to get these days," the driver said.

"Yeah. I guess I'll take a chance." The man kept the gun. He put it on the car floor boards. The car traveled fast and turned often.

Doc Savage was a bronze giant of a man who somehow fitted in with the turmoil which had occurred—he had caused it—in the street. He appeared from the entranceway of the skyscraper, from which point he had thrown the explosive grenade and the smoke bomb.

Doc crossed the sidewalk, dived into the cab with Monk and Ham and began cranking up windows.

"Get the windows up," he said.

His tone was imperative without being loud or excited. He started the cab engine and meshed gears. He finished cranking up the front windows while spinning the steering wheel to bring the machine around in the street.

By this time the bomb smoke, with a high tear-gas content, had spread until it shrouded the entire upper end of the street. To trail the killers, they would have to try to get through the stuff.

The cab was not air-tight. Some of the gas came in, and, because it was potent stuff, even a small quantity rendered driving unsafe. Their eyes became blurred with agony and leaked tears.

The bronze man twisted the cab in to the curb. He said, "They must have got away in a car. Get a description of it."

He flung out and ran into a drugstore and entered one of a battery of telephone booths. He called police headquarters, dialing the unlisted number of the radio room direct, and gave them—he first identified himself, since he held a high honorary commission on the city police force—a description of the three killers, the scene of the crime, the direction which they must have taken.

Ham came in. "Man across the street saw the car. Light-gray coach." Ham named the make of car and gave the license number.

Doc Savage relayed that information to the police, using sentences that were short, conveying clear detail.

Then he went back to the cab, started the machine and drove carefully around the block, sounding the horn frequently because his eyes were stinging wetly.

Monk asked, "How did you get wise?"

"You notice a new newsstand across the street?" Doc asked.

"Didn't have time to notice anything."

"The newsstand proprietor is an observant ex-detective who lost both legs in an accident," the bronze man said quietly. "We have him on salary."

"You mean this sleuth in the newsstand is hired to stay there and keep his eyes open for what looks like trouble around the building? It's a good idea. This ain't the first time we've been waylaid near headquarters."

Doc Savage said, "The detective telephone that four men seemed to be watching the place. Renny, Long Tom, Johnny and myself have been taking turns keeping an eye on the four."

Monk nodded. Renny was Colonel John Renwick, noted for his big fists and his engineering knowledge. Long Tom was Major Thomas J. Roberts, electrical wizard, and not as feeble as he looked. Johnny was William Harper Littlejohn, eminent archaeologist and geologist, and a walking dictionary of the largest-sized words. These three, with Monk and Ham, made up a group of five men who were associated with Doc Savage in his unusual profession.

Doc stopped the cab near the body of the man who had carried the long blue gun. There were two policemen and a crowd.

"He was hit twenty times," one of the policemen said. "He died as quick as they ever do."

Doc said, "We would like to examine his clothes."

The policeman agreed. "I imagine it will be all right, Mr. Savage. As soon as the morgue wagon gets here. I'll have them undress him inside it, and send his clothes right up."

Doc nodded. "Tell your homicide squad that four men attempted to assassinate my associates, Monk and Ham. We do not know why. This one got some tear gas, and could not escape. One of the others shot him, probably to keep us from questioning him."

"I'll tell homicide," the officer said.

Chapter 8
WATCH RUTH DORMAN

Some years ago when Doc Savage began the unusual career for which he had been trained, he had started equipping the headquarters which he now occupied on the eighty-sixth floor of the midtown building. The establishment took in the eighty-sixth floor, and was divided in three sections, the first section being a reception room, a small chamber furnished with little more than a huge safe and a rather startling inlaid table of rare woods and some comfortable chairs. A much larger room was the library, packed with scientific volumes. But the largest section of all was a laboratory which, as was well known to men in advanced science, contained some of the most advanced equipment in existence.

In the reception room, Doc Savage waved Monk and Ham to chairs. "You two fellows disappeared following the torpedoing of the *Virginia Dare*. When the survivors were landed at Buenos Aires, we naturally expected you to be accounted for. But when we sent a cablegram to Captain Kirman of the *Virginia Dare*, we received an answer saying that you two had never been on his liner."

Monk and Ham both had open mouths. "You say Captain Kirman cabled that we had never been on the *Virginia Dare*?" Ham muttered.

Doc Savage nodded. "That is what caused the delay in finding you. We had no idea what had become of you. We finally put a worldwide detective agency to work trying to find you. Just a few days ago, they located both of you in that South American jail."

Doc Savage's metallic features were composed, his flake-gold eyes expressionless. "Suppose you tell the complete story."

Monk said, "It's some story."

Ham said, "It's a story about a golden man they found floating in the ocean. It will sound kind of goofy."

"Proceed."

Ham went back to the beginning of the story. He did not use many words. Twice, Monk interrupted to bring in facts which Ham had overlooked.

"And we had never seen those men who tried to waylay us in front of this building a while ago," the lawyer finished.

The silence that followed lasted some moments. Then Doc asked for certain repetitions of the story, as if to verify points that he considered significant. "You filled a jug with the luminous water which had surrounded the *Virginia Dare*, but the jug was broken and the water lost?" he asked.

"Yes. The jug rolled off the table in our stateroom and broke," Ham explained.

"But you are not sure the ship was rolling enough to really tumble the jug to the floor."

"That was what puzzled us."

Doc Savage's expression did not change. "Did this unusual golden man make *any* prediction which did not come true?"

Monk answered the query. "Everything the guy predicted happened. The villa in Maderia being sold to the ship's physician, the ship being torpedoed, the rescue vessel showing up—all like he said."

"And the golden man knew you two by sight, although you had never seen him before?"

"Yes."

"You barely mentioned a Mr. Sam Gallehue," Doc Savage said. "Was there anything particularly outstanding about him?"

Monk's head shook a negative. "Naw, he was just one of these sirupy clucks that was so agreeable he got in your hair. Affected a phony English accent. Liked to hang around us, and run around after Captain Kirman."

"In other words, the kind of a man who cultivated the company of important people, whenever he happened to be?" Doc suggested.

"That's right."

Ham said, "Definitely a snob, is what I would call Mr. Sam Gallehue."

"Clever man?" Doc asked.

"Oh, no. Just a fawning dope of a guy."

Doc Savage got up, moved to one of the windows and stood looking out through the thick bulletproof glass. He asked, "This unusual person—the fellow you call the golden man—did he seem entirely willing to come to New York so that we could examine him?"

"Quite willing to come," Monk agreed.

"And it was shortly after he agreed that you began having your troubles?" Doc said in a tone that was half question and half remark.

"Eh?" Monk stared. "You think maybe *that* was why we were framed in South America?"

Without answering, Doc Savage slightly shifted the line of inquiry by stating, "This golden man said the sea was his mother and the night was his father, you say?"

Monk made an it-seems-goofy-to-me-too face. "And here's something else, Doc. When we got off the plane a while ago, we saw a woman that Ham claims is one of the big bombs in society around here. She was wearing a funny ring with a black-star setting. I asked her about it—"

Ham interjected, "Yes, and when he asked her, I expected Mrs. van Stigh to sick a chauffeur or a secretary on him. But instead, she said something about the sea being a mother and the sky a father and something about ectoplasm. She positively beamed on Monk while she said it."

Ham's tone implied that anyone who could beam on Monk must have something drastically wrong with their mental mechanism.

The bronze man made no comment. He turned from the window slowly.

Monk continued, "But to get back to what we want to know—who got us in all that trouble in South America? The first guy I want to see about that is Captain Kirman!"

"Captain Kirman of the *Virginia Dare*. You suspect him?"

"He's our bird," Monk agreed.

A buzzer whined softly, a red light flashed, and Doc Savage moved over to the inlaid table and touched a button which caused a television image to appear on a wall panel. The image showed the corridor outside, and a policeman with a bundle of clothing. Doc opened the door.

The policeman explained, "That man who was machine-gunned in the street—one of our homicide men knew him. He had a record as long as a giraffe's neck."

Doc said, "It might be a good idea if the police started picking up his known associates for questioning."

"We'll do that," the officer agreed. He put the bundle of garments on the table. "This is the stuff he was wearing when he was shot."

The officer departed, and Doc opened the bundle of redly-damp clothing.

The garments were on the cheap, flashy side. A billfold, containing four hundred and twenty-odd dollars, led Monk to remark, "A lot of green stuff for a mug like him to be packing around. Whoever he was working for must pay off."

The only written or printed document in the clothing was a slip of paper, coral-pink in tone, on which had been pen-printed in blue ink three words.

The words:

Watch Ruth Dorman.

While they were looking at the bit of paper, the buzzer whined again and the red light flashed—the gadget was a protective alarm which prevented anyone setting foot on the eighty-sixth floor without their knowing it—and three men entered.

The first of the newcomers was extremely tall and thinner than it seemed any man could be and still live. He wore, dangling from his lapel, a monocle that was obviously a magnifying glass. Staring at Monk and Ham, he said, "I'll be superamalgamated. An ultraauspicious eventuation."

Monk grinned. "I see you've still got the words, Johnny."

The second arrival was small, with a complexion that would have gone well with a mushroom cellar. He was Major Thomas J. Long Tom Roberts, the electrical wizard, and his appearance of feebleness was deceptive. Not only had he never been ill, but he could whip nine out of ten football players on an average campus.

The third man had fists. Fists that would not go into quart pails. His face was long, with a habitual funeral-going expression. Physically, he looked bigger than Doc Savage, although actually he was not. He was Lieutenant Colonel John Renny Renwick the engineer.

These three, all associates of Doc Savage, shook hands heartily with Monk and Ham.

"Holy cow!" Renny jerked a large thumb in the general

direction of the street below. "The cops just told us there was a Fourth of July down there a while ago."

"We can't figure it out," Monk said.

Long Tom asked, "Where have you two lugs been? Why did you disappear for three months?"

Doc said, "Tell them the story, Monk."

Monk described the affair again taking more time and using more words than Ham had employed earlier in reciting the same details to Doc Savage. The bronze man listened intently, but Monk brought out nothing that Ham had not mentioned, so he made no comment and asked no question.

Renny looked at the sheet of paper from the machine-gunned man's clothing. "Who's Ruth Dorman?" He used his normal-speaking voice, which was loud enough to make bystanders instinctively want to put fingers in their ears.

Doc Savage passed the slip of paper to Renny. "You might start tracing it," he suggested. "Johnny and Long Tom can help you."

The big-fisted engineer nodded.

Monk and Ham had gone into the laboratory, where there were equipment lockers. They returned with supermachine pistols. These weapons, resembling oversized automatics, had been developed by Doc Savage. They could discharge an astounding number of bullets in a minute—either high-explosive slugs, mercy bullets, gas pellets, or smoke slugs.

"I'm ready to hunt Captain Kirman," Monk announced. "Wonder where we'll find him?"

Doc Savage said, "We can try the steamship line which owned the *Virginia Dare*. They may have information."

Chapter 9
DEATH BY IMPOSSIBILITY

The building stood on Broadway, south of Wall. There were seven steamship lines listed on the bronze plaque beside the entrance, and *Intra-marine Lines, 20th Floor,* was second from the top.

There was dark marble and indirect lighting on the twentieth floor, and wide double doors that admitted into a large room where many clerks and stenographers were at work. They made themselves known. Not more than a minute later, Doc Savage was shaking hands with a Mr. Elezar.

"Captain Kirman?" said Mr. Elezar. "Oh, yes. One of our most efficient commanders. Had a brilliant career. Went to sea at the age of ten, won first command before he was twenty-five. We were very sorry to lose him."

"Lose him?" Doc asked.

"Yes. Didn't you know? He has quit the sea. Oh, yes, indeed. Seemed broken up over the loss of the *Virginia Dare,* although he did not say so. Said he was just getting old, and thought he would like to try it a spell ashore. Ridiculous idea, too. He is no older than I am." Mr. Elezar looked to be about fifty.

"Is Captain Kirman now located in the city?" Doc asked.

"Oh, yes. Yes, indeed. Hardly two blocks from here. He has rented and furnished an office suite."

"Can you tell us what kind of business he is in?" Doc asked casually.

"Rare fish."

"You mean that he has become a dealer in rare tropical fish?"

"That's right."

Doc Savage nodded. "Thank you very much," he said. He reached out and took Mr. Elezar's hand and shook it, and, still holding the man's hand, turned it over and looked at the ring he had noticed.

"Unusual ring."

Mr. Elezar did not say anything. He seemed uncomfortable.

Monk craned his neck and saw that the ring contained a setting which was in the shape of a black star with blood-red edging.

"An extraordinary ring," Doc Savage said thoughtfully. "Believe we have heard of another ring of this type."

Mr. Elezar pulled his hand away. He looked as if he was about to break out in perspiration.

Doc said, "Can you tell me about that ring?"

Mr. Elezar said, "I'm sorry, but Captain Kirman suggested—" He bit his lower lip. "I'm . . . er . . . I have no information about the ring. It . . . it's just a thing I picked up in a pawnshop. Yes, that's it. I got it in a pawnshop."

"Could you give me the name of the pawnshop?" Doc asked. "I would like to get myself a ring like that one."

Mr. Elezar seemed desperate as he put on an act of trying to remember, then said, "I'm sorry, but I can't seem to recall. It was one of those places on the Bowery. There are so many."

Doc Savage was silent as they rode down to the street in an elevator.

But Monk growled angrily. "Mr. Elezar and the ring," he decided, "will bear looking into."

Ham had expected Doc Savage to go directly to Captain Kirman's office, and he was surprised when the bronze man turned into a downtown telephone office.

"What now?" Ham asked.

Doc said, "When you got in trouble in South America, you say the commandant talked to Captain Kirman, and *he* said he did not know you?"

Ham nodded. Monk put in, "And that ain't all, Doc. Captain Kirman bribed the radio operator to fake a radio message from you that denied we were who we claimed to be."

"Are you sure it was Captain Kirman?"

"The man answered his description."

"That," Doc explained thoughtfully, "is the point."

The bronze man entered a telephone booth where he remained for some thirty minutes.

His expression was unchanged when he finally came out of the booth, but Monk and Ham got the idea he had learned something interesting.

"I was fortunate," Doc told them. "The commandant was in his office. However, the telephone connection to that part of South America could be improved."

"What on earth did you telephone South America for?" Monk demanded.

"To ask the commandant the location of the scar on Captain Kirman's head," Doc explained.

Monk's small eyes narrowed. "And where was it?"

"Under the left eye."

Monk exploded. "But Captain Kirman's scar was on top of his head"—Monk wheeled to stare at Ham. "Say, the commandant didn't talk to Captain Kirman at all. Captain Kirman didn't bribe the radio operator. It was that other cuss, the man who sold us the Spanish shawls that got us into jail."

Ham nodded gloomily. "I remember how the case of mistaken identity occurred. One of us asked the commandant if Captain Kirman had a scar on his head, and the commandant said he did have, and that it was the result of a mine fragment in the World War. Captain Kirman's scar came from that cause, and we just took it for granted the commandant had talked to Captain Kirman."

"Dang it, now we're without a clue!" Monk complained. "Captain Kirman was my suspect!"

Doc said, "There is the matter of that star ring Mr. Elezar was wearing. Judging from Mr. Elezar's confusion, the ring had some connection with Captain Kirman. We might still talk to Captain Kirman."

Captain Kirman's office girl was a sensible-looking middle-aged brunette. When she learned their business, she went away through a door, but came back shortly.

"Captain Kirman is on the telephone," she said. "He will see you soon."

Doc Savage moved over to examine some of the tanks of rare fish. Monk joined him. They peered at an array of tanks, filters, aerators.

Monk squinted at the fish. "They're kind of fancy fish to be so small," he remarked. "They worth much?"

Doc said, "Some of them probably sell for more than a hundred dollars each."

Monk gasped. "You mean that a fish an inch long will bring a hundred bucks?"

"Or more. Collector's items," Doc explained. "You take these two fish in this tank, for instance. They are *mistichthys luzonensis,* native of the Philippine Islands, where they are called *Sinarapan* by the natives. They are very small, rarely more than half an inch long, and they are rare because they occur in Lake Buhi, far in the interior of the islands, a place so remote that it is almost impossible to bring out any living species."

"Then they're high-priced because they're scarce?"

"Something like that. However, in the Lake Buhi district of the Philippines, they are so plentiful that the natives catch great quantities of them in nets and make them up into little cakes which they serve with their rice—"

A buzzer sounded and the office girl picked up the telephone. She was not, something about her indicated, a woman who had been an office girl all her life. There was a polish in her manner, a confident ease, that indicated she was a woman who had possessed money and social position. She put the telephone down.

She said, "You may go in now."

Captain Kirman's office was large and the windows were wide. The windows faced the bay, so there was a view of ships sailing, ferries drawing long white wakes after them, tugs working. In addition to the door through which they had entered, there were two other doors—one door on each side—which were closed.

Captain Kirman looked different. It was not the absence of his uniform—Captain Kirman seemed worried and strained. His face was not as ruddy as when Monk and Ham had seen him last.

And his voice was bluff and hearty after the fashion of an actor with stage fright.

"Well, well, well!" Captain Kirman said. "Imagine seeing you fellows. Imagine! This *is* a pleasure."

Monk took the captain's hand, and it was cool and clammy, like holding a live frog.

Monk said, "I never expected to find you in the fish business, skipper."

"Oh, it's a very profitable business," Captain Kirman said vaguely. "By the way, what have you fellows been doing with yourselves?"

"That," Monk explained, "is what we wanted to talk to you about."

"Me?" Captain Kirman seeming puzzled, absently rubbed the scar on his bald spot.

"Yes. You see, something happened to us in South America."

Captain Kirman said vaguely, "I did wonder what had become of you and your friend, Ham Brooks. You disappeared rather suddenly. I presumed that you had decided to stay over, or something. I missed those frightful quarrels you two used to have."

'We didn't stay voluntarily," Monk said.

"The hell!" Captain Kirman's eyes flew wide. "What do you mean?"

"We were jobbed. Framed. Somebody got us thrown in jail on a fake charge. Then, today, when we got back to New York, somebody tried to kill us."

"The same one who framed you?"

"We don't know," Monk said. "But we got some very large suspicions."

Captain Kirman passed a hand through his hair. He seemed to be growing pale. "Why are you talking to me about this?"

"Remember that golden man who got found in the ocean?" Monk inquired.

"Why—of course. Naturally."

"Recollect the black star that was in the sky just before he was found?"

"I—yes. Yes, I recall."

"Well," Monk said, "we want to ask you about some rings that have black-star settings. For instance, we want to ask you about one particular ring, worn by a friend of yours—named Mr. Elezar—"

He did not finish because a man cried out in horror in an office somewhere upstairs, cried out shrilly, "Stop him! He's jumping out of the window."

Doc Savage and the others, turning instinctively toward the window, were in time to see the body fall past.

The cry from the office above, the cry to stop someone who was jumping out of a window, was not loud, but it had arresting quality of horror. It jerked all eyes to the window, so that all of them saw the form tumble past the window.

"A suicide!" Ham gasped. The dapper lawyer jumped to the window. There was no screen, but a glass shield across the lower part kept papers from blowing out. Ham leaned across the shield and peered downward. His voice became stark. "Look!" He pointed.

About ten floors below there was a ledge that was part of the architecture of the building. The figure they had seen fall past the window was sprawled out on this. There was no retaining wall to the ledge and, although the ledge was wide enough that the body could not very well have missed landing on it, there was nothing to prevent the victim toppling over the edge of the ledge, if much moving about was done. That would mean a fall of another ten floors to the street.

While they were staring at the body, it moved. The victim doubled one arm. A leg drew up, and the contorted figure turned half over.

"He's alive!" Monk gasped.

"If he moves, he'll roll off that ledge!" Ham breathed.

Captain Kirman said sharply, "We've got to do something. You get down there and see if you can reach the ledge. I'll telephone the police."

Captain Kirman snatched up the telephone.

Doc Savage, Monk and Ham rushed out of the office. As they passed through the reception room, the office girl gave them a bewildered stare. They did not stop to explain.

Doc Savage took the stairway down; Monk and Ham waited for an elevator. However, all of them reached the floor, ten stories below, at about the same time. Evidently that entire floor of the building was unoccupied. None of the doors was labeled with firm names.

Doc tried a door. It was locked. He put force into twisting and a shoving, and wood groaned and the lock tore out. Inside there was a large room, comprising most of that floor of the building. It had been in disuse for so long that dust was a layer over the floor. The windows across the room was huge expanses of soiled, uncurtained glass.

Monk looked out of a window. And always remembered how he felt. An eerie sensation. He later tried to think of the feeling as like the time Ham put an oyster down his collar, which did not describe it exactly, however. The man was lying there on the ledge, dead now. And it was Captain Kirman.

They stared at Captain Kirman's body, and it was impossible to believe. They had left Captain Kirman in the office ten floors above after they had seen the body here on this ledge. They had seen a body fall past the window. It had not been Captain Kirman. It could not have been. Captain Kirman had been standing in the room with them at the moment. But Captain Kirman was lying here dead.

Monk pulled in a deep breath so charged with astonishment that it whistled.

"He must have a twin brother," he said.

Ham reached for the window lock.

Doc Savage said, "Wait." The bronze man examined the window lock closely. It had not been touched recently. There was dust, and the dust had not been disturbed. No visible indication that the window had been opened for weeks. Doc scrutinized the floor, bending down so that the light slanted across the dust. There were the tracks they had made in the floor dust, but no others.

Ham said, "No one has been in or out of this place for some time." His voice was strange.

Doc opened the window. There was a layer of soot and city grime on the ledge. But there were no tracks. The only marks were a smear or two close to the body, where it had moved a little after it had fallen.

Monk, looking at the body, suddenly paled.

"What's the matter?" Ham asked.

"Remember that scar on top of Captain Kirman's head?" Monk asked.

"Yes."

"Look."

Ham stared. "The same scar on the top of this man's head." *"This is Captain Kirman!"*

Doc Savage suddenly wheeled, raced back across the room,

into the hallway, and took the stairs upward. He kept climbing at full speed, until he reached the floor where Captain Kirman's office was located. The climb did not greatly quicken his breathing, but his metallic features were strangely set as he entered the office.

The middle-aged, competent office girl glanced up. "Yes?" she said.

"Has Captain Kirman gone out since we left?" Doc asked.

She shook her head. "No." She made a move to rise. "Do you wish to see Captain Kirman again? Shall I announce you?"

"Never mind," the bronze man said.

Doc shoved open the door of Captain Kirman's private office and entered. The captain was not there. The window was up, the way they had left it, and nothing appeared to have been disturbed.

Going to the window, Doc looked down. He could see the body lying on the ledge, and Monk, who had climbed out and was standing beside it.

Doc went back to the reception room. He asked the office girl, "You are *sure* Captain Kirman did not leave his office?"

She stared at him for a while. She was puzzled. "Positive," she said.

The bronze man was quite motionless for a time.

Then: "Captain Kirman," he said, "is dead."

The woman seemed to tighten all over. "How?"

"By impossibility it would seem," the bronze man said.

Chapter 10
BEAUTY AND A SPHINX

Ham Brooks arrived in the office, his chest heaving and perspiration popping from the race up the stairs. He gasped, "Was Captain Kirman here?"

"Captain Kirman is the man lying dead there on that ledge."

Ham swallowed. He seemed to become stiff. He said, "That couldn't happen."

Doc turned to the office girl. "Did you hear any strange sounds from the office?"

She tried twice before she could answer. "You mean—after you men rushed out?"

"Yes."

"No."

"You heard nothing?"

"Nothing."

"And you are certain that Captain Kirman did not leave his office."

She nodded. "He was in there after you left."

"How do you know?"

The woman said, "I tried the door. It was locked. I wanted to ask Captain Kirman why you had rushed out in such a hurry. The door was locked. I knocked. He said he did not wish to be interrupted. I heard his voice distinctly."

The flake-gold of the bronze man's eyes seemed to stir with strange animation.

"The door was locked when you tried it?"

"Yes."

"It was *not* locked," he said, "when I came back a moment ago."

She stared at him. She continued to stare, much too fixedly. Then, rather slowly her eyes unfocused, and one turned off slightly to the right, and the other turned up, both showing whites. Her lips parted. Her breath came out slowly and steadily as if her lungs were emptying themselves to the utmost. While she was sagging, Doc caught her. He lowered her to the floor. Her eyes closed.

Ham asked, "Fainted?"

"Yes."

"Why?"

The bronze man did not answer. He put the woman on a desk. He went back into Captain Kirman's office. The other two doors from the office were still closed. He opened the one to the right. It admitted to a small closet. Doc examined the plaster walls of the closet, and found them solid, undisturbed.

The other door let him into another room, larger than the closet, which had one window. There were fish tanks in the room, and fish swam in some of them.

In one of the tanks a cloud of small, brilliant orange-black-blue fish dashed out of sight among water plants the moment the bronze man appeared.

Doc Savage looked at the orange-black-blue fish. He moved over to the tanks, peering into them. A few of the tanks were labeled, but most of them bore no markings. The orange-black-blue fish fled when he came close to them. Some remained motionless in the water and watched him with popeyes.

Doc looked around. Only two fish tanks seemed to be empty. Those two tanks had water and plants like the others. But no visible fish.

Ham came to the door. "What are you doing?"

Doc Savage did not answer immediately. Finally he said, "Looking at the fish."

Ham was puzzled.

"Fish can't tell us anything."

Doc pointed. "Two tanks seem to be empty."

Without commenting on this remark, Doc went back to the office where they had left Captain Kirman. Doc gave attention to the window, then put his head out and examined the walls of the skyscraper. Other windows were closed. Directly across, was the blank brick wall of a building which must be a storage warehouse, judging from complete lack of windows. The bronze man's gaze swept the vicinity, searching for staring faces at windows, but there were none. Nobody appeared to have witnessed the weird death.

Ham said, "This thing couldn't have happened!" And his voice was hoarse.

Doc went to Captain Kirman's desk. There was a long letter opener of ivory lying there. He picked up the opener and returned to the small room which held the fish tanks.

Doc went to the two tanks which seemed to hold no fish.

There proved to be fish in the tanks. When he thrust the paper knife down into the plants, tiny fish flashed into view, and fled madly around the tank, so swiftly that only close observation showed their presence until they again sought cover.

There seemed to be satisfaction on the bronze man's features as he replaced the letter opener on the desk where he had found it.

"Well?" Ham asked.

"Murder," Doc said.

"But how?" Ham demanded. "How did he get killed?"

The bronze man said, "We might call it a case of death by impossibility, for the time being."

Ham stared at him. But Doc's expression, as far as Ham could see, was one of unchanged seriousness.

"What . . . what do you mean, Doc?"

Doc Savage seemed not to hear the question. So Ham did not repeat his query. Ham was acquainted with the habit which the bronze man had of becoming conveniently deaf when he was asked something which, for a reason, he did not wish to commit himself by answering.

The telephone rang. Doc picked up the instrument. "Yes. . . . Yes, speaking," he said.

Doc used Captain Kirman's voice.

Ham gave a violent jump, then looked sheepish, deciding his nerves must be going bad. But it was eerie to hear Captain Kirman's voice speaking in the room—or an imitation of the captain's tone and delivery that was of startling fidelity. Ham hurried over and pressed his ear close enough to hear what came over the wire.

Doc listened to a woman's voice say, "This is Elva Boone, captain."

"Yes," Doc replied.

"Listen, I've stumbled onto something," Elva Boone said. "I think it may be what we have been hunting for. I think your life may be in danger."

"That is interesting," Doc Savage said.

The girl—the feminine voice was young—asked, "Where is Ruth Dorman?"

Doc Savage—although memory must have flashed through his mind of the phrase *"Watch Ruth Dorman,"* written on the bit of paper in the pocket of the man who had been machine-gunned—did not hesitate. He said, "I do not know where she is just now."

"Can you find her?"

"Well—not immediately, I am afraid."

Ham was spellbound by admiration for the voice-imitating job. He had heard Captain Kirman talk a great deal while they were on the *Virginia Dare,* and he knew the perfect imitation of the captain's voice which Doc Savage was managing was uncanny.

Elva Boone asked, "Can you meet me right away?"

"Yes."

"Good. I will be at Ruth Dorman's apartment."

Doc Savage, without changing expression, said, "If I am in danger, it is possible I am being watched. Maybe it might be better if we did not meet at Ruth Dorman's apartment. Perhaps a place near there would be better."

"How about the drugstore on the corner two blocks down the street?"

"What corner would that be?"

"Eighty-sixth Street and Broadway," said Elva Boone.

"Oh—are you uptown now?" Doc asked.

"Yes."

"That's funny," Doc said. "I saw a woman a while ago that I thought—what are you wearing? A brown dress?"

"A gray suit," Elva Boone said.

"It wasn't you, then," Doc told her. "Well, I will be there in twenty minutes."

He hung up.

Ham said admiringly, "You used a nice trick to find out what she would be wearing."

They took a subway uptown. Because the subway was faster, and they happened to catch the rearmost car, whereupon they moved to the back, where there was privacy.

Ham said, "I had a last look at the office girl. She will be all right. Just fainted."

Monk muttered, "I wonder why she fainted."

"Guess it was just shock over finding out her boss had gone out of the window," Ham said.

Monk frowned at the dapper lawyer. "You think he committed suicide?"

"Captain Kirman?"

"Well—he was the dead man, wasn't he?"

Ham said, "When the body fell past the window, Captain Kirman was in the office with us."

"But the captain is dead on that ledge."

"A man can't be dead, and still stand and talk to you."

Monk rubbed his jaw, and felt of his necktie as if it was tight. It was a gaudy necktie, one he had chosen to offend Ham's taste. "Captain Kirman *did* talk to us, didn't he? He told us to get down there and keep the man from rolling off the ledge, while he got busy and telephoned the police. Isn't that what he said?"

"Something like that."

"Well, what happened?"

Monk looked uneasy. "Stop harping on it!"

"Well, how could a thing like that happen? A man can't be dead and still stand and talk to you," Ham said.

Monk said, "You remember that golden man they found in the ocean?"

Ham grimaced. "It will be a long time before I forget *him.*"

"Well," Monk reminded, "there were some strange things about him. He foretold the future. He knew things it didn't look like any man could know. He was unnatural. Spooky."

Ham stared strangely at Monk, but he did not say anything more.

There was a girl in a gray suit waiting in the drugstore at Eighty-sixth and Broadway so they decided she must be Elva

Boone. She was a tall girl, and there was a curved delight about her that caused Monk to shape a whistling mouth of admiration, but no sound, and scowl sidewise at Ham.

There was actually more than prettiness about this girl. There was strength under her curves, strength of spirit and of will and of ability. She had dark hair. Her eyes were blue, like clear Christmas skies. Her mouth was a warm full-blown rose.

Monk strode forward and took the elbow of the girl in the gray suit before she was aware that he was in the neighborhood.

He asked, "You are Miss Elva Boone, I presume?"

The girl stared at them.

She shook her head.

"I'm sorry," she said. "My name is Jalma Coverly. You have made a mistake—or you are crazy."

Monk looked foolish.

Ham burst out in a chuckle, Monk looked so foolish, while Monk grew red-necked and sheep-faced and peered at him malevolently. They were going to have trouble over this girl, both of them suspected.

Doc Savage turned partly away. He was good at ventriloquism, but no one is ever perfect at it, particularly when imitating an unfamiliar voice while at the same time getting a ventriloquial effect. Doc imitated Captain Kirman's voice, and made it low and excited. "Run, Elva! Run!" he said imperatively. "It's a trick!"

Fright flashed over the girl's face. She half turned in an effort to escape. Doc's hand leaped out and trapped her wrist.

"You gave yourself away," the bronze man said quietly. "You are Elva Boone."

Ham, his face getting sober, said, "We had better go somewhere and talk this over."

Elva Boone was glaring at them to cover fright. "You must be crazy!" she said.

Ham shrugged. "We might be. If we are, it would explain some of the things that have been happening."

They moved out of the drugstore before Doc Savage spoke, then the bronze man said, "Miss Boone, you have some information. We want it."

The girl was not impressed. "I'll tell you nothing," she said defiantly.

Doc Savage had no idea of the exact location of the apartment of the mysterious Ruth Dorman, although it must be somewhere within two blocks of this spot. The neighborhood was a section of large apartment houses. An area of two blocks radius would include thousands of apartments.

Doc addressed Elva Boone.

"We will go to Ruth Dorman's apartment and talk this over," he said confidently, as if he knew perfectly well where the place was.

The complete casual confidence in his voice worked. The girl was fooled, and she led them to Ruth Dorman's apartment.

There was one incident before they got to the apartment.

They met a policeman.

Elva Boone tried to have them arrested. "Officer, these men are kidnaping me!" she gasped.

Doc Savage drew the patrolman aside and produced from his billfold a card which identified him as a high-ranking police official. The patrolman examined the card, and in addition recognized Doc Savage, so he was satisfied. He grinned at Elva Boone and walked away.

The girl got the wrong idea of what had happened, for she had seen the billfold.

"You bribed him!" she said angrily.

Chapter 11
SISTERS

Ruth Dorman's apartment proved to be an eleven-room duplex that was a semipenthouse, with ceilings that were high, the furniture all period stuff, and good. On the library wall was a Persian animal rug that was typical of the apartment—it was a rug made in silk and silver, a rug which had taken decades to weave, and which was very old, and which had cost a small fortune even when first woven.

"Good taste," Ham said, glancing about appreciatively.

Doc Savage pocketed a tiny, ingenius metal probe with which he had picked the apartment lock. He moved through the rooms, searching, but found no one.

"Servants?" he asked Elva Boone.

She glared at him. "You should know. You have been watching the place for days!"

Doc asked, *"We* have been watching this apartment?"

"Yes!"

A trace of grimness came over the bronze man's face, and he turned to Monk.

Monk said, "Doc, if this joint is being watched, maybe Ham and I had better find out who is doing it."

But Doc Savage shook his head. "We will put Long Tom, Johnny and Renny on that job."

The bronze man found a telephone and got his headquarters on the wire. Renny, answering, said, "Holy cow! Doc, you remember that piece of paper you gave us to trace? The one with 'Watch Ruth Dorman,' written on it."

Doc asked, "Have you traced it?"

"Well, to some extent. It was a narrow piece of stationery of good quality, and we decided it was probably torn off a sheet of hotel stationery. You know hotels generally supply their stationery to the guest rooms in wide and narrow sheets. Well, we concluded this was a narrow sheet. The only trouble with the theory was that this paper was coral pink. The high quality suggested a swanky hotel, so we began calling the snazzy hotels and asking if their stationery was coral pink. It turned out to be the Royal Rex."

"How about the blue ink with which the note was written?" Doc inquired.

"The Royal Rex supplies blue ink to its guest rooms," Renny said. "Do you want us to go to the hotel? That's not the biggest hotel in town, but it comes pretty near being the most ritzy. I don't know how on earth we would find the person who wrote that note."

"Here is what I called you about," Doc said. He gave the address of Ruth Dorman's apartment. "It is possible someone may be watching this apartment," he said. "So you and Long Tom and Johnny come over here and search the neighborhood. But be careful."

"Have you found out what this is all about yet?" Renny asked.

"Not yet."

Ham came in from another room. He had been searching the apartment.

"A man lives here," he announced.

Elva Boone stared at him. There was surprise in her aquamarine-colored eyes. "And where else," she asked, "would you expect my sister's husband to live?"

Ham held his mouth open for a moment. "Your *sister's* husband?"

"Of course," said the girl.

"Ruth Dorman is your sister?"

"Yes."

"Go on."

She stared at him. "What do you mean—go on?"

Ham explained patiently, "We are after information. You have some that we need."

The girl compressed her lips, and did not say anything. Her manner indicated she did not intend to answer.

Doc suggested, "We might look in her handbag."

At that, the girl's lips parted, and she made a gesture of half lifting her hand, but she did not speak.

Doc found the usual woman-litter in her handbag—and one other article. The article was a pin of yellow gold with a setting in the shape of a black star that was edged with crimson. It was exactly same kind of star that they had seen in the two rings.

Doc showed the girl the star. "What does this mean?" he inquired.

She would not answer.

An hour later, they had got nothing out of her except stubborn refusals to talk. Then the police arrived with Mrs. Ruth Dorman—alias the office girl from Captain Kirman's office. Mrs. Dorman was pale, but not hysterical. Her composure, as a whole, was good.

Doc Savage consulted the policeman in charge, asking, "What did you learn?"

The officer shrugged. "Practically nothing." He glanced sidewise at Mrs. Dorman. "I'm not sure but that this woman doesn't know more than she is telling, though. But she is an important person—or her husband is—so we can't just lock her up on suspicion."

"Important? In what way?"

"Money."

"She is wealthy?"

"Her husband is."

"Then why was she working as Captain Kirman's office girl?"

"Just to learn about fish, she says. She was interested in rare fish, and was working there to learn about them. Or so she claims." The officer frowned. "That was a little funny, too. Captain Kirman didn't know anything about rare fish."

Doc Savage was thoughtful for a moment. "You mean that Captain Kirman was not particularly interested in rare fish?"

"Matter of fact, he didn't own those fish in the office, even the fittings in the place. Another guy had financed him."

"Who was Captain Kirman's backer?"

"Old codger named Benjamin Opsall."

"Have you learned anything about Opsall?"

"We haven't talked to him. Opsall's butler said he wasn't home. But we've inquired around. He is a rare-fish dealer, all right, one of the biggest."

"How about Mrs. Dorman's husband?"

"Fred Dorman is his name."

"What is his business?"

"Broker. Big business man. As dough-heavy as they come."

"How long has Ruth Dorman been married to him?"

"Little over two years."

"Children?"

"One. It's adopted. Boy. About five years old. He's away at boarding school."

That was about all the information the policeman could give. He departed.

Chapter 12
TRAIL TO THE WIZARD

Where Elva Boone got her two dueling pistols was something that forever remained a mystery—but she got them, and they were loaded. It nearly cost Monk his left ear to learn about their being loaded, the bullet missing the ear by no more than an inch or so. Elva Boone had refused to talk. Mrs. Dorman likewise had refused. It had become more and more obvious that both women were scared out of their wits—not frightened of Doc Savage and his men, but afraid of something else.

The mystery of where the guns came from was doubly confounding because, although Elva Boone had moved around a little, Monk and Ham had watched her. It was a pleasure to watch her.

But suddenly she was pointing two dueling pistols at them, which was no pleasure. The guns were short and blue. The girl's voice was elaborately calm. She said, "You men will get down on the floor and stretch out."

Monk then had the bright idea which he later regretted. He said,

"Nobody ever keeps dueling pistols loaded while they're lying around the house."

Elva Boone, her voice like fine metal, said, "You wouldn't believe me if I told you these are loaded, would you?"

"No," Monk said.

The girl then pulled the trigger of the left-hand gun, and it made such a shocking noise that a vase full of flowers upset on a side table. Monk squawked, dodged so violently that he nearly followed the vase in upsetting.

"The other one is also loaded," the girl said. She backed toward the door. "Ruth, you come with me," she ordered.

Mrs. Dorman put her fingertips against her teeth. She was pale. "But, Elva, is this wise—"

"Come on," her sister said grimly, "I have an idea."

Mrs. Dorman obeyed. The two women backed out. The door was slammed, and the lock clicked.

Ham said, "There's a back door!" and whipped through dining room, kitchen and storeroom, to get to the rear door. But as he approached it, he heard the lock clicking.

"They got here ahead of me," Ham roared angrily. "We're locked in!"

He rushed back, joined Monk and his eyes hunted for Doc Savage. "Where'd Doc go?" he demanded.

Monk pointed.

The bronze man had jacked up one of the window screens, and had swung out on the window ledge. There was hard concrete sidewalk and street more than twenty floors below. The building was not of brick, but of block-stone construction, with a space at the joints. But not much space. Hardly safe purchase for fingertips. Doc started up.

Monk moved over to the window—looking at the wall Doc was scaling, peering down onto the street—and had the feeling that his hair was standing on end. He knew Doc possessed fabulous physical strength. He had seen the bronze man do things that looked impossible. But that did not keep ice out of his veins.

The bronze man reached the roof. There was a small superstructure there which housed the elevator mechanism. The door was hasped shut, but not locked. He got inside.

The machinery of one elevator was operating. Doc stopped it.

Ten minutes later, when Elva Boone and Ruth Dorman hurried out of the apartment house—the elevator had stopped dead between two floors, and it had been necessary to send the building superintendent to the roof before it could be started again—Doc Savage, Monk and Ham were out of the building. They were at the far end of the block, waiting in a taxicab.

"That good-lookin' gal has got that pistol in her purse," Monk said grimly. "Notice how she carries the purse, her hand in it."

The two women headed in the opposite direction, walking fast.

Ham asked, "See any sign of Renny, Long Tom or Johnny? They should be here and watching this place by now."

Doc Savage pointed. "Notice the telephone lineman."

"Eh?"

"In the center of the street."

New York City telephone lines are carried in underground conduits which can be reached in most cases, through manholes in the pavement, which accounted for the fact that the "lineman" was seated on the rim of an open manhole in the center of the street. A regulation telephone company truck was parked at the curb, and a protective railing and red warning flags had been erected around the manhole.

The "lineman" sat there with an acetylene cutting torch in his hand. He wore the kind of hood that welders wear, and he was going through the motions of welding something below the lip of the manhole.

Ham chuckled. "Long Tom, isn't it?"

Monk said, "That's a slick disguise he's thought up. I didn't even recognize him."

A cab cruised down the street, and Elva Boone hailed it quickly. The two women got in.

Doc said to the driver of their own machine, "Trail that cab— the one that the two women just got in."

The driver looked around. He was suspicious, and not afraid. He said, "What is this, pals?" in a tough voice.

"We're detectives," Monk told him, altering the truth a little.

That made it different, and the driver put the cab in motion. They proceeded to follow Elva Boone and Mrs. Ruth Dorman south and east to Central Park.

Doc Savage made no move to stop the two women. Monk and Ham did not question him as to his reasons. They had seen Doc do strange things before. They had seen him let a suspected person apparently get away, and lead him to the higher-ups.

"What about Renny, Long Tom and Johnny?" Ham asked.

Doc said, "They can stay where they are. If anyone is watching the Dorman apartment house, they may be able to spot whoever it is. Anyway, we have no means of communicating with them without attracting attention."

Monk eyed the bronze man. "What do you think is back of this, Doc? Don't it look as if it hitches up, in some way, to that golden man they found in the ocean?"

"Apparently it does," Doc admitted.

The taxi they were following moved slowly. When the machine was in the park, the two women abruptly alighted and dismissed the cab. They walked for a while, seemingly doing nothing but strolling.

Doc and his men kept out of sight.

Without having done anything except stroll, the two women took another taxi.

"What was the idea of *that*?" Monk pondered. "Did they just take a walk to calm their nerves?"

Doc Savage said nothing.

Elva Boone and Mrs. Ruth Dorman ended their trip in front of a building of distinctly startling appearance. The structure was near the swanky Murray Hill section, one of the old brownstones. But fire escapes and every hint of ornamentation had been stripped from the face of the structure, and the building was painted a somber black.

The two women talked to their cab driver for a while. The driver shook his head—some money changed hands—and there was a little more conversation. The driver nodded.

When Monk glanced at Doc Savage, the bronze man was watching the two women through a small pocket telescope which Monk happened to know was powerful for its size.

Doc said, "They told the taxi driver they are going into the black building, then through an alleyway to a side street, where the driver is to pick them up."

Startled, Monk was about to demand how Doc had found that out. Then he understood. The telescope—Doc Savage was a skilled lip reader.

"Monk, you keep an eye on the front of the place, in case we were mistaken," Doc suggested.

Monk nodded. He waited until Elva Boone and Ruth Dorman had entered the black building, then got out of the cab. Doc and Ham rode around to the opposite side of the block. Doc said, "Ham, you stay in the cab, two blocks down the street, and watch for signals." Ham nodded, moved away in the machine.

A moment later, Doc himself was in the street, crouching back of a parked car for concealment.

Elva Boone and Mrs. Dorman had stepped out of an areaway. They seemed familiar with the vicinity, and glanced about for their cab. The hack was not there. The women waited for a few moments, obviously growing more nervous. It dawned on them that their cab driver had gotten the idea there was something wrong, and had decided not to have anything more to do with them.

Elva Boone and Ruth Dorman walked to a drugstore, where they ordered soft drinks. They sat at a table.

The drugstore had a side door. Doc got through the side entrance and into a booth without being observed. From that spot, he could watch the faces of both women, and, although it was impossible to hear what they were saying, he could read their lips without difficulty.

Elva Boone was talking energetically, driving home some kind of an argument which ended, "—so that we can keep you out of this, Ruth. The fact that you were in Captain Kirman's office when he was murdered—I'm convinced he was murdered—was unlucky as the dickens. But the police don't suspect you. Or if they do, they certainly don't suspect the real facts. You can tell your husband you were merely working there to learn about fish."

"I wish," said Ruth Dorman, "that we could tell the whole evil truth."

"We couldn't prove any of it, Ruth."

"I know. Only—"

"And *you* don't want your husband to find out about it."

Ruth Dorman shuddered. "No, Fred mustn't even guess."

Elva Boone said, "However, if you were smart, you would tell him."

"No, no! You know Fred—the way he believes. And the way he would feel about a thing like this."

Elva Boone frowned at her sister. "You were an idiot, Ruth, to get involved in it."

Mrs. Dorman nodded dumbly.

Elva reached over impulsively and squeezed her sister's hand. "However, I think my plan will work. Doc Savage and his two friends trailed us—trailed us right up to the Dark Sanctuary. They will think we went there, so they will investigate the place. Investigate it—that's what we want them to do."

Again Mrs. Dorman nodded.

Elva added, "Let's get out of this neighborhood. We've led the bloodhounds to the rat hole where we think they should do their digging. Now we can sit back and see what happens."

"I hope you're right, Elva."

"It can't hurt anything," said the positive young woman. "From what I've heard about Doc Savage, if anyone can crack this nut, he can."

The two women left the drugstore and hailed a taxicab. While they were doing that, Doc Savage stood where the sisters could not see him and signaled Ham, semaphore style, with a handkerchief.

"Follow them and RARHQ," Doc wigwagged.

Ham acknowledged that he understood. The code letters RARHQ meant, "Report to the automatic recorder at headquarters." In the bronze man's skyscraper laboratory was a gadget connected to the telephone wires which automatically recorded incoming calls together with whatever the caller said.

Chapter 13
DARK SANCTUARY

Monk Mayfair was standing in front of an apartment house with a pencil and paper in hand pretending to be a newspaper reporter in search of material for a feature story about the strange things that apartment-house doormen see. Standing there, Monk could see the black building which Elva Boone and Mrs. Dorman had pretended to enter.

"Where's my pet hog?" Monk asked Doc Savage.

"With Ham in the cab," Doc explained. "Ham is trailing the two women."

Monk joined Doc, and they walked down the street. Monk said, "I asked that doorman about the black building. He says it's the Dark Sanctuary."

"The what?"

"Dark Sanctuary."

"Did he tell you what it is?"

"I asked him, but he said he didn't know. He said a lot of limousines and chauffeured town cars drive up there in the course of a day, though."

"The two women want us to investigate this Dark Sanctuary."

"That's why they led us here?"

"Yes."

"It ain't a trick, maybe? The dames didn't maybe hope to lead us into a trap?"

The bronze man remained silent on that point. As they approached the severely plain-black front of the building, a car was just pulling into an arched driveway which penetrated into one side of the building and out the other. The machine was a fifteen-thousand-dollar imported town car with chauffeur and footman in uniform.

Monk said, "Hey, they sure have the ritz around the place."

Doc headed straight for the door.

Monk was uneasy. "You figure on barging right into that joint, Doc?"

Doc Savage nodded.

By the way of preliminary precaution, Monk took his trouser belt up a couple of notches, so that he would not lose that essential garment if the action became brisk. He altered his necktie knot, tying in a knot of his own invention which was not fancy to look at, but which had the very good virtue that, if a foe grabbed hold of the necktie in a fight, the necktie would come off Monk's neck instead of choking him.

"Well, let's hope it's a keg of nails," Monk said.

The door was of some type of black wood, and the use of black coloring at the portal, together with the black coloration throughout, had achieved an effect of dignity. There was no effect of garishness about the place—nothing theatrical, nothing carnival. But it was impressive.

At the door stood a man in a black uniform, a uniform not completely black, but touched off with deep scarlet.

Monk stared at the scarlet touches on the uniform, and remembered the black star with the crimson edging.

Monk said to the doorman, "We are newspapermen. We have orders to get a story out of this place for our paper."

A forbidding expression came over the doorman's face. "Nothing doing, pal!" he snapped. He must have touched a button, because three other men, dressed like himself, and husky, appeared. The doorman said, "You two birds clear out."

Doc Savage's voice was quiet. "Possibly," he said, "this might make some difference." He displayed credentials which proved he was a police official.

The doorman hesitated. Finally he told one of the men he had summoned, "Go get Gallehue."

"What the hell is cops doing here?" the man asked.

"Go get Gallehue."

The man went away.

Out of a mouth corner, Monk said, "You hear that, Doc? Gallehue. There was a Sam Gallehue on the *Virginia Dare*. Reckon it's the same bird."

Still with no expression on his metallic features, Doc Savage turned to the doorman and asked, "You are sending for Mr. Sam Gallehue?"

"Yes," the doorman said shortly. "What about it?"

Monk said, "It's lovely. We're old pals."

Mr. Sam Gallehue thought it was lovely, too; at least he told them so effusively while he pumped their hands—Monk's first— and said, "Oh, how delightful. Quite. I'm so glad to see you, really I am."

Monk returned the handshake as enthusiastically as if he had hold of a dead fish and said, "This is the chief—Doc Savage."

Mr. Sam Gallehue additionally was delighted no end, he said. He had heard of Doc Savage, he added, and now that he was meeting the bronze man, it was one of the moments of his life. Really a pleasure. Would they have some cocktails? He consulted his wrist watch. There was a swell place around the corner which was especially nice at this hour.

Monk, with not too much tact—courtesy was not Monk's long shot—said, "It's this funny black building we're interested in."

Mr. Sam Gallehue blinked. "Beg pardon?"

"What kind of a joint is it, Sammy?"

"Joint?" Mr. Gallehue was horrified. He glanced about nervously. "Suppose we go to my private office," he muttered.

The private office was not black, but it was darkly wooden in tone. Nothing was gaudy, but also nothing was very cheap. The effect was one of rich dignity.

Sam Gallehue pulled out chairs and patted the seats as if to make sure they were soft enough for his visitors. But he did not look happy.

"I hope, I sincerely hope"—Gallehue was looking at Doc Savage—"that you are not here in your official capacity."

Doc asked quietly, "What would my official capacity be?"

"Or—by that, I mean"—Mr. Sam Gallehue ran a finger around the inside of his collar—"that I have heard you are a man who, and I can say so without exaggerating, is known extensively— known in the far corners of the earth I may truthfully say—as one who devotes himself, his energies and the services of his organization to righting what are considered to be wrongs."

Monk put in, "Then we're to take it there's a wrong around here you're afraid we might try to right?"

Sam Gallehue sprang up in alarm. "Oh, my! My, no!" He popped his eyes at them. "Surely, you're kidding me! Surely!"

Monk watched the man and thinking that this was the first instance, in the time that he had known Mr. Sam Gallehue, that he had heard the man disagree with anyone.

"Just what kind of racket you got here?" Monk asked bluntly.

Sam Gallehue paced over nervously and opened the door, looked out, then closed it. There was no one listening, if that was what he had wanted to find out. He faced them and opened his mouth, but, instead of speaking, walked over and got a drink of water. Finally, "You remember the golden man found in the ocean?" he blurted.

Monk blinked. "I'll say I remember the golden man!"

"You recall also," said Sam Gallehue, "that he was an . . . ah . . . shall we say—unusual person."

"There was plenty screwy about him."

Mr. Gallehue was displeased. "That is—blasphemy!"

"Blasphemy!"

"What the heck!" Monk scowled. "Who you trying to kid?"

Mr. Gallehue's tone became dignified and firm. "The golden man," he said, "is a person with powers beyond those of mortal ken."

The manner in which the statement was made, coupled with the quietly rich atmosphere of the room, was so impressive that Monk discovered himself glancing uneasily at Doc Savage, then at the floor. "You trying to tell us," Monk muttered, "that he's . . . he's—"

"No—not a supreme deity," Mr. Sam Gallehue said with effective dignity. "I have never put forth a flat statement on that point." He hesitated, then added solemnly, "It is my own personal conviction that such must be the case, and I did not arrive at such a conviction lightly, I assure you. In the beginning, I was a skeptic, like yourselves. But I assure you solemnly that I am no longer a skeptic."

Monk scratched his head. "I don't get this."

Mr. Sam Gallehue said, "In the beginning, I realized that this golden man from the sea was not an ordinary mortal. I was, I think, his first follower. The first believer. And I am now his business manager and backer."

"You put up the money for this place?" Monk indicated their surroundings.

"Yes." Mr. Sam Gallehue nodded for emphasis. "And for the Mountain Sanctuary as well."

Doc Savage, who had spoken almost no words, now entered the conversation. "You handle the money?" the bronze man asked.

"Yes."

"Do you charge fees?"

"No."

"Then how do you get the money?"

"Everything," said Mr. Sam Gallehue proudly, "is voluntary donation."

"Then this is a cult?"

"I do not like that word—cult," the other replied in an injured tone.

"But if we wish to be vulgar, we might call it a cult?"

"I— Yes."

Doc Savage stood up. "In that case, I believe we would like to talk to this golden man."

Mr. Sam Gallehue shook his head hurriedly. "I am sorry, indeed I am, but you will have to make an appointment, and I must warn you that it will be several days before you can expect an audience—if you are so fortunate as to get one at all."

Doc Savage's flake-gold eyes fixed on Gallehue intently. "Take us to him. And never mind announcing us in advance."

"I—" Gallehue was perspiring.

Monk put in a growled warning. "There's several things this golden wizard of yours better clear up. There's the mystery of who got me and Ham locked up in a South American jail. There's the question of how Captain Kirman was murdered. And there's more about Ruth Dorman and Elva Boone." Monk scowled. "How would you like for us to run you and your cult into jail?"

"I—" Gallehue shuddered. "Jail! You couldn't do that. We are not guilty of anything."

"You would have a chance in court to prove that."

Gallehue wiped his face. "I— Come with me," he said finally.

They followed Gallehue. Monk, walking close to Doc, muttered, "So my friend Gallehue brought the golden man to New York and set him up as a cult leader. Smart idea. They been makin' dough, too. From that limousine trade, they must be hookin' the big-money trade."

Doc said, "Mr. Gallehue."

"Yes."

"Do the members of your cult wear black star rings or pins as insignia?"

Gallehue complained, "I wish you would not refer to it as a cult."

"Do the members wear a black star insignia?"

"Yes. That is the way our—believers—identify themselves."

Doc Savage had never seen the golden man before—Doc was *sure* of that—but the golden man arose from where he was sitting in a darkly dignified chair in a darkly dignified room and extended his hand and said, "I am very glad to see you, Mr. Savage."

Doc, amazed, said, "You know me?"

The golden man seemed not to hear the inquiry. He studied Doc for a few moments, then said in a deeply impressive, solemn voice, "Since that stormy night when you were born on the tiny schooner *Orion* in the shallow cove at the north end of Andros Island, you have done much good, and many things that are great."

Doc was floored, figuratively. Not by the praise—praise did not impress him, and it was always embarrassing—but by the fact that this golden man knew the exact place of his birth. It was astounding. Doc himself had known of no living man who had those facts. His five aides did not know. It was in no written record.

The golden man added, "You will be grieved to know your friend, Baron Orrest Karl Lestzky, is dying in Vienna tonight. He will be dead in another three hours, and, as you know, it will be a great loss, and very sad. Lestzky is one of the few great surgeons who really understands your new brain-operating technique, as I know you are aware."

Doc Savage, trying not to be impressed, *was* impressed.

Doc asked, "You know Lestzky?"

"Only as I knew you—if he would walk into this room." The golden man seemed to be weary. He leaned forward, took his face in his hands. He sat there. Doc watched him, studying him with rigid intentness.

"It is sad," the golden man said dully. "Very sad. I am tired in my soul."

Then he got up and walked out of the room. He said no more. The door shut behind him. They could hear his footsteps, heavy, for a time, going away. Then silence.

Doc got up and moved through rooms to the street exit, saying nothing, and left the Dark Sanctuary.

Monk followed. Monk didn't know what to think.

Chapter 14
THE FISH MAN

Benjamin Opsall met Doc Savage and Monk Mayfair on the semicircular driveway that was like a tunnel in the front of the Dark Sanctuary. A limousine and chauffeur stood there, and Opsall was walking back and forth, looking completely delighted with the world and with himself.

When he saw Mr. Sam Gallehue—Gallehue had followed Doc and Monk to the exit—Opsall dashed forward, saying, "Oh, there you are, Mr. Gallehue!" Opsall thrust a slip of paper into Mr. Sam Gallehue's hands. "I want you to have this!" Opsall exclaimed. "It's a small expression of my gratitude!"

Gallehue looked at the slip of paper, which was a check. The figures for which it was made out were large. Gallehue glanced apologetically at Doc Savage, then took Opsall's elbow, and the pair moved to one side.

From the corner of his mouth, Monk whispered, "String figures on that check looked like the tail of a comet."

Doc Savage studied Benjamin Opsall. Opsall had large moist eyes and a large moist mouth, and he was wide and solid. His skin was clear with health, drowned by the sun—or sun lamp—and, even without the limousine, he would have looked prosperous. Around fifty was his age.

The Gallehue-Opsall conference broke up when Sam Gallehue pocketed the check, then shook Opsall's hands and patted Opsall on the back.

Doc Savage said, so that only Monk could hear, "Trail this Opsall."

"Eh? Why?"

"He is the man who set Captain Kirman up in the rare-fish business."

"Oh!" Monk pulled in a deep breath. "I forgot that."

Trailing Benjamin Opsall proved unexpectedly easy, for Opsall came over to Doc and Monk. He grabbed their hands. "Two more *Believers*, aren't you? That makes you friends of mine." He laughed delightedly. "We're all friends in a wonderful peace, aren't we?"

"Let's hope so," Doc Savage said conservatively.

Opsall smiled at them. "Are you coming? Going?" He held open the door of his limousine. "Can I give you a lift?"

Doc Savage said, "That would be very kind."

The bronze man got into the limousine, and Monk followed. There were jump seats which folded down, and the chauffeur lowered one of these for Monk. Opsall climbed in, and the big machine got in motion.

Opsall proceeded to talk a blue streak. "I've been a *Believer* for over a month now, and I'm more sincere now than on the day I became one."

He effused for some minutes about the wonders of the golden man, and the spiritual benefits of being a *Believer.* There were financial benefits, too, he imparted—and the story of what was behind his joy came out. It seemed that the golden man had informed him several days previously that a certain European nation was going to confiscate the foreign property of an American company. This had happened on schedule, and the stock of the company had naturally tobogganed. Opsall, having sold a great deal of the stock short, naturaly had made money from the debacle. "A cleaning!" he declared.

"This being a *Believer* must be profitable," Monk said.

"Oh, enormously." Opsall leaned forward and patted Monk's shoulder. "But, mind you, I would be a *Believer* even if there wasn't a damned cent of profit in it. By the way, would you gentleman care to drop in at my place of business for a spot of tea?"

"What sort of business have you?" Doc asked innocently.

"I deal in rare fish."

"Tropicals?"

"Yes. Maybe you might like to see my stock. It is one of the most complete in existence."

"That would be interesting," Doc admitted.

Monk grinned.

The Opsall rare-fish establishment was impressive, there being large showrooms with tanks containing species of aquarium fish— dwarf gouramis, betta fighting fish, and other bubble-nest builders; platys, helleri, and various types of live bearers, together with egg-layer types such as cichlasomma meeki, neon tetras and white cloud mountain fish. Opsall recited the names of the fish rapidly, leading Monk to mutter, "Sounds like Greek to me."

"Your terminology on chemistry would sound as confusing to me," Opsall assured him.

Doc Savage asked, "Mr. Opsall, are you acquainted with Captain Kirman?"

Opsall looked up quickly. "Oh, yes."

"Known Captain Kirman very long?"

"Well, only a few weeks."

"Business associate of yours?"

"Not exactly."

"But you set him up in the tropical-fish business?"

Opsall nodded slightly. "May I ask why you seem so interested?"

Monk answered that question. "Captain Kirman died today. It was no natural death."

Opsall showed distress. "Damn it, he owes me—" He hesitated, then said apologetically, "I . . . I'm sorry that the first thing I thought of was the money he owes me. I suppose I'm vulgar and mercenary."

He gestured for them to follow him, and moved away. "We will go to my private office," he explained. "I'm distressed by this news. I need a drink."

They entered the private office, Opsall opening the door and stepping inside and turning to hold the door ajar for them.

"Some place!" Monk exclaimed.

"My private greenhouse," Opsall said. "I use it to grow plants to augment our displays of rare fish."

One wall of the office was glass, and beyond was a view of a small private greenhouse filled with colorful tropical and semitropical flowers. A second wall was a huge aquarium in which fish of all colors and sizes swam among water plants that were as exotic as the fish. The other two walls were ordinary plaster.

"I'll say it's some place!" a distinctly unpleasant voice informed Monk.

Men with guns—there were four of them—had been standing, two on each side of the door, and they now fanned out quickly so that, if necessary, there would be room for bullets.

"Señors, you are slow getting back," one said. He was a thin man with a scar under his left eye.

Opsall ogled them. "But I don't know you!"

"Hey, Doc!" Monk was pointing at the man with the scar. "Doc, this is that guy who framed me and Ham in South America."

Doc Savage remained silent, although he could have added another pair of the four men to the identified list. The pair had been members of the group who had tried to waylay Monk and Ham in front of the skyscraper headquarters.

The thin man with the scar went to a desk which stood in the center of the floor. When he turned, he had a tray and glasses. Water was in the glasses.

The man uncorked a bottle, poured a part of its contents into each of the glasses.

"This will only put you to sleep, señors," he said. "Drink it. No harm. Good. *Mucho bueno.*"

Doc and Monk had caught the odor of the stuff. They knew what it was. Poison, which would be working slow if it took more than five minutes to kill them.

Doc Savage spoke three words in a strange language. The words translated into, "Hold your breath."

The language was ancient Mayan, a vernacular spoken by the Central American civilization of Maya centuries ago, but now a tongue so lost in the civilized world probably no one but Doc Savage and his associates understood or could speak it. Doc and his men used it for communication without being understood by others.

Doc, after he spoke, and as if afraid of the menacing guns, lifted both arms slowly so that his hands were above his head. His arms were not straight up, and the right one was doubled and tight as if it was making a muscle. The bulge of biceps sinew swelled up against his forearm until there was crunching sound as a fragile container inside his sleeve was crushed. It was a small noise, and no one noticed.

He waited. The gas released from the container he had broken was odorless, colorless, potent—it would induce harmless unconsciousness with uncanny speed. And it had an additional quality of becoming ineffective after it had mixed with the air for slightly more than a minute.

Unfortunately, the anæsthetic gas did not first bring down the thin man with the scar. It was one of the others, and he was very susceptible to the gas, because it got him before the others had breathed enough to be greatly affected. The man caved down slowly.

The scarred man yelled. He fired his gun straight at Doc Savage's chest. Then he sprang backward, fleeing wildly.

The bullet knocked Doc back, although he was wearing a bulletproof undergarment of alloy mesh. That protection was at best an emergency one, and the bullet struck a blow greater than any fist.

Monk threw out a hand, clutched a chair, and hurled, all in one move. The chair hit a foe. The fellow reeled, upset, lay where he fell—either the chair had knocked him senseless, or it was the anæsthetic gas, for he had fallen where the gas should be strongest.

Doc got back his balance, then leaped forward, making for the thin man with the scar. The thin man fired his gun, but missed completely. Somehow that must have given him the idea Doc was bulletproof. He took to flight. The quickest escape route was through the glass wall into the greenhouse, so the man put his hands over his face and plunged into the glass wall. Glass broke, came down in jangling sheets.

That left only one assailant in the room. Monk made for that one. Monk's hands were big and hairy and hungry in front of him. The intended victim saw Monk, tried to escape. He was slow. Monk's fist made a sound like a fistful of mud falling on a floor, and the man walked backward, senseless, making waving movements with his arms, into the falling glass of the greenhouse wall.

The anæsthetic gas had by now become ineffective from mixing with the air.

Opsall still stood rigid in the same tracks he had occupied when it all started. The anæsthetic gas had not affected him—he must have been so scared that he was holding his breath.

Reinforcements arrived. Other men—they had been hidden in the greenhouse—joined the action. These men had kept hidden behind the flowers, the luxuriant tropical plants, in the little private greenhouse.

They leaped up, three together—then two more—and a sixth.

The man with the scar screamed, "Watch out—they let loose gas!" He went flat on his face, knocking over flowerpots.

One of the six reinforcements was a dark man with a weapon peculiar to South America. A bolas. Three rawhide thongs, tied together at one end, with iron weights on the free ends. A bolas, but one that was more compact than those used by pampas cowboys to trap the legs of cattle and throw them.

The man was good with his bolas. He took a slow windup, the bolas weights whistling, then let fly. Doc saw it coming, tried to leap clear. His jump was about a foot and a half too short—one of the thongs went about his arm; then with lightning suddenness, both arms were tied to his chest by layers of rawhide. His strength, developed as it was, could not break the thongs.

The impact of the bolas, coupled with the loss of his arms for balancing, caused Doc to upset.

The bronze man, sprawling on the floor, rolled in a melee of upsetting flowerpots. A gun began crashing; its uproar was deafening. Doc rolled as best he could without use of his arms, until he was in a narrow aisle lined by crockery pots and long troughs which held plants.

There was no skylighting in the greenhouse. The flowers were cultivated entirely by fluorescent lighting, and the fluorescent tubes were glowing nests of rods in the ceiling.

Doc Savage, still on the floor, rolled over on his back, got a heavy flowerpot between his heels, and tossed it upward. He aimed at the fluorescent light tubes, at the nest of contacts at one end of a bank of them. The pot hit the target, and electric blue flame showered.

It was suddenly dark in the windowless place.

He had managed to short out the light circuit and blow fuses.

In the darkness, a man came charging across the greenhouse floor, upsetting things, groping and cursing. Pure luck led him to stumble over Doc Savage. Doc struck with a leg; the man yelled. Doc lunged, grabbed with both legs, scissors fashion, and got hold of the man. Using the enormous muscular strength of his legs, Doc hurled the fellow away, and there was noise of objects upsetting and the man howled in pain.

Bullets were going through things, making various kinds of racket. Back in the office, there was a fight, a violent fight between several men, one of whom was Monk. Doc listened to it while he struggled to get the rawhide bolas thongs loose from his body. Then Monk's angry roaring suddenly stopped.

A man puffed, "Gimme a knife or gun, somebody! The leg of the damned chair broke when I hit him."

The voice of the man with the scar came out shrilly over the uproar, demanding, "Have you caught one of them?"

"Yeah. The one they call Monk."

"Do not kill him!"

"But, hell—"

"Keep him alive!" yelled the scarred man. "If we fail to get Savage, we can use this Monk."

"I'm damned if I—"

"Take Monk and get out!" yelled the leader. "If Savage does not stop bothering us, we'll kill his damned friend."

A moment later, a new voice—it must have been a lookout they'd had posted outside—began howling that police were coming.

"Clear out!" shouted the scarred man. "Run, hombres!"

Doc seized another flowerpot with his feet. He did not throw it. He put it down. The distance was too great. There were too many of them and they had too many guns for him to tackle unless his arms were free. Some of them were still shooting, driving bullets at random, while others searched for those who were casualties.

"I thought there was supposed to be gas in here," a man said.

"There was," the leader growled. "I do not know what happened to it. Get a move on. The police are close!"

"What about Opsall?"

There was a moment of brittle silence.

"Knock him senseless," the leader said finally, "and leave him. He does not mean anything to us."

Doc Savage lay prone and helpless, struggling with the tangled rawhide, while they left, taking Monk with them.

Chapter 15
DECEIT

The police were not very patient with Benjamin Opsall. They thought it was strange that the gang had staged the ambush in Opsall's private office in such an extensive fashion. They were inclined to wonder if Opsall had led Doc Savage and Monk into a trap.

"But it wasn't my doing," Opsall assured them. "Practically the last the leader of those men said was to knock me senseless and leave me, because I had no value to them."

Disgruntled policemen made a complete search of the vicinity.

While Doc Savage was waiting around for the police-made excitement to subside, he did one peculiar thing. He happened to find a revolver lying in the greenhouse wreckage. It was an ornate gun with elaborate pearl grips and some gold-inlay work on the barrel.

The gun was the one which had been carried by the thin man with the scar under his left eye. The fellow must have dropped it during the fight.

Doc pocketed the weapon. He did not say anything to anyone about finding it.

The police failed to locate Monk. They did find an eyewitness who had seen the homely chemist tossed into a car. The car had then departed the neighborhood at high speed. Monk had been unconscious at the time, the witness believed. He was also bleeding from the mouth.

Having done all they could do, the police departed.

After they had gone, Doc Savage left Opsall's rare-fish establishment, and found a telephone. He got in touch with his headquarters and found that Ham Brooks was there.

"Anything to report?" the bronze man asked.

Ham said, "Elva Boone and Mrs. Ruth Dorman went back to their apartment and Renny, Long Tom and Johnny are watching the apartment house. So far, they have not been able to discover anyone shadowing the place."

"Anything else?"

"Yes. Remember that steamship company official who was a friend of Captain Kirman's—the one who told us where Captain Kirman's office was located? I mean the fellow who was wearing the black star ring, and wouldn't tell us anything about it."

"I know who you mean."

"I got him on the telephone," Ham said, "and when he found out Captain Kirman was dead, he jarred loose with some information. Here's how he got the ring. At Captain Kirman's request, he had joined a kind of cult that hangs out in a building uptown called the Dark Sanctuary. Black stars with red borders are the insignia of this cult. That cult sounds interesting. The cult leader is a strange golden man. And the cult business manager is none other than our friend, Mr. Sam Gallehue. That's something, isn't it?"

"You say the steamship official joined the cult at Captain Kirman's request?"

"Yes."

"Why?"

"Captain Kirman wanted him to investigate the cult."

"Did Captain Kirman want it investigated secretly?"

"Yes, secretly."

"Why was Captain Kirman so interested in the cult?"

"The steamship man didn't know."

Doc Savage said, "Ham, will you come to Opsall's fish establishment? Meet me at a tobacco store a block south and a block east."

* * *

Twenty minutes later, a dark-skinned man with curly yellow hair and a rather unhealthy cast to his skin, a lumpy left cheek and a nose with distended nostrils, approached Doc Savage at the cigar store a block south and a block east of Opsall's fish establishment.

"How do you like it?" the unusual-looking man asked.

"Good enough, Ham," Doc said.

Ham Brooks said, "I found this make-up stuff at headquarters. Not bad, eh? Wax in one cheek. Gadgets up my nose to make it flare. And skin dye."

Doc said, "You will watch Opsall."

"Where is he?"

"In his place of business. But be careful, Ham. Be careful with your trailing. But do not fail to follow him."

Something in the bronze man's tone impressed Ham.

"What are *you* going to do, Doc?"

The bronze man's voice took on grimness. "We are not making much progress in this thing," he said. "So it seems we will have to start some bombing operations."

Doc's first bombing operation came off without complications.

The bronze man crept into Opsall's rare-fish establishment by way of a rear window; eventually he managed to reach the semiwrecked private greenhouse without being observed. In the office, visible from the greenhouse, Opsall sat. Doc watched him. Opsall was straining his hair with his fingers and smoking a new white meerschaum pipe.

Doc tied a long string to the doorknob and kept hold of the other end of the string.

Then the bronze man got out the inlaid, pearl-decorated revolver. When Opsall's head was turned just right, Doc took careful aim, resting the gun on a flower trellis, and shot the meerschaum pipe out of Opsall's teeth. The gun report was deafening. But, if possible, Opsall's astonished howl was louder.

Doc then made some noise of his own. He fell down on the floor, out of sight of Opsall, and knocked things over. In his own voice, he shouted, "Drop that gun, you!"

In an imitation of the voice of the man who had the scar under his left eye, he yelled, "Get away, damn you!"

Doc then fired the gun twice more, kicked over a row of plant boxes, threw a flowerpot against the wall, hurled another at the ceiling. He drove a fist into a palm to make a loud blow sound. He groaned and upset a bench.

Slapping his hands against the floor, he made a fair imitation of a man taking flight. Then he jerked the string, causing the door to slam. He kept pulling the string, and it slipped off the doorknob. He hauled it in, rolled it up and thrust it in a pocket.

The whole thing had been a fair imitation of an attempt on Opsall's life which Doc had thwarted.

Some moments later, Doc arose to his feet. He made himself tremble, and felt the back of his head as if he had been hit there.

Opsall approached empty-handed and frightened.

Doc demanded, "Which way did he go?"

"W-who?" Opsall gulped.

"The man was trying to kill you."

"He gug-got away through the duh-door." Opsall swallowed. "H-how did you happen to tuh-trail him?"

Doc said, "Oh, I was keeping a watch on this place. Afraid those raiders would decide you knew too much, and send somebody back to kill you."

"W-which one was it?" Opsall asked.

"Hard to tell. One of them had a scar on his face, didn't he?" Doc exhibited the gun. "This is the gun that was dropped."

Opsall's eyes were about as wide as they could get. He was speechless.

Doc handed him the ornate gun. "You better keep this for self-protection," he said.

"Thuh-thanks!"

"Do you know of any other reason why they should kill you?"

"I—no. No, of course not!"

After assuring Opsall that he did not think the raiders would be back soon, Doc Savage left the building. He re-entered secretly at once by the back door, got into the basement, and found the telephone junction box. He tore the wires out, disrupting all telephone service to the building.

Then Doc Savage joined Ham.

"Follow Opsall if he goes anywhere."

"Right."

"If Opsall is mixed up in this," Doc explained, "he now has something to think about, and he will want to talk to the others about it. He can't telephone, so he will probably go to them. And wherever he goes, you follow him. Make your reports by short-wave radio."

"I'll be tied to his shoestrings," Ham said grimly.

Renny Renwick was sitting behind the counter of a candy store. Through the window of this store, he could watch the entrance of the apartment house where Mrs. Ruth Dorman lived, and munch chocolate cherries at the same time.

"I rented this job for the day," Renny told Doc Savage. "I have a car parked close to here, in case we need it. Johnny is around at the back of the apartment house. Holy cow, they got good candy here!"

"Is Long Tom still welding manholes in the middle of the street?" Doc asked.

"No. He has tapped the Dorman woman's telephone wires. He's listening in on that."

"Has he heard anything?"

"Nothing."

Doc Savage said, "It is time we started some action. Can you get Long Tom and Johnny?"

Renny grabbed a fistful of candy, then came around from back of the counter. "I'll fetch 'em."

Five minutes later, Renny was back with Long Tom and Johnny. Doc gave instructions.

"Long Tom, you and Johnny watch a place called the Dark Sanctuary." He gave them the address of the establishment. "Long Tom, you tap the telephone wires as soon as possible."

"Want me to try to rig microphones in the place, so we can eavesdrop?" Long Tom asked.

"If you see a way of doing that, it would be a good idea," Doc admitted.

"Shall we watch for anybody in particular?"

"Two men. One of them is the unusual golden man who is the cult leader. I want to know what he does and where he goes. The other man is Sam Gallehue, the business manager of the cult. Report his movements, too."

"Report to the recorder at headquarters?"

"Yes."

"Where's Monk?"

"They got him."

"Who did?" Johnny gasped.

"The same scar-faced man who got Monk and Ham thrown in jail in South America."

Johnny and Long Tom departed, grimly silent, deeply concerned.

Doc Savage told Renny, "We will call on Elva Boone and Mrs. Dorman and see if we can get them to talk sense."

* * *

Elva Boone answered the doorbell of the Dorman apartment, then tried to slam the door, but Doc pressed inside. Renny followed.

"That was accommodating of you to lead us to the Dark Sanctuary," Doc informed the angry young woman. "Unfortunately, we did not get much information from the place."

The girl was startled. She hesitated, then shrugged. "I thought I fooled you," she said curtly. "You knew I was leading you there. So what?"

Doc said, "How about a complete story?"

"And a true one," Renny added.

Elva Boone glanced over her shoulder at her sister. Mrs. Dorman shook her head frantically. "No, Elva! We can't tell anyone!"

Elva Boone looked at Doc Savage. "We've been discussing you," she said. "We could use the brand of help you dish out."

Her sister gasped. "Please, Elva! If my husband ever found out—"

"Ruth, you fool, you're already mixed up in Captain Kirman's murder."

"But—"

Doc said, "Let's have the story."

Elva Boone hesitated, finally nodded. "My sister was married several years ago and thought she had divorced her husband," she said. "There was one child. Later she married Mr. Dorman, but she was a fool. She never told Mr. Dorman about being married before, because her first husband was—well, a trashy kind. Mr. Dorman is a snob, but my sister happens to be in love with him. Then she found she wasn't divorced. It was kind of a problem, and it bore on her mind.

"To bring the story up to date—a little more than a month ago, Ruth got all worked up over this cult that hangs out in the Dark Sanctuary. She became what they call a *Believer*. She was impressed. She actually thinks this strange golden man who is head of the cult is—well, not an ordinary mortal. In justice to Ruth, I'll have to say that it's hard not to think otherwise.

"But to make the story still shorter, Ruth told the golden man about her other husband, and her divorce she didn't get. She asked advice—and she got it."

"What was the advice?" Doc asked curiously.

"To make a clean breast of it to Mr. Dorman. The golden man told her that if Mr. Dorman wasn't man enough to forgive and forget, he wasn't man enough to be a husband."

"Good advice," Doc said.

"I agree. But it would have lost my sister her husband, as sure as anything. Ruth didn't take the advice."

"Then what?"

"Blackmail. About a week later. A man delivered a note from Ruth's ex-husband, demanding money, or he would go to Mr. Dorman with the story."

"Has Ruth paid anything?"

"Yes." Elva nodded. "She decided to pay. But I talked her into trying to ferret out who was at the bottom of the blackmail, at the same time. I helped her."

"How did you do the ferreting?"

"I suspected the cult, so I watched the Dark Sanctuary. I discovered another man watching it, and one day, I accosted him, and he turned out to be Captain Kirman. He told me that he, like myself, was trying to get evidence against the cult."

"You and Captain Kirman joined forces, I presume."

"Yes." Elva nodded. "Ruth went to Captain Kirman's office to work and help in the investigation whenever she had spare time. To tell the truth, about all she did was take care of the business while Captain Kirman was out investigating. But that was a help."

"Did you get evidence against the cult?"

"Not a bit."

"Why was Captain Kirman so interested in the cult?"

Elva Boone grimaced. "That's a funny thing. He would never tell us. But he was interested. *Very* interested."

Doc said, "Would you care for some advice about your sister?"

"I would welcome it," Elva Boone said fervently. "We're at our wits' end."

Doc asked, "Does your sister have an out-of-town relative she can visit in a hurry?"

"Why, yes. Our Aunt Lorna, in Detroit."

"She should visit Aunt Lorna."

"You mean—get her out of the way until this is settled?"

"Yes."

Elva turned to her sister. "Ruth, I think you had better do that."

They got Ruth Dorman aboard a Detroit-bound plane which left LaGuardia field at six o'clock that evening.

The automatic recorder which receives messages in Doc Savage's skyscraper headquarters had abilities that were almost human. If a stranger called the bronze man's establishment, a mechanical voice from the device said, "This is Doc Savage's office, but no one is here at the moment. This voice is coming from a mechanical device. If you wish to leave a message, whatever you say will be recorded automatically, and Doc Savage will receive it upon his return."

After Ruth Dorman had been shipped off to Detroit, Doc Savage returned to headquarters with Renny and Elva Boone. He turned on the recorder to see what messages had been received.

There was a report from Ham. It was, "Watching Opsall's place. Nothing has happened. No sign of Monk. That is all."

The last message was from Johnny.

Said Johnny's voice, "Johnny reporting, Doc. Mr. Sam Gallehue left the Dark Sanctuary at five-twenty. He went to a large apartment building on Park Avenue. He has an apartment there. He is now in the apartment. The building is across the street from that snazzy club Ham belongs to. Long Tom is watching the Dark Sanctuary. He has tapped the telephone. No sign of Monk. That is all."

Doc Savage switched off the apparatus.

"Do you know some good actors?" he asked Renny.

"Actors?" Renny was puzzled. "Holy cow! What do you want with actors?"

"Do you know any?"

"Yes. Male or female?"

"Male. Men who will do a rather tough job if they are well paid."

"The actors I know," Renny said, "would play Daniel in a den of real lions for cash money."

"Get hold of three of them," Doc said grimly.

"What are you going to do?"

"Toss another bomb, and see what happens."

Chapter 16
MURDER IS AN ACT

Mr. Sam Gallehue, answering his doorbell himself, wore a long purple robe, comfortable slippers, and his fingers fondled a dollar cigar.

When he got a good look at his visitors, Gallehue nearly dropped the cigar on the expensive rug. He was not disturbed so much by the visitors as by the way they were holding their hats. They carried the hats in their hands in such a fashion that the headgear concealed shiny revolvers from the elevator operator, but allowed Gallehue a distressingly unobstructed view of the weapons.

"Invite us in, Sammy," one man said.

Gallehue went through the motions of swallowing a hard-boiled egg, then said, "Cuk-come in."

The two men entered and closed the door.

"I . . . I don't know you!" Sam Gallehue gasped.

"Sit down," said one of the men.

"But—"

"Sit down!"

Sam Gallehue sat down. His hands twisted together. He quailed involuntarily while one of the men searched him for a weapon and found none.

"What—who—"

"One more word out of you," one of the gunmen said fiercely, "and we'll knock about six of your teeth out."

Gallehue watched in silence as the men went to work. A little at a time, his expression changed. One of the gunmen kept a close watch on Gallehue.

The other gunman opened the window, shoved his head out and looked upward. It was quite dark outside.

"O. K., Gyp," the man said.

From a window above, a voice called down cautiously in the darkness. "All set?"

"Yes."

"Are you boys down below?"

"Yes."

"Did they get an apartment right under this one?"

"Two floors above that ledge, nine stories below us," said the gunman. "Go ahead and drop the wire down to them."

A moment later, a thin wire with a weight on the end sank past the window. The gunman reached out and steadied it in its descent. "All right," he said finally. "They caught the end of the wire down there. They'll make that end fast to something in the room."

From the night overhead, the voice whispered, "Now we better tie the dummy on this end of the wire, eh?"

"Go ahead."

"How is Gallehue dressed?"

The gunman turned around to look at Gallehue—the cult

manager had become practically as pale as he could get—then wheeled back to the window. "He's wearing a purple dressing robe."

"We ain't got nothing like that up here to dress the dummy in."

"What kind of clothes you got?"

"A blue suit."

The gunman withdrew his head again, and prowled around the apartment until he found Gallehue's closet, from which he dragged a blue suit. "Put it on," he ordered Gallehue.

"But—"

"Put it on!"

When Gallehue had drawn on the blue garment with shaking fingers, the gunman went back to the window once more.

"All set," he called upward to his companion. "He's got on a blue suit now. Put the blue suit on the dummy, so everything'll be cocked and primed."

"O.K."

The gunman, whispering upward, gave full instructions about how the murder was to be committed.

"When you hear Doc Savage in this apartment, toss the dummy out of the window, so it will land on the ledge below. Doc Savage will see it fall past the window, and see it on the ledge. The boys downstairs will have the end of the wire, attached to the dummy, and they'll give it a jerk or two to make it look as if the dummy is about to fall off the ledge. Savage will rush down there to save the dummy. As soon as he is out of the room, we'll knock Gallehue on the head and toss him out of the window, and his body will land on the ledge. The boys downstairs will then haul the dummy back up out of sight—and Doc Savage will have another impossible death to puzzle about."

"Right."

The gunman withdrew his head, and stepped back to eye the window appraisingly. "There should be more light outside," he remarked. "But the man upstairs will yell that somebody is about to commit suicide, and that'll get Doc Savage to look at the window, so he will see the dummy fall past."

Gallehue tried two or three times to speak, and finally croaked, "Yuh-yuh-you're going to *murder* me?"

"Them's orders."

"W-who gave such orders?"

The gunman laughed in a way that made Sam Gallehue's hair

seem to move around on his scalp. "You poor fool. You put a lot of trust in your pals, don't you?"

"I don't understand what you mean," Sam Gallehue said.

"Didn't it ever occur to you that someone else might want the split you've been getting?"

While Sam Gallehue was getting paler, the doorbell rang. The two gunmen looked at each other. "Doc Savage," one whispered. "He's about due here."

The other gunman jammed his revolver muzzle into Sam Gallehue's ribs. "Don't let on we're here," he snarled. "If you let out one peep about us, we'll blow you to pieces."

The two gunmen then moved into an adjoining room. They left the door open a crack, so that their weapons still menaced Gallehue.

The doorbell rang again. Sam Gallehue admitted Doc Savage. Gallehue was wet with perspiration, afraid to try to make a break. Doc Savage stepped into the apartment. Big-fisted Renny followed the bronze man.

Doc eyed Gallehue. "Is something wrong?" the bronze man asked.

"I—no," Gallehue croaked. "No, nothing is . . . is—"

Doc Savage's flake-gold eyes moved over the room, then he approached a chair. He took hold of the chair, as if to change its position.

Gallehue suddenly broke.

"Two gunmen!" he shrieked. He pointed at the side door. "In there!"

Doc Savage hurled the chair at the door which concealed the two gunmen. The chair hit the door with a crash, Doc Savage following it. The gunmen, however, got the door shut before Doc reached it. They did not fire their revolvers.

"Renny!" Doc rapped. "Head them off! The hall!"

Renny raced for the hall.

The bronze man himself hit the door with his shoulder. It crackled. The third time he slammed his weight against it, the lock tore out of the door, and he plunged through.

There was the pound of running feet. Angry words.

Mr. Sam Gallehue staggered over to a chair and was a loose pile of paleness in it. He did not entirely faint, although he held both hands against his chest over his heart.

It was fully five minutes before Doc Savage and Renny returned to the room.

Both men looked disgusted.

"They got away," Doc reported.

"Thu-thank goodness!" Gallehue gasped.

"What were they doing here?" Doc asked.

"They were gug-going to murder me."

"How?"

Mr. Sam Gallehue told them how the murder was to have been committed. He told them exactly what had happened in the apartment, and what had been said, and nothing more.

Doc Savage and Renny Renwick, leaving the apartment house half an hour later, were somewhat silent, as if disappointed. At the corner, three men joined them, two of these being the gunmen who had menaced Sam Gallehue, and the third man their companion who had carried on the dialogue from the window overhead.

Doc Savage said, "Renny recommended you as very good actors, and he did not exaggerate. You did an excellent job."

Doc paid them.

"Thank you, Mr. Savage. I believe we put it over, all right. Gallehue was completely fooled." The actor hesitated and looked uneasy. "But what if he reports this to the police?"

"Both Renny and myself are honorary police officials," Doc explained. "So we can explain it, if necessary. What you were doing was actually a piece of detective work."

The three actors, satisfied with themselves and the pay, entered a taxicab and drove away.

Renny said, "Doc—that business about the dummy body—are you sure that was the way Captain Kirman was murdered?"

"As positive as one could reasonably be," Doc said.

"How did you happen to solve Captain Kirman's murder? It looked like an impossible death—a body falling past a window, and the body turning into that of a man who was standing in the room with you."

Doc said, "You recall that a room adjoined Captain Kirman's office. The killers were hiding in that room while we were in the office. Captain Kirman knew they were there, but he did *not* know they were going to kill him, so he gave no alarm."

"How'd you figure that out?"

"The fish."

"Eh?"

"There were two tanks in the room which contained very timid fish. These fish had been recently scared. It was a reasonable surmise that they had been scared by the killers of Captain Kirman hiding in the room."

"But how did the killers get out of the small room after they threw Captain Kirman's body out of the window, and their colleagues in a downstairs office hauled the dummy off the ledge? They didn't leave through the door. Mrs. Dorman was in the outer office."

"Probably stepped to the window ledge of the adjoining office—or climbed a rope ladder. It was not difficult, probably. And no one would have seen them because the building opposite was a warehouse which had no windows."

"How come Mrs. Dorman didn't know the men were there?"

"Captain Kirman must have sent her out on some small errand to get her away. Or he brought the men in when she was out. Or they sneaked past her somehow. There are several ways."

"Holy cow!" Renny sighed and eyed his big fists. "Well, that's one danged mystery cleared up—all but why they killed him. But we didn't get any concrete results with out gag we pulled on Gallehue, did we? You think he is guilty."

"We scared him, and we deceived him."

"But he did not act guilty."

A long, thin piece of shadow, and a small shapely one, joined them, and Johnny's voice said, "Miss Boone and I got the Gallehue telephone tapped. It's hooked onto a recording device, so that any calls Gallehue makes will go on to a record."

"Good," Doc Savage said. "Johnny, you continue watching Gallehue. If he leaves his apartment, trail him."

"Right. You want me to keep in touch with you by radio?"

"Yes."

"What do you want me to do?" Elva Boone asked. "I'm beginning to like this excitement."

"Come with me and Renny," Doc told her.

"What are we going to do?" she inquired. "Another bomb?"

"Yes, another bomb," Doc agreed. "If we keep it up, the law of averages should bring us some kind of a result."

Chapter 17
THE EMPTY BUSHES

The night sky was a dark path for ponderous black clouds that slunk like marauders, almost scraping bellies against the higher buildings. The air was so heavy that one was conscious of breathing it; it was like perfume without odor. Street traffic was listless and made vague discontented murmurs, while far down in the bay a steamer embroiled in some harbor problem kept hooting long distressed blasts mingled with short excited tooting.

The Dark Sanctuary was a swarthy mass of dignified masonry. Next door, however, leaped up an apartment house with lighted windows that were many bright eyes in the murk of a depressing night.

Doc Savage and Renny and Elva Boone located Long Tom Roberts in the shadows.

Long Tom asked, "Any trace of Monk yet?"

Long Tom said grimly, "The place is as quiet as a grasshopper in a hen yard. There were some lights at the windows, but they all went out about eleven o'clock, and a lot of men left. They looked like servants and attendants, because they all wore uniforms. The golden man is still in there."

Doc Savage said, "Keep an eye on the place. In about twenty minutes, you should get a radio call from me. If you do not, use your own judgment."

"You mean—if we don't hear from you, bust into the place?"

"That might be the best idea."

Doc Savage entered the lighted apartment house next door to the Dark Sanctuary. He talked awhile with the doorman, and showed his police credentials. Eventually he was conducted to an empty sixth-floor apartment.

A few minutes later, Doc Savage swung out of the window of the empty apartment and went down a thin-silk cord which was equipped with convenient handholds. The end of the cord was tied to a collapsible grapple, and the grapple was hooked around a radiator pipe.

A slowly descending shadow, he reached the roof of the Dark Sanctuary, then searched rapidly. All skylights and roof hatches were steel-barred, and locked, he found. He had hitched to his back with webbing straps a pack of some size. He shoved a hand into this, felt around, and brought out a bottle.

The contents of the bottle hissed and steamed when he poured it on the ends of half a dozen skylight bars. He waited about five minutes, then grasped the bars one at a time and broke them apart without much effort. The acid he had used was strong stuff, and he was careful in replacing the bottle in the pack, because it would eat through flesh as readily as through steel.

The glass panes in the skylight were large, and it was not much trouble to remove one near the edge. He hooked another silk-cord-

and-collapsible-grapple device over the rim of the skylight, then went down into darkness.

He searched.

The Dark Sanctuary was empty except for the golden man.

The golden man was asleep in a second-floor room, sleeping placidly, snoring a little.

Doc uncorked a small bottle and held it under the sleeping man's nostrils. After a while, the snoring became more loud and relaxed. Doc reached down and shook the figure, to make sure the golden man was now unconscious.

Doc Savage made another quick search of the building in order to make certain no one else was there. The most impressive part of the place, he discovered, had been shown to him on his previous visit.

From the back pack of equipment, Doc Savage removed a tiny radio of the so-called "transceiver" type which had both transmission and receiving circuits in a space little larger than that of a camera.

"Long Tom, report in," he said into the microphone.

From somewhere in the street outside, Long Tom Roberts advised, "All quiet out here, Doc. Renny and Elva Boone are here with me. What shall we do?"

"Keep a watch on the place," Doc said. "Warn me if anyone comes."

"Right."

Into the radio, Doc said, "Ham, report in."

Ham's voice, rather faint, said, "All quiet."

"You are still watching Opsall's tropical-fish place?"

"Yes."

"Opsall has not gone anywhere?"

"No, he is still there. He sent someone out, and they came back with several men in work clothes. I presume they are workmen he hired to straighten up the damage to his office and greenhouse."

"Report any developments at once."

"I will."

Doc said, "Johnny, report in."

Johnny's voice—he never used his big words when speaking directly to Doc Savage—said, "All quiet here, too. Gallehue has not stirred from his apartment. He has made no telephone calls."

"You report any developments, too."

"Right."

The bronze man left the receiving part of his radio outfit

switched on and placed the instrument on a table near the head of the bed on which the unconscious golden man lay.

Opening the pack, he spread the contents out on the floor. There were chemicals, various instruments used in diagnosis, and lighting equipment.

He put up the light reflectors first. They were clamp-on style type, and when he switched them on, the fuse immediately blew. He found the box and substituted a heavier fuse. There was an enormous amount of intense white light.

There was a deceptive quality about his movements, for they seemed slow, although actually he was working at high speed. He laid out instruments and chemicals.

The portable X-ray was one of the first instruments he used. That and a fluoroscopic viewer so that it was unnecessary to take photographs. Probably fifty times, he shifted the X-ray about the golden man's head and body. He took blood samples and put those through a quick analysis; he did the same with spinal fluid. The fact that the golden man was under the influence of an anæsthetic handicapped to some extent the checking of the nervous condition.

Nearly two hours later, he finished with his diagnosis, and studied the notes he had made. He seemed to be making a complete recheck.

Finally, with the same sure and unhurried movements that had characterized his diagnosis, he mixed three different batches of chemicals. He administered these, two in quick succession, and one later, with hypodermic needles.

He went to the radio.

"Long Tom," he said.

"Yes."

"Everything quiet?" Doc asked.

"It seems to be," Long Tom replied over the radio. "Some guy is throwing a masquerade party down the street, and there are a few drunks stumbling around the place."

Doc Savage got reports from Ham watching Opsall, and Johnny a Gallehue's apartment. Neither man had anything to announce.

"It is vitally important that I am not to be interrupted for the next two or three hours. If anyone tries to enter the Dark Sanctuary, stop them. Use any means you have to, but stop them."

"I take it you're about ready to toss the next bomb?"

"About."

"Nobody will get in there," Long Tom said.

During the two hours following, there was no one but Doc Savage in the room where the floodlights made intense glare, and Doc was glad of this, because what happened in the room was not pleasant to see or hear. Doc's metallic features were inscrutable in the beginning, but toward the last they changed and his neck sinews turned into tight strings of strain and his cheeks became flatly grim and perspiration crept out on his bronzed skin.

He was busy most of the time, at first being in great haste finding stout sheets and blankets and ripping them in wide strong sections which he folded into flat bands that were as strong as canvas straps. With these he tied the golden man. The bed was strong, but he made it stronger by removing a heavy door from its hinges and placing it on the bed and arranging a pad of quilts, then lashing the golden man to that.

By then the golden man had become hot, feverish, moist with perspiration. He twisted restlessly. He made muttering noises. His condition grew rapidly more delirious. His body twitched uncontrollably and at times strained against the confining straps, the effort making knots of muscle crawl under the skin of his arms and legs like animals.

When his screaming became loud, Doc Savage applied a gag.

There were hours of that, until past midnight, when the golden man became quiet, except for some nervous shaking in his hands. Eventually he opened his eyes.

He said, so very weakly that it was hardly understandable, "It was the agent at Lisbon. No one else knew what plane I planned to use."

"All right," Doc Savage said. "Everything will be taken care of."

He gave the golden man something to make him sleep, and the man slept.

A clock somewhere was finishing striking two o'clock in the very black night when Doc's radio receiver began hissing, indicating one of the short wave transmitters used by his aides had come on the air.

Ham's voice said, *"Doc!"* excitedly.

The bronze man leaped for his radio, but before he reached it, Ham said wildly, "Those workmen who went into Opsall's place—they weren't workmen. They've grabbed Opsall! They just carried him—"

Ham's voice stopped. There was a report—it might have been a gunshot, a quick blow, or someone might have kicked the other microphone. Then there was a loud, metallic gnashing that indicated the microphone had been dropped, and other noises that were made by feet, and by the radio being kicked about.

"Now—slam him one!" a voice grunted. "But watch out for that sword-cane!"

There was a blow, then silence.

"Ham!" Doc said sharply.

He heard a voice, evidently belonging to a man who had put Ham out of commission, say, "What the hell is this box thing?"

"Must be a radio," another voice said.

That last voice, Doc Savage was positive, belonged to the thin man with the scar under his left eye.

The first speaker growled, "We'd better put the radio out of commission." There was a crashing, and the radio suddenly went off the air.

Almost instantly afterward, Long Tom Roberts was on the air demanding, "Doc, what had we better do about that? They got Ham, it sounded like."

Doc Savage asked, "Is your car close?"

"Parked about half a block away. I can get—"

Then Long Tom's voice also stopped. It ended instantaneously, with a lifting snap to the last word that indicated intense alarm. Followed fully half a minute of silence.

"Long Tom! What happened?" Doc asked.

When Long Tom's voice did come, it was a yell of warning at Renny. "Renny!" he roared. *"Renny!* Watch out for those guys! They're not drunks!"

Not from the radio, but from the street outside came the sound of six shots, very closely spaced. From the street in front of the Dark Sanctuary.

Doc Savage lunged for a stairway and went down in long leaps. The uproar in the street was increasing. It must be very loud, in order to penetrate to his ears in such volume. A supermachine pistol turned loose. The unusual weapon belonged to either Renny or Long Tom, of course. It made a sound that might have come from a great airplane engine.

Doc reached the front door of the Dark Sanctuary and flung the door open.

Renny dived inside almost instantly. He had Elva Boone in his arms—under one arm, rather—and he dropped her and put a fresh magazine into his supermachine pistol. He aimed into the street. The gun made its great bullfiddle roaring, the recoil shaking Renny's fist.

Doc shouted, "Where's Long Tom?"

Renny, his big voice an angry rumble, said, "They grabbed him. If it hadn't been for his warning, they would've got me, too."

"Who?"

"Remember we said there was a drunken party in progress down the street? Well, they weren't drunks."

Elva Boone said, "The drunks proved to be plenty sober, and they were watching *us*. They got all set—and then they closed in."

Renny finished emptying his supermachine pistol into the street, then did something that was rare with him—he swore. "It's no use," he said.

Doc Savage looked through the door. Two trucks were in the street. Huge ones. Van bodies, with sheet steel inside, apparently, and solid-rubber tires that bullets would not ruin. And bullets could not touch the motors, because both machines were backing down the street. They came slowly, angling toward the door of the Dark Sanctuary.

Doc said, "They have prepared for this. Renny, take the girl. We may manage to get away by the back door."

Renny growled some kind of a protest—he was never anxious to retreat in a fight—and in the middle of his muttering, there was an explosion from the back of the building. Wood crashed. Then men ran and a voice said, "Get those masks on! And fill this place full of gas!"

"They've blocked the back door!" Renny rumbled.

Doc said, "Try the roof!"

Half up the first flight of stairs, Doc heard charging feet in the hall above. There was a rear stairway; men had rushed up by that route to head them off.

Doc wheeled, went back. He found the entrance switch—the master switch which controlled all current in the building; it was the type which mounted the fuses in blocks that could be pulled out—and yanked out the fuse blocks, and ground them underfoot, rendering them useless.

He started back through the darkness, and met a man.

Doc whispered, "Did Doc Savage go this way?"

"Oh," said the man. "I didn't know you were one of us—"

Doc struck him with a fist. Because it was too dark to depend on repeat blows, the bronze man hit very hard at the middle of the body. The man doubled. Doc grabbed him around the neck and used fists some more. The fellow was wearing a gas mask, and the mask came off and skittered across the floor.

Upstairs, there started a great bear-bellowing which, with blows, rending clothing, cries that denoted various degrees of agony, indicated Renny had gone into action.

Along with that noise, there was a quick series of mushy explosions that were undoubtedly gas grenades.

Renny's fight noise stopped as suddenly as it had started.

"Is he dead?" a voice asked.

The voice was muffled and unreal, indicating the speaker was wearing a gas mask of a type that permitted conversation to be carried on.

"Don't think he's dead," another voice said. "I banged him over the head with a gun, that's all."

"Keep him alive. Put hin in one of the trucks."

"What about the girl?"

"Put her with him."

Upstairs, there was an anxious voice shouting, "They've done something to the golden man! He's dead! There's floodlights rigged up in his bedroom, and all kinds of instruments scattered around. He's lying here on the bed, dead."

Doc saw faint ghosts reflected from flashlights and heard feet going up the stairs to the golden man's bedroom.

"Hell, he's only asleep!" They had evidently examined the golden man more closely.

"But you can't wake him up!"

"Well, he's unconscious, then. He's got a pulse. Take him out, too."

"Want him put in the trucks?"

"Yeah—put him in the trucks."

Doc Savage withdrew quickly, moving back until he was beside the man he had knocked unconscious. He found the gas mask where it had fallen on the floor, and placed it beside the senseless man, then ground a foot on the mask to give the impression that it had been ruined in a fight.

By now, the gas had started penetrating to this spot. The bronze man's eyes stung; it was tear gas. Doc brought out of a pocket a transparent hood, air-tight, which he drew over his head. Elastic at the bottom held the hood tightly about his neck. It was a contrivance that served as temporary gas mask, waterproof container, or other uses, as need required.

He heard pounding feet approach, and a man calling, "Bill, what happened to you? Where are you?"

Doc Savage stepped through a nearby door and waited there, hidden.

A lunging flashlight beam appeared, and located the man senseless on the floor.

"Bill!" The man with the flashlight dropped beside the form on the floor. "Damn the luck!" he said.

Doc Savage lifted the rim of his transparent hood until only his mouth was exposed. He asked, imitating as closely as he could, one of the voices he had heard upstairs, and making the voice sound far away, "Is Bill alive?"

"Yeah. Just knocked out. Broke his gas mask."

Doc said, "Roll him in something so the gas won't hurt his eyes. Use a rug. Then get some of the men to help you carry him out to a truck. Keep him wrapped up so the gas won't get to his eyes."

"Right," the man said.

The fellow hurriedly rolled the unconscious Bill in the rug. The rug, an eight-by-ten size, made a compact covering. Then the man dashed away to get help in carrying the burden.

Doc came out of his hiding place and unrolled the rug, lifted the unconscious man and dumped him into a closet. Returning to the rug, Doc grasped one edge and rolled it about himself. Then he waited.

Very soon, men arrived and laid hold of the rug. Doc was tense all the while he was being carried—but luck was with him, and the rug did not unroll.

He heard a man join them, cursing the fact that they had found silken cords dangling from a forcibly opened skylight, and another silken cord from the roof up to a window of the apartment house.

"Savage escaped that way," the man snarled. "It looks like we shook an empty bush."

Doc, still inside the blanket, was dumped into a trunk.

Sounds told him that the golden man was placed in the other truck.

There was noise of a police siren, followed by perhaps twenty pistol shots. After that, the trucks rolled rapidly and the police siren did not follow. On the truck floor, Doc bounced quite a lot.

Chapter 18
THE SHOCK CURE

After the truck had rumbled along for ten minutes or so, a man dropped beside Doc Savage and began tugging at the rug. "You come out of it, yet, Bill?" the man asked.

Doc made his voice weak and different and muttered, "Go 'way! I'm all right. Lemme alone!"

He knew by then that it was intensely dark inside the van body of the truck. He moved impatiently, growled again, "Lemme alone! You wanna bust in the face!"

The man who had come to him growled something about an ungrateful so-and-so, and went away.

Someone shouted at the driver, "Damn it! Is that as fast as this thing will go? The town will be alive with cops looking for us in another ten minutes!"

"Keep your shirt on," the driver snapped back. "We're driving out on the wharf now."

A wharf, Doc decided, meant a boat. He hastily unwrapped the rest of the rug, but remained where he was, holding the rug about him.

The truck stopped, the rear doors were thrown open, but practically no light penetrated. The night was amazingly dark.

"Unload and get everybody on the boat," a voice ordered. "Make it snappy. Don't show any lights."

Doc Savage threw the rug down. He fished hastily in his pockets, found a pencil, and began scribbling on the interior of the van body. He wrote by the sense of touch alone, printing at first, then using longhand because that was faster.

To further insure his message being found, he located a crack and stuck the pencil into it, leaving it there.

"Bill?" somebody demanded. "You able to move?"

"Lemme alone," Doc growled. "I'm coming."

He climbed out of the truck. There was not enough light to distinguish faces, but he could make out, faintly against the river water, the outlines of a boat. It was a power cruiser, evidently near eighty feet in length. The vague impression of it indicated speed.

Doc walked aboard and felt around until he located a lifeboat. He discovered there was a canvas cover over the boat. He unlaced that and climbed in.

He heard another conveyance drive out on the dock. The driver of this car had switched off his lights and was guided by a lighted cigarette which a man waved in a small circle. It was a passenger car.

Sam Gallehue's voice spoke from the machine. "I've got that one called Johnny," Gallehue said. "How did it come out?"

"We got everybody and everything but Doc Savage."

"How did he get away?"

"Through the roof. The police were coming, and we had no time to follow him."

"We've got all of his men now?"

"Yes. They're all aboard."

"That ain't so bad," Sam Gallehue said. "We'll keep his damned men alive for a while and try to use them for bait in a trap that will get him."

Mr. Sam Gallehue was evidently a versatile individual; previously he had given the impression of being a rather timid man who was overanxious to agree with everyone, a man who was inclined to fawn on people. The Sam Gallehue who was talking now had snakes in his voice.

Doc Savage judged that the big boat made in excess of thirty knots while it was traveling down the bay and out through the channel—the channel lights kept the bronze man posted on their whereabouts—to the open Atlantic, and thirty knots must be cruising speed, because the motors were not laboring excessively. The boat was probably fast enough to outrun a naval destroyer, if necessary.

No lights were shown.

Before things had time to settle down, Doc left his lifeboat hiding place. He moved along the deck. Twice, men passed him, but he only grunted agreeably and stepped aside to let him pass, since it was too dark for recognition.

A little rain began to fall. There was no thunder, and, best of all, no lightning. The rain was small drops, warmer than the sea spray which occasionally fell across the deck like buckshot.

Doc took a chance.

"Where'd they put the golden man?" he asked a shadowy figure on deck.

"Stern cabin," the figure said. "Who're you?"

"Bill."

"How's the head?"

" 'S all right," Doc muttered.

There was no one at the door of the stern cabin, and no one in the corridor outside, although the corridor was lighted. Doc Savage took a deep breath, shoved open the door as silently as he could, and entered. He closed the door behind him, and kept going.

The one man in the cabin—he was the thin man with the scar under his left eye—stood at a bunk on which the golden man lay. He half turned. His mouth flew open, so that his jaw was loose and broke under Doc's fist, although Doc had intended only to render him senseless. The man fell across the bunk. Doc lifted him off and put him on the floor.

On the bunk, the golden man's eyes were open. He asked, "How much longer is this mess going to last?" His voice was still weak.

Doc turned one of the golden man's eyelids back to examine the eye. "How do you feel?"

The other grimaced feebly. "Terrible."

"The treatment you underwent tonight accounts for that," Doc explained. "But with your constitution, you will be all right in a few days."

The golden man shut his eyes for a while, then opened them. "Treatment?" he asked.

Doc said, "You had amnesia."

"Loss of memory, you mean?"

"Amnesia is not exclusively loss of memory," Doc Savage explained. "In your case, however, it did entail the misfortune of not being able to recall who you were, what you had been doing, or anything about yourself. But it also included a semidazed state, in which condition you could not rationalize thought processes. That sounds a little complicated. Your trouble was partly amnesia, and partly a form of insanity brought on by physical shock. Mental derangement, we can call it."

The golden man breathed deeply. "I seem to remember having an awful time earlier tonight."

Doc said, "That was the treatment. You underwent what is sometimes called the shock treatment for mental disorder."*

"Could shock have brought on my trouble?"

"Yes."

---

* The method of treatment for insanity to which Doc Savage is referring is well known to mental specialists under various names and methods. One of the most widely used being the treatment of insanity by inducing high fever in the patients—a sort of kill-or-cure process which, as less stringent methods are developed, is gradually falling into disuse.

"Then I guess it happened when the bomb went off in my plane."

Doc Savage asked, "You remember everything that has happened?"

The golden man nodded. .

"Suppose you give me an outline of the story," Doc said. "And try to compress it in three or four minutes. We may be interrupted."

The golden man lay still, breathing deeply. "My name," he said, "is Paul Hest. I am chief of intelligence for"—he looked up slyly—"let's call it an unnamed nation, not the United States. We learned that an American liner, the *Virginia Dare*, bringing refugees from Europe, was to be torpedoed. The torpedoing was to be done by the U-boat of another nation, disguised as a submarine belonging to my country. The idea was to build up ill feeling in the United States against my country."

Doc nodded slightly, but said nothing.

Paul Hest continued, "We wanted to warn the *Virginia Dare*, and at the same time lay a trap for the submarine. We could not radio a warning to the *Virginia Dare*, because the message would have been picked up. So I flew out by plane to drop the warning on deck. But there was a bomb in my ship. A counter-espionage agent put it there. I think I know who it was—a man in Lisbon. But that is not important. What is important is that the bomb blew up, and the shock gave me amnesia."

Doc Savage reminded, "You were found floating in the sea, naked."

"I guess I came down by parachute and took off my clothes so I could swim."

Doc said, "I understand there was a strange black star-shape in the sky above you."

"Yes, I remember that faintly. It was just smoke from my plane, after the explosion. The star shape was—well, an accident."

Doc said, "There was also a glowing material in the water. It followed the *Virginia Dare* after the liner picked you up."

The golden man smiled faintly. "That happens to be a war secret of my country, so I can tell you only in general terms what it was. It was a substance which has the chemical property for glowing, like phosphorous, and which is also magnetic, in that it will cling to any metal, providing that metal is not nonmagnetic. It is a substance for trapping submarines, in other words."

"The glowing material," Doc said, "can be put in depth bombs and dropped near submarines, and it will then follow the sub and reveal its location. Is that it?"

Nodding, Paul Hest replied, "Yes, that is it. I was carrying bombs of the stuff to use on the sub that intended to torpedo the *Virginia Dare.* I told you we intended setting a trap for that U-boat."

Doc Savage listened intently. Someone was coming down the corridor.

Paul Hest said, "I imagine the star and the glowing stuff—and my crazy talk about being born of the sea and the night—was kind of eerie."

The footsteps stopped at the door and the door opened and a man entered.

Doc Savage had moved and was standing behind the door; he pushed against the panel and shut it instantly behind the man who had come inside; then Doc put his hands on the neck of the man, all in one fast chain of motion. The struggle between the two of them made them walk across the floor in different directions for a few moments, then Doc got the man down and made the fellow senseless.

"Better finish that story in a hurry," Doc told the golden man.

Paul Hest shrugged. "What else do you want to know? After the plane explosion, I was goofy. I couldn't remember a thing about myself, although I had no difficulty recalling some information. I had heard of you and your men, of course, and I knew a great deal about you—I have a complete dossier of yourself and your men in the files at headquarters. I studied your methods, too, which accounts for the great knowledge of you which I recall having displayed."

Doc said, "Numerous times, you showed you knew things that apparently no man could have known."

Paul Hest smiled faintly. "The intelligence departments of most leading nations know things that apparently no one could know. I happen to have a prodigious memory—or did I say that? Anyhow, that accounts for my knowing your men, knowing you, knowing about your friend who was to be killed in Vienna—that was a projected political murder of which we were aware months in advance. As for knowing the *Virginia Dare* was to be torpedoed, naturally I was aware of that, and I also knew what ships would be in the vicinity. We had arranged for an agent of ours on the steamer *Palomino* to fake a distress call from the *Virginia Dare* in case the ship actually was torpedoed, which accounts for my knowing the *Palomino* would turn up for the rescue that night. My agent used gas on the *Palomino* radio operator to get the fake S O S into the captain's hands. Remember?"

Doc Savage said, "Did Sam Gallehue actually think you were a—well, shall we say a wizard?"

Paul Hest nodded. "I believe he actually did. At any rate, he was quite sincere in taking me to New York and setting me up as a cult leader."

"Gallehue was sincere?"

"I believe so."

"But Gallehue has staged all this," Doc advised. "He got Monk and Ham consigned to a South American prison, so he could get hold of you. He hired men to try to kill Monk and Ham. And he has been fighting us tooth and nail."

Paul Hest grimaced. "I said he was sincere—I didn't say he was honest."

"Did Gallehue start the cult with his own money?"

"No, it was Opsall's money."

"Did Gallehue start the cult as a method of getting information which he could use to blackmail the people who became so-called *Believers* in the cult?"

Paul Hest considered. "I don't think so. I think Gallehue was sincere. A crook, but sincere. The cult was making a lot of money. It was a gold mine. Why should Gallehue resort to blackmail?"

Doc Savage was silent for a while.

"If anyone comes in," he said, "you act as if you are out of your mind. Make them think you knocked these fellows unconscious." Doc pointed at the pair on the floor.

Chapter 19
THE CRASH

The big boat was still plowing along in complete darkness. One man was at the wheel, and the binnacle inclosing the compass presented a small wedge of light in front of him.

Doc Savage, moving up to him casually, asked, "Where did they put the prisoners?" in a low, guttural voice.

"Fo'c's'le," the man said gruffly.

Doc moved around beside him, reached out as if to take the wheel, but instead took the man. The man was bony and not overly strong, and Doc crushed him against the wheel, holding the throat clamped shut against any sound, until he could locate nerve centers at the base of the skull. Pressure there, while not as quick as a knockout, produced more lasting senselessness.

Doc put the limp figure on a cockpit seat, and pulled a blanket over him, so that it might appear the fellow was asleep.

Holding his watch close to the binnacle, Doc read the time. There were other instruments which flooded briefly with light when he found a panel switch. He noted the boat's speed off a log that read directly onto a dial. He did some calculating.

Later, he changed the course, veering it sharply to the left, then straightening out the craft so that it was headed toward a destination of his own.

His flake-gold eyes strained into the night, searching.

He left the wheel briefly to search the helmsman he had overpowered. Of the stuff he found, he took a gun, cartridges, two gas grenades and a pocketknife.

It took a long time, and he was showing signs of intense strain—before he picked up a light. It was a bit to the starboard far ahead. He watched the light, counting the number of seconds between its flashing.

The wheel had a locking screw which would clamp it in any position. He set the course carefully, locked the wheel, and walked forward.

A man was sitting on the forecastle hatch. He wore oilskins, judging from the slashing noise when he moved, and he was disgruntled.

"Everything quiet down below?" Doc asked.

"Hell, yes," the man snarled. "What the devil do they want to keep a guy out here for? In this rain! Everybody in the fo'c's'le is tied hand and foot, anyhow!"

Doc Savage said, "Here, let me show you something," and leaned down until he found the man's neck.

A moment later, Doc got the forecastle hatch open. He listened, then dropped the guard's unconscious body inside, and followed.

"Monk!" Doc said in a low voice.

A gurgle answered him. Monk sounded as if he was gagged.

Doc felt around until he found Monk's form. He cut the homely chemist loose. "Get circulation back into your arms," Doc ordered. "Then cut the others free." He stabbed the blade of the knife into the bunk mattress and pressed Monk's fingers against it. "Use this knife. You able to do that?"

"Sure, Doc," Monk said with great difficulty.

Doc said, "When the boat hits, jump over the bow and swim ashore—all of you."

The boat hit the beach at a speed of about thirty knots, which was nearly thirty-four miles an hour, and the beach was sloping sand, so that the craft crawled up a long way before it stopped. In spite of that, the shock was violent enough to bring crashing down, everything that was loose, and throw Doc Savage, who was in a braced state of semiexpectation, against the wheel so hard that the spokes broke out and he was forcibly relieved of his breath.

Doc had located in advance the button which controlled the boat siren. He sent a hand to this as soon as he could manage, but the siren remained silent; the circuit had been disrupted somewhere. Neither would the lights work.

It seemed to Doc that the first real sound after the crash was Monk's elated howl from the direction of the bow.

"We're off, Doc!" Monk bawled. "We're off the boat!"

Doc Savage was relieved, and sprang for the rail himself.

Then the searchlights came on. They blazed on as he gained the rail. They plastered upon the boat a light as white as new snow, and spread a calcimine glare over the sea. Searchlight beams came from five directions, X-ing across each other at the grounded boat.

Three of the searchlights were from State police patrols on shore, and two from coast guard boats on the sea nearby.

Doc tossed the tear-gas bombs on deck for good measure, then dived overboard. He swam ashore without trouble.

A State policeman put a flashlight on him, then asked, "You're Doc Savage?"

"Yes."

The cop said, "The New York police found a message written inside a truck in pencil. It said to plant an ambush at four places along the coast of New Jersey, Long Island, Connecticut and the Hudson River. You are supposed to have written that message."

Doc admitted having written it.

The State policeman picked up a riot gun. "Come on, gang," he said to his brother officers. "Some of them birds may try to swim ashore."

Doc Savage had been standing at the window of the coast-guard station, watching Sam Gallehue and his gang being loaded into police cars.

Long Tom and Johnny came in.

"I'll be superamalgamated," Johnny declared. He dropped in a chair. "Opsall just broke down and confessed. That sure surprised me."

Doc asked, "Opsall was doing the blackmailing?"

Johnny said, "Yes, Opsall admitted the blackmailing. He worked it as a side line, and Gallehue didn't know anything about it. Opsall had a man or two working in the Dark Sanctuary, and had a microphone or so in the place. He gathered his information that way."

Long Tom interrupted, "You know what set them against each other, and caused the blowup, Doc?"

Doc suggested, "Our so-called bombs?"

Long Tom grinned faintly. "That's it. You made Opsall think Gallehue had sent a man to kill him, and that set him against Gallehue. You made Gallehue think Opsall had tried to kill *him*. The result was the blowup—Gallehue went wild and grabbed Opsall and everybody else he could lay hands on. He was heading for a spot up on the Maine coast where he had fixed up a summer layout for his cult, as near as we can make out."

Johnny said, "Right now, he's headed for assuetudinous statuvolism."

"What's that?" Long Tom asked.

Renny said, "Another word for jail."

PERIL IN THE NORTH

Contents

Chapter 1
THE BLUE DOG

The man was in a wild hurry. He came across the street with his head back and his feet pounding. A taxicab nearly hit him.

He dived into the crowd in front of the Ritz-Astoria Hotel like a bowling ball going into a set-up of pins. He elbowed the elegant doorman of the Ritz-Astoria in the stomach when that resplendent mass of gold braid and brass buttons got in his way.

"Gosh!" he gasped. "Mr. Savage! Wait!"

Doc Savage was signing autograph books by the score as they were thrust in his face. The Ritz-Astoria bellhops and assistant managers were indignantly trying to shove a swarm of other autograph hunters aside and open a lane to the door.

"Mr. Savage!" panted the hurried man. "We've got rats!"

Doc Savage looked at him.

"Rats?" Doc said.

The man nodded. "Rats," he gasped. "Dozens of them."

The man was round, red-faced, perspiring. He trembled.

"What about these rats?" Doc Savage asked him.

The man pounded his chest to help get air into it.

"My pal is sitting there with a gun!" he exclaimed.

"With a gun?"

The panting man said, "He watches the rats."

Doc Savage considered the point.

"You mean," he said, "that your pal sits there with a gun and watches the rat holes for the rats to come out?"

"Oh, no! That ain't it." The man shook his head violently.

"How is it, then?"

"The rats are in glass bottles," the man explained.

Doc Savage said, "Why does your associate not pour water into the bottles and drown the rats, if he wishes to be rid of them?"

"That ain't it. You don't get this right."

"No?"

"He's afraid. My pal's scared."

"Afraid of what?"

"I don't know."

Doc Savage said, "You are not making this very clear. By any chance are you wasting my time? I am sorry, but there is a reception for foreign notables and army commanders here at the hotel, and I am supposed to be in the receiving line. If this is not important, I will have to ask you to excuse me."

"Oh, gosh!" the man gasped. "Wait!"

He jammed a hand into a pocket, fumbled and brought out a piece of paper, which he unfolded.

"Here!" He thrust the paper forward. "Maybe that will explain. My pal wrote it."

Typing on the paper read:

> Have given my diabetic rats arteriosclerosis and returned them to normal several times. Now complications have come up. Would you be interested?
>
> Bill Browder

Doc Savage shoved the paper in his pocket. "Can you take me to this pal of yours?"

"Sure!"

"Do it, then," Doc Savage said. "And quick."

A gentleman in a full-dress suit with medals and a red ribbon across his chest wailed, "But, Mr. Savage, you are supposed to help entertain! And we hoped for a speech. The ambassador wants—"

"I am sorry. This happens to be important," Doc Savage said.

They wedged through the crowd. Because the sidewalks were jammed, they took to the street.

The man glanced up at Doc Savage.

"Gosh!" he said.

His awe was understandable. Doc Savage was *big*, but it was only when you walked at his side or saw him in a crowd that you realized his size. His development was remarkably symmetrical. His skin was tanned by tropical suns a deep-bronze hue, and his hair was only slightly darker.

They ran to a car, climbed in and sped away. The big bronze man drove expertly.

Doc Savage said, "This pal of yours—what do you mean when you call him a pal?"

The man grinned. "He's a swell guy. I'm janitor of the house where he lives. I keep his furnace going and mow his lawns. He's a great egg."

"Then you are not a business associate?"

"Me? Oh, no. Not so you would notice it. He don't mow lawns and attend furnaces for his living."

"What does he do?"

"Them rats, mostly," the man said. "He puts in his attention on the rats."

"Where is he now?"

The man gave the address. It was beyond the city, in a suburb.

They whipped along in silence for a while. The man caught a glimpse of Doc Savage's eyes, and he was impressed. The bronze man's eyes were probably his most remarkable characteristic. They were like pools of flake gold, strangely stirred, as if by tiny winds.

The man said, "I've heard a lot about you, Dr. Savage."

The bronze man made no comment.

"I understand you're a great scientist and a great doctor," the man said. "I've heard a lot about that. And you help people out of trouble, don't you? Guys who are in a mess, and the law don't seem to be able to help them—you pitch in for them, don't you?"

Doc swung the car into a long, wide express highway.

"Sometimes," he said.

"I think Bill Browder and his rats are in trouble," the man said.

The city fled away behind them. Business buildings became smaller, turned to houses. The houses grew scattered. There were no stoplights on the express road. Traffic did not interfere with them. Cars gave them a wide berth.

"What makes the cars shy away from us?" the man asked. "I noticed, back there in town, everybody gave us the right of way."

"Red police lights on the front of the car," Doc replied briefly.

"You a cop?"

"We have honorary commissions on the force," the bronze man said. "Both myself and my associates."

"I've heard about them helpers of yours," the man said. "Five of them, ain't there? They're quite some guys, themselves."

Doc Savage did not answer. He was, as a rule, not exactly a fountain of information. In fact, he was not free with words. He almost never conducted a conversation merely for the sake of carrying on one.

They rushed along for about five miles.

Doc abruptly asked a question. "How did you happen to be so out of breath when you reached me?"

"Oh, that?" The man grimaced. "Bill Browder told me you were going to be at that hotel. He said you would get there a few minutes before nine o'clock, because the reception was due to start at nine. So I rushed. I rushed like the devil. But I made it."

Doc Savage made no comment.

They turned in at a brick bungalow in a modest-home section that was near a more pretentious residential district.

The man touched Doc's arm. "Say, will you tell me something?"

"What?" Doc asked him.

"What is it them rats have got—arteriosclerosis? What is arteriosclerosis?"

Doc Savage said, "Scientists for a long time have been experimenting in giving arteriosclerosis to diabetic rats, on the theory that a disturbance of fat metabolism allows plaques of fat to be deposited in the arteries, thus causing one of the principal diseases of old age. If Bill Browder has given it to diabetic rats, then cured them of it, and given it to them again, he has discovered what will be one of the great things of this generation. He has discovered the thing so many medical scientists have been searching for."

The man looked baffled.

"I still don't get what arteriosclerosis is," he said.

"Hardening of the arteries," Doc said.

"Oh!"

Bill Browder met them at the cottage door.

"Thanks, Snooker," he said to the man who had brought Doc. Snooker went away, vanished in the night.

Bill Browder said, "Mr. Savage, I'm delighted and flattered."

Doc Savage said, "Where do you get your fat metabolism, Mr. Browder? Do you get it by retorting quinine?"

Bill Browder hesitated.

"Why, yes, I use that method," he said. "It's an old method, but I use lots of old ones."

Doc Savage's flake-gold eyes became a little more animated.

"That method," he said, "would be a new one. It would be more than that. It would be amazing."

Bill Browder's jaw fell. "What do you mean?"

"I mean that fat metabolism and retorting and quinine haven't the slightest possible connection with each other," Doc Savage told him. "Which would automatically prove that you know nothing whatever about medical research. So you would not be able to tell whether a rat had arteriosclerosis. I doubt if you would recognize a diabetic rat as such."

Bill Browder swallowed. "You didn't take long to trick me," he said.

Doc Savage's flake-gold eyes were intent on Browder.

"If you contemplate any ventures with that gun Snooker mentioned," he said, "you might give it a second thought."

Browder licked his lips. "I was not thinking of that, I assure you."

Doc Savage said nothing.

Bill Browder blinked, changed his weight from one foot to another. He looked more and more uncomfortable.

He took a gun out of his coat pocket and handed it to Doc Savage.

"Here," he said. "Take it. I don't want you to get the wrong idea about me. Now that you're here, I'm probably safe without a gun, anyway."

"What makes you think that?" Doc asked him.

Browder grinned slightly. "I've heard a little about you and that crew of men you work with."

"You know nothing of medicine?" Doc asked.

"Practically nothing."

"How did you learn about science experimenting with giving arteriosclerosis to diabetic rats?"

"Oh, I copied that out of a newspaper item," said Bill Browder. "I looked the word up in the dictionary. You have no idea how hard it is to pronounce a word like that."

"The idea being to get me to come here?"

"Sure. I'd heard you were one of the world's leading experimenters in medical research. I knew a thing like that would bring you here in a hurry, particularly if it was connected with a little mystery."

"You are clever."

Bill Browder grinned briefly. "I haven't been told that very often."

"How much of your story was genuine?"

"The mystery," Bill Browder said sincerely. "There's plenty of that."

Browder was a young man who went to width rather than height. He was not fat. His hands were knobby and strong. There were freckles on his nose. His eyes were blue, with crinkles at the corners, and he had brown hair and rather large ears. But there was, as a whole, nothing freakish about him.

Doc Savage finished inspecting him more closely.

"No rats," the bronze man remarked.

"No, no rats," said Bill Browder.

"But there *is* a mystery?"

Browder was suddenly serious. "Plenty of that," he said.

"Suppose we hear about it," Doc said.

Browder rubbed his jaw uncomfortably. "You . . . er . . . are not angry with me? I mean, about getting you out here with that gag about the funny rats?"

Doc Savage said, "I am not particularly amused by it. If it was justified—if there was a good reason for what you did—that would be different."

"There's this mystery."

"I have asked you to tell me about that."

Bill Browder grunted and wheeled. "Better than that, I'll show it to you." He walked toward the rear of the house. "It's due around here about this time."

Doc Savage strode beside him. "What is due about this time?"

"The blue dog," explained Bill Browder.

Chapter 2
STRANGER'S WARNING

Doc Savage strode along with Bill Browder until he saw that the young man was going to leave the house. Then the bronze man got in front of Browder and said, "I think you had better tell me more about this right now."

Browder pointed at the back door. "The dog will be out there." He consulted a wrist watch. "Yes, it's almost ten o'clock. The dog comes around ten every night."

Doc stood aside. "A blue dog?"

Stepping to the door, Browder said, "Yes."

He opened the door. There was a brick stoop outside. It was very dark. Browder went out on the porch.

Doc followed him. The bronze man was alert. "The dog is blue, you say. You mean that there is something unusual about the color."

Browder closed the door behind them, and it was darker than ever. "I'll say the dog is unusual."

Doc Savage stepped to one side. It was no accident that his back was against a brick wall. He gave his opinion. "This has stopped sounding unusual and begins to sound silly."

"Wait until you see the dog. That's the silliest thing of all." Browder fumbled around in the darkness. "Here's a chair. We might as well sit down. We may have to wait a few minutes. The dog doesn't come exactly at ten every—"

He stopped. *"Sh-h-h-h!"* he warned.

Doc already had heard the sound. It was out somewhere in the backyard. An animal. Judging from the sound, the animal was exploring a garbage can.

Browder came swiftly to Doc's side. "I've rigged up a homemade floodlight," he whispered. "That's so you can see the dog. I'll turn it on."

"You think that is the dog?"

"Yes, it must be," Browder whispered. "Wait. Here's the switch."

The next instant, light spouted over the scene. The backyard was a mediocre one with untrimmed shrubbery and a lawn that needed mowing.

The dog was *blue!* There was no question about that. The color of the animal was distinctly azure.

Whirling, the dog showed teeth. It was a big animal, with almost the shoulder height of a great Dane, but with more the aspect of a wolf. Reflected light came from its eyes redly, as if it had the orbs of a dragon.

The dog suddenly shot away into the darkness. Where another animal would normally bark, it did not make a sound.

"You see!" breathed Bill Browder.

Doc dropped a hard grip on Browder's arm. "What are you trying to pull? That dog is not remarkable. It is simply a big police dog with freak coloration."

Browder moved in the direction the dog had taken. "Come on! You haven't seen anything, yet."

He sounded so earnest that Doc went with him.

Then the dog barked at them. It was a low, rather fierce woofing sound.

"He'll keep doing that," Browder whispered. "We can follow him by that noise." He opened a yard gate. "You say that color is actually natural?"

They walked down an alley. The dog moved ahead of them. It was intensely dark.

Doc said, "A freak of nature. In the case of plants, they call a peculiarly colored specimen a sport."

Browder stumbled over a rut. The dog barked hoarsely again. "I've followed this dog before," Browder said.

"You mean that you just saw it, became curious and followed it?"

"Yes."

"What happened?"

"The next day, someone tried to kill me," Bill Browder replied. "And they've tried twice since then to kill me."

Doc Savage yanked to a stop. Not so much because of what Browder had said did he stop. There was another reason, a reason who had popped up in their path with a gun! It was a girl.

The girl had a small flashlight, the beam of which she turned on her gun long enough for them to notice the weapon. The revolver was shiny and cheap.

"Please stand still," the girl said.

They stopped, because of the obvious fact that a cheap gun will shoot just as violently as an expensive one.

She had come from behind a bush. She was tall, but the backlight from her flash had not disclosed much about her face.

"Bill!" she gasped. "Bill, you can't do this!"

"Huh!" exploded Bill Browder.

The girl blazed her flashlight in their eyes.

"Go back!" she urged. "Give this thing up, Bill. You've got to!"

"Great blazes!" said Bill Browder.

"Bill, you've *got* to stop," said the girl. "I don't know who this man with you is, but you're trying to get him mixed up in things. You can't do that. This has got to end, I tell you!"

There was deep, almost tearful vehemence in her speech. Completely serious.

She made one more statement.

"This is the last chance I'm giving you," she said. "You'd better stop, Bill, before it is too late."

Then she began backing away. She put her flashlight on her gun. While the weapon was in the light, she cocked it, obviously so they would realize she meant business.

Her light went out. They could hear her running away.

Bill Browder let the air out of his lungs in a windy rush.

"Whew!" he exclaimed.

"Who was she?" Doc Savage asked.

Browder snorted.

"I never saw that girl before in my life," he said. "Isn't that the strangest thing?"

Doc said, "She called you by name."

Browder gulped. "That's what makes it queer."

Doc said, "You stay here. Do not move from this spot, you understand."

Bill Browder grabbed Doc Savage's arm and snapped, "Here, here! You can't—"

Doc Savage took Bill Browder by the neck, and they struggled for a while. Doc gradually worked his fingers around to the young man's neck, and Browder, apparently realizing something drastic was about to happen to him, struggled furiously. Doc located the nerve centers he was seeking, put pressure on them and Browder became limp.

Doc put him on the ground. Browder was unconscious. The effect of the nerve pressure was about the same as a knockout blow, although senselessness would grip him longer; and there would be no great feeling of discomfort after he revived.

The bronze man followed the girl. He was not breathing hard. He was not excited; at least he showed no signs of excitement.

Doc traveled fast. The lay of the ground was unfamiliar, but the girl was still within hearing, still running. He pursued the sound.

They left the alley, went across an open lot which was studded with brush and trees. Doc heard limbs crackling under the girl's feet several times.

She reached a street. A car engine started. The motor came to life suddenly with an urgent roar, and gears gnashed iron teeth.

Doc put on speed. He whipped out of the trees, felt a sidewalk underfoot and reached the street.

The car was plunging away. Its headlights were not on, but the machine was a dark shape like an elephant with no legs against a distant street light.

Sprinting madly, Doc got his hands on the cold, slick metal back of the machine. There was no spare tire. He located the gadget which held the license plate. It was fragile. But under that was the handle which locked the turtleback, and the handle was stronger. And the bumpers projected some distance.

He got on the bumper. It was no small feat in gymnastics to do so. And he could not remain there long, particularly if the driver went over rough streets.

He tugged out his handkerchief, swung down and jammed it into the end of the exhaust pipe. Almost at once, the car began to slow as the exhaust gas crowded back into the machine and choked the motor.

Before the car had fully stopped, he was around to the front and had jerked open the door on the driver's side.

The fat girl glared at him.

"The very idea!" she said. "What *is* the idea, anyway?"

Doc Savage's flake-gold eyes narrowed. This was not the girl he had started out to pursue. This one was older, had a different voice, and there was certainly nothing comparable in their figures.

This girl would weigh considerably more than two hundred pounds.

Like all fat girls, she looked jolly. But there was nothing jolly about the swing she aimed at Doc's jaw. He barely got out of the way.

"You . . . you woman-frightener!" yelled the fat girl.

Doc said, "Stop that!"

She went silent. The bronze man's voice had a way of conveying emphatic power, without rising in tone, that was effective.

"Why were you in such a hurry?" he asked.

She stared at him. "I heard you running through the trees toward me," she said. "What girl wouldn't get scared?" Her voice grew indignant again. "Here I am walking home across that vacant lot from my friend's house, and—"

"Who is your friend?"

"Anna Stringer," snapped the fat girl. "She lives over there"—she pointed beyond the empty lot—"and her brother is a policeman, in case that means anything to you."

"Your name?" Doc asked.

She scowled. "It's none of your business."

Doc said, "Your name, please." He said it so she jumped.

"Er—Fern Reed," she said.

"Did you see anything of a girl with a gun?" Doc Savage asked.

She gaped at him. "Of course not!"

The bronze man nodded. "It is possible I made a mistake," he said.

The fat girl snorted. She pressed the starter button, and her car motor whirred.

Doc Savage fished in a pocket and drew out a glass vial holding not more than a large tablespoonful of liquid. He stepped back, waited for the car motor to start.

When the engine began firing, Doc hurled the glass vial against the side of the car. It broke. The contents, a liquid, splashed over the car.

Doc watched the car go away. He made a mental note of the rather strange point that the car had no license plate on its holder.

* * *

Bill Browder sat up, took hold of his neck and groaned a groan which contained more astonishment than anything else.

"What'd you do to me?" he demanded.

Doc Savage did not answer.

Browder said, "You did something to my neck. Made me pass out." He frowned. "Yeah—that's what you did. You're a surgeon and doctor, and you would know how to do such things."*

Doc said, "You have not been hurt."

Browder lurched to his feet. "I guess not. Say, you did that because you don't trust me, didn't you?"

"As a precaution, rather," Doc corrected him.

"While you went to look for the girl?"

"Yes."

"Did you find her?"

Doc Savage said, "Do you know a very fat girl named Fern Reed?"

Bill Browder chuckled. "Fern Reed? That name sure doesn't sound like a fat girl. No, I don't know her."

"She is working with the girl who accosted us, I think," Doc said. "The fat girl was posted in the vacant lot at the end of the block to decoy me away from the other girl. I fell for their trick, unfortunately."

Browder shook his head. "That seems fantastic."

"Have you a neighbor named Anna Stringer?"

"Stringer? No, of course not," said Browder. "No one by that name in this neighborhood."

"Fern Reed said she had been visiting Anna Stringer," Doc said. "That merely verifies my suspicion she was lying."

Out of the darkness nearby came a hoarse woofing noise.

Browder whirled to the sound.

"Great blazes!" he exclaimed. "That dog is still hanging around!" He started forward. "Come on!"

Doc gripped his arm. "You are still going to follow that dog?"

"Of course," Browder said. "Come on. You'll see something

---

* The causing of unconsciousness by such means is not new. It is, however, quite dangerous in unskilled hands. There was one case recently, at an Atlantic coast bathing resort, of a lifeguard who produced this unconsciousness for amusement, in various victims who agreed to submit. He was not experienced. He held the pressure too long, with the result that his "hypnotism," as he was calling it, became a death. He faced charges of manslaughter.

fantastic. You'll see what I've gone to so much trouble to bring you out here to see."

Browder pushed ahead. Doc moved at his side. For a while, they heard nothing. Then the dog's bark came again, ahead and to their left.

Doc listened closely to the dog. He was as silent as he could be and still keep pace with Browder until he heard the dog bark again.

Then the bronze man flung out a hand and stopped Browder. "That is not a dog; it is a man," Doc said. "Do you know anything about that?"

"Man?" Browder blurted. "But we *saw* the dog!"

"It was a dog in the beginning. Now, it is a man." When Browder tried to go on, Doc held him. "You said something earlier about someone trying to kill you."

Browder sounded earnest.

"Yes, twice," he said. "Three times, I mean. Once it was poison in my milk; I caught it that time because the milk tasted queer. Then a car tried to run me down. And someone heaved a knife at me last night. It just missed me."

"Who did all that?" Doc asked.

"I don't know. So help me, I don't." Browder groaned. "But it started happening after I followed that strange blue dog and found out that the lives of two hundred and fifty people are at stake."

Doc Savage tightened his grip on Browder's arm.

"Two hundred and fifty people?" he said. "Their lives at stake? What are you talking about?"

Browder breathed inward hoarsely.

"That's why I'm going to such lengths to get you interested in this," he said.

The grip which Doc Savage was holding on Bill Browder's arm was tight enough that Browder squirmed uncomfortably, tried to loosen the bronze man's fingers, but failed.

"This is the truth about two hundred and fifty people," gasped Browder. "Please believe that. I know I lied to you about the arteriosclerosis and the rats. But it's the truth about all those people."

The dog barked again. Evidently the "dog" was getting impatient, because this bark was not as good an imitation as the others had been.

"Two hundred and fifty people," Doc said. "How are they in danger?"

"I don't know."

"Are their lives in danger?"

"Yes. They'll die if something isn't done."

"Where are they?"

"I don't know."

"What menaces them?"

"I don't know."

"Apparently," said Doc Savage, "there is a great deal you do not know—or are not telling."

Browder squirmed. "Look, here's how it happened," he gasped. "I follow the dog, see? I'm only curious, because it's so funny-looking. That blue color, you know. This is four nights ago, and I don't have nothing to do but follow the dog and satisfy my curiosity."

He paused while the woofing of the "dog" came from the darkness again.

He continued, "Four nights ago, see? I follow the dog to a house, a big house over there"—he pointed toward the south—"in the woods. I hear men talking. They are outside the house, in what I guess is the garage. There are three of them, and they are firing questions at a fourth guy. They are asking this fourth guy where a Bench Logan can be found. The fourth guy says he don't know no Bench Logan. The others think he is lying, and they say so. They talk back and forth rough to each other. It comes out that two hundred and fifty people are going to die if this Bench Logan cannot be found."

Bill Browder paused to swear.

"Right then, this blue dog barks at me," he added, "and I have to take out like a rabbit. The men all hear me, and they give me some chase, I can tell you. I think I get away, but I guess I don't, because right away begin these mysterious attempts to knock me off."

Doc Savage was silent for a moment.

"There is one big hole in your story," he said. "Unless you can clarify that, the thing is not believable."

"What hole?"

"Why you did not go to the police?"

Bill Browder grunted in surprise. "Why, I left that out," he said. "I forgot to say that I heard these men say that nobody but this Bench Logan could save those two hundred and fifty people. And Bench Logan is wanted by the police. If Bench Logan is arrested, he can't help those people. So—well, what would you do? I didn't go to the police. I racked my brain. I was worried about it, I can tell you. Finally, I thought of getting you. You are supposed to be the kind of a man to go to when something like this comes up."

There was silence. Then, coming into existence almost imperceptibly, a trilling. It was a low and weird note which traced a definitely musical, yet tuneless, pattern in the darkness. The trilling was the sound of Doc Savage, a thoughtless thing which he did in moments of mental stress.

"Browder," he said, "in the darkness ahead is a man barking like a dog. He is trying to decoy us somewhere. I am going to follow him and see what happens. Do you wish to go with me, or return?"

Browder pulled in a shaky breath.

"I'll go along," he said.

They moved on together.

The "dog" kept ahead of them, barking a little more happily, now.

Chapter 3
THE ELUSIVE MR. LOGAN

The man who was barking like a dog did not lead them into a trap.

Astonishingly enough, it was the other way around. The man walked into one himself.

Almost in mid-bark, as it were, the man was interrupted. There came a sudden, dull sound, as if a blow had hit him. The man yelled. There was nothing nice in the yell. It was filled with agony and astonishment.

Then an automatic pistol blasted itself empty! Its bullets knocked bark off trees, dug at the ground not far from Doc Savage and Bill Browder. Browder made a barking noise of his own and dived behind a tree.

Ahead, the fracas continued. There were blow sounds, profanity, men falling down! Someone turned on a flashlight, but the light was shattered before the beam revealed anything except vague dodging bodies.

Doc Savage watched and listened with interest. Mostly, he listened. There was not much to be seen in the darkness. But the sound—plenty of it—told him that one man was fighting three or four others. The one man was doing a bearcat job of it. He did not, obviously, need help.

The terrific fighter was the man who had been doing the barking. The others had jumped him without warning.

"Mr. Browder," Doc Savage said, "what do you imagine this means?"

"Gosh!" said Bill Browder. "I never expected anything like it."

He sounded amazed.

Suddenly the terrific fighter got the best of all his opponents. He tore off through the darkness, running like an animal.

Doc Savage had been waiting for this. He went into action himself.

He pursued the man, and did it silently. He did not set out directly on the man's trail, but headed rather at an angling course to the right. He did this for two reasons. First, to get ahead of the runner. Second, there was a street light far ahead, and against its glow he could see such obstacles as trees and dodge them.

Within two blocks, Doc was ahead of the runner.

The bronze man took anæsthetic grenades out of his pocket. He was wearing the full-dress suit—getting somewhat mussed by now—in which he had intended to attend the affair at the Ritz-Astoria.

Naturally, the pockets of the dress suit had not been full of the gadgets which the bronze man was in the habit of using when he went to the Ritz-Astoria. But trouble found him at unexpected times. So he kept a supply of his more common gadgets in his car. He had, when the strange business about the diabetic rats came up, prudently transferred some of the devices to his pockets.

The anæsthetic grenades had to be carried in a metal case because they were so breakable. Thin-walled glass globules which contained chemicals, they would shatter readily and the liquid contents would vaporize almost instantly.

Doc heaved grenades ahead of the runner. It was a tough job, because the runner was traveling fast. Three of the grenades had no effect. But the fourth did better, and the headlong pace of the runner slackened.

Shortly thereafter, he stopped. Then he sank down, as if sleepy.

When Doc reached him, he was snoring. The snoring was one of the effects of the harmless, but potent, anæsthetic.

The victim was a lean, tall young man. Doc struck a match and let the light shed over the fellow's face. The face was flat-cheeked, not unhandsome. There were hollows under the eyes, evidences elsewhere of a long period of strain.

The man had not come unscathed from the fight. His lip was

split, his jaw skinned; he would have a black eye, and a quantity of skin was missing from his hard brown knuckles.

One thing stood out about the man—his violent physical force. He gave the impression, even while unconscious, of a stick of dynamite with a fizzing fuse attached.

Doc picked him up. How the fellow had been able to whip a number of assailants was instantly apparent. His muscles were hard. Even the biceps were as firm as tendons.

Doc carried him to his automobile, put him inside. The car, innocent though it looked, was armor-plated and had bulletproof windows. It would hold the young man safe, once it was locked.

The car stood under trees where it was intensely dark.

Doc was in a hurry. As soon as he had tossed the unconscious man into the machine, he slammed the door, turned the key and left. He ran back toward Bill Browder.

Bill Browder was being very still. The other men, however, were moving around. Doc Savage stood in the darkness, listening to them, for a while. Then he moved boldly.

"Gentlemen," he called, "what is going on here?"

Instant silence fell.

A man broke it with, "It must be a policeman!"

Doc said, "It is not a policeman. I am Doc Savage, and my companion, who is around somewhere, is Bill Browder. We witnessed that fight a moment ago. As a matter of fact, we were following that fellow who got away from you."

A new voice came out of the darkness. It had authority, and it took charge of the other end of the conversation.

"I am amazed," the voice said. "Is it all right if I come forward and talk with you?"

The man had a slight accent, as if he were a foreigner speaking English, or an American who had been in a foreign country a great deal.

Doc Savage got more of his anæsthetic bombs ready.

"Come ahead," he said.

A huge blob of the adjacent darkness became a man. He was enormous. The fact that he had short legs had little bearing on the impression he gave of size. It was fat size. Bulbs and balloons of flesh that bounced and shook. A human blimp.

"As I said," remarked this elephant, "I am amazed."

Extremely fat men are usually funny. This one wasn't. If extremely fat men are not funny, they are usually pitiable. But there was nothing pitiable about this one.

He was an elephant, and he conveyed the feeling of being just about as effective as one, in anything he might undertake.

"I am Thomas J. Eleanor," he said.

Doc Savage had trained his memory to retain a great quantity of general information. He had heard of Thomas J. Eleanor. The man was an international financier of some note, and about whom not a great deal was known. The man had lived much of his life abroad—Paris, London, Rome, Berlin, Budapest—which would account for his accent.*

Doc asked, "The Thomas J. Eleanor who controls World Zone Airways?"

The fat man chuckled. "Right," he said. He thumbed on a flashlight briefly, so that the glow revealed Doc. He chuckled. "You are the Doc Savage of whom I've heard, I can see that," he added. "This astounds me. How did you happen to be here?"

Doc seemed not to hear the question. He listened to footsteps approach. Four men. Thomas J. Eleanor turned his flashlight on them.

The four men were, by their clothing, a butler, two chauffeurs and a gardener. They looked as if their employer had picked them while hunting men who would not be afraid of anything.

"My servants," said Thomas J. Eleanor. "You need not be alarmed by them."

Doc Savage turned his head.

"Bill Browder," he called. "You might as well join us."

There was a silence. Then Browder came forward cautiously out of the night. He had a flashlight, and he turned this on the group.

"Hey!" Browder exploded. "These are the guys I saw questioning that fellow about where they could find a man named Bench Logan."

Thomas J. Eleanor was suave and polite. He stepped forward and looked at Browder.

"I never saw you before," he said. "I don't understand— Oh, I think I do, too! Did this happen four nights ago?"

---

* The amazing quality of Doc Savage's memory—his whole mental equipment, too—is a never-ending source of wonder to his friends and associates. Those who have followed the bronze man's past adventures know of the scientific training which he received, and which is responsible for his unusual development. Doc was placed in the hands of scientists at childhood, by his parents, and received unending training for many years. Naturally, he became a mental genius and a physical marvel. When you train and study like that, you are bound to become good. Naturally also, this life has had its handicaps. Doc is really a fellow who has missed a lot of fun—as you and I know fun.

"Yes," Browder said.

"Then you're the fellow who ran when the dog barked at him that night," said Thomas J. Eleanor. "We have wondered who that was."

Bill Browder snorted.

"You're being mighty dang polite about it," he said. "But how about the three attempts to kill me? How about *them*?"

"I have no idea what you're talking about," said Thomas J. Eleanor.

He sounded properly incredulous.

Doc Savage said, "I trust you will not say you have no idea about the fellow you just attacked, Mr. Eleanor."

The enormously fat man was silent.

"That man," he said abruptly, "might have told us where to find Bench Logan."

Browder exclaimed triumphantly, "There, Mr. Savage! Didn't I tell you they were hunting a man named Bench Logan?"

Thomas J. Eleanor seemed lost in thought for a while. "That fellow we were trying to capture—the one who got away a few minutes ago—do you suppose there is any chance of our finding him?"

"Very little chance," Doc Savage said.

"That is too bad," Thomas J. Eleanor said with feeling.

A police siren sounded out of the distance. It approached. Someone had finally called the police to investigate the gunfire, apparently.

"It might save endless questions if we were not found here," suggested Thomas J. Eleanor. "Suppose we . . . er . . . walk to my home. It is only a short distance. We can talk there."

Bill Browder did not act enthusiastic about this. But he finally accompanied Doc Savage, Thomas J. Eleanor and the other men.

The home of Thomas J. Eleanor was as large as a hangar for a trans-Atlantic airplane, and considerably more ornate. There were maids, housekeepers, footmen and more chauffeurs in evidence. Everything functioned discreetly.

In a great study, paneled with teak, Eleanor faced them. He produced excellent cigars and drinks, which Doc Savage declined. Bill Browder accepted.

Doc was studying Thomas J. Eleanor. The man undeniably had enormous personal magnetic power. There was something strange about this. He was not a man you would enjoy being with, or a man you would laugh with as a buddy.

As a whole, one got the feeling that Thomas J. Eleanor had devoted his whole life so intensively to getting things he wanted, and getting tasks accomplished, that he could not be any other way. He was a master of men, and everything about him said so. His slight foreign accent only enhanced his dynamic, mysterious character.

Thomas J. Eleanor took a pose. Lights in the study were low.

"Mr. Savage," he said, "I do not know why you are here, but I do know your reputation. You have the name of a man who rights wrongs and punishes evildoers in the far corners of the earth. I have heard much of you in my—in my past life. As I say, I do not know why you are here, but I want you to help me."

Doc Savage said, "We rarely help individuals."

"When you say *we*, you mean yourself and your five associates, I presume. Actually, you have six associates, because there is a young woman, a cousin named Patricia Savage, who occasionally helps you."

The bronze man nodded.

Thomas J. Eleanor frowned. "What do you mean when you say you rarely help individuals?"

"When *one* person only is in trouble," said Doc Savage, "it usually means that he or she got into it because of greed, selfishness, or some other unpleasant motive. Usually, when one man is in trouble, it is his own fault. Not always, but usually. When a number of people are in trouble, it is usually the other way around. Some one man is usually responsible for their predicament."

The huge, dynamic man nodded. "Very well put, and very true. And that will bring me, without delay, to making a statement. The statement is this: Two hundred and fifty people, approximately, are going to die if I do not find a man named Bench Logan."

Bill Browder exploded. "You see!"

The dim lights in the room made it hard to distinguish the expression on Thomas J. Eleanor's face, if there was an expression.

Doc said, "Two hundred and fifty people."

"Approximately."

"They will die?"

"Unless we get Bench Logan."

Doc Savage shook his head patiently. "You will have to be more specific than that," he said.

* * *

One of the servants had kindled a fire in the fireplace, and it blazed up brightly. Thomas J. Eleanor moved out of the glow it cast.

"The thing can be put very simply," he said. "I want you to find Bench Logan and turn him over to me. I know you do not take pay, but I will donate any reasonable amount you name to any charity you designate."

"What would you consider a reasonable amount?"

Thomas J. Eleanor shrugged.

"Would one hundred thousand dollars strike you as reasonable?" he asked.

Bill Browder gasped in astonishment.

"You must want Bench Logan badly," Doc said.

Eleanor shook his head. "I don't want him at all," he said. "Those two hundred and fifty people who are going to die want him badly. They have to have him, or they will stop living. All of them. You see how it is?"

"I do not see at all how it is," Doc Savage told him. "We are doing a great deal of talking and getting nowhere. Where are these two hundred and fifty people?"

"I cannot tell you that."

"What can you tell me?"

"Anything you want to know."

"What menaces these two hundred and fifty persons?"

"Death!"

"What form of death?"

"Sudden!"

"What is its exact nature?"

"I cannot tell you that," said Thomas J. Eleanor.

"What are the names of these people?"

"I cannot tell you that."

"When will they die?"

"Very quickly. Some of them may be dead, now."

"Can you produce their bodies?"

"No."

"Or show me where they can be found?"

"I cannot do that, either," said Thomas J. Eleanor.

"Just what can you tell me?"

"Anything," said Thomas J. Eleanor, "about Bench Logan."

"Who is he?"

"He is the young man we attempted to seize a short time ago and who got away."

"What connection has he with the two hundred and fifty people whose lives are in danger?"

"I'm sorry, but I cannot tell you that."

Doc Savage walked over to the light switch at the end of the room and punched it. Bright light flooded the room. Instantly, Thomas J. Eleanor moved, lifting a hand and turning his face.

One of his men sprang forward and switched off the lights.

"Bright light hurts Mr. Eleanor's eyes," the man explained.

Doc Savage walked toward the door.

"Come on, Browder," he said.

Bill Browder stared. "What? Are you leaving?"

"We are walking out of here," Doc Savage told him.

Thomas J. Eleanor bounced forward with surprising agility for such a big man.

"You can't do that!" he yelled. "After all, you haven't learned anything about this yet."

"I have been asking questions, and getting what actually amounts to no answers at all," Doc Savage said.

Bill Browder bleated, "What about who tried to kill me? I haven't found that out. I want to know."

"I'll tell you everything," said Thomas J. Eleanor.

Doc swung on the fat man.

"Where are these two hundred and fifty people?" he demanded.

"I cannot tell you that," said Eleanor.

Doc whirled to the door.

"Come on, Browder," he said.

Chapter 4
THE WORRIED GIRL

They walked out of the mansion without the slightest interference. Thomas J. Eleanor merely stood and stared at them.

The fat man seemed, for some reason or other, very pale.

Doc Savage swung down the winding walk toward the estate gate, and Bill Browder trotted at his side.

"I wonder who tried to kill me," said Bill Browder. "I wish I could have found that out."

Doc made no comment.

Browder complained, "We didn't learn anything, did we? We didn't find out a thing about the blue dog, or about the two hundred and fifty people."

Doc walked in silence.

Browder said, "But one thing sure, you know now that I was telling you the truth about all this."

The bronze man still said nothing.

"I wonder what became of Bench Logan," pondered Bill Browder.

Doc spoke. He said, "Browder, go home."

"Huh?"

"Go home," directed the bronze man. "Lock your doors and stay inside. Better still, if you have a friend or a relative, go and stay with him. Telephone me your new address."

"Gosh!" exclaimed Browder. "Do you think I'm in danger?"

"By your own confession, you have been the victim of three attempts on your life. What makes you think the attempts will now stop?"

"I hadn't thought of that."

"Go home."

"Listen, I ain't afraid!" Browder declared. "I want to go with you. I'd like to see you work. I've heard you're a wonder. I think I would be safer with you, too."

Without another word, Doc Savage took Bill Browder by the neck.

Browder was instantly horrified.

"Wait! Wait!" he squawked. "I'll go home! Don't do that to me again! I'll go!"

Doc released him. Browder galloped off into the night. His feet hit the sidewalk hard for a while, then silence fell. Doc glanced around. The night was, if possible, darker than before. Three or four blocks distant was a small drugstore on a lighted corner. The establishment seemed to be open.

Doc Savage walked to the store and entered. There were no customers, and the proprietor looked up vaguely.

The bronze man went to the telephone booth. The telephone directory dangled from a chain on the outside of the booth. He killed some time looking at the directory.

A slight sound came from the rear of the store. The proprietor wriggled his nose like a rabbit, but did not turn his head toward the sound.

Doc whirled and entered the rear of the store. It was a storeroom littered with boxes, and it contained a table at which Bill Browder was just seating himself.

Browder was in the act of adjusting a telephone headset over his ears.

Bill Browder emitted a howl of fright an instant before Doc Savage got hold of his neck. That was the only vocal sound he made. His other noises were futile blows and a clatter as he kicked over a packing case in his struggles.

When Browder was unconscious, Doc placed him on the table. The bronze man walked back into the front of the store.

The druggist was the color of old canvas. He had not moved more than a foot from where he had been standing, and he did not look at Doc Savage. He did not stir or look up while Doc entered the telephone booth, or while the bronze man was telephoning.

A young woman with a very pleasant voice answered the telephone. Doc seemed surprised.

"Pat," he said, "what are you doing at headquarters?"

"Oh, I just like to sit around the place," Patricia Savage told him. "I sit here and think of all the exciting things that have happened in the past and hope more of them will happen."

"How did you get in?"

"Oh, I snitched Monk's key out of his pocket. He doesn't know that, yet."

"Where is Monk?"

"Uptown," Pat said. "Monk, Ham, Johnny, Long Tom and Renny are all getting ready to throw you a birthday party. They have everything all set. The trouble is, they haven't been able to find you. Where have you been? They thought you would be at that doings at the Ritz-Astoria. Monk and Ham went down to get you, but you weren't there. What's up?"

Doc Savage spoke rapidly. "Get hold of them," he said. "Have Monk and Ham investigate a man named Bill Browder." Doc gave Browder's address.

He added, "Have Johnny and Long Tom find out everything possible about Thomas J. Eleanor, the international financier. The fellow is something of a mystery-man. I want everything they can dig up on him."

"Whee!" said Pat gleefully. "Something is breaking!"

Doc said, "Have Renny check up on a man named Bench Logan. I know nothing about Bench Logan, except his name, which is probably spelled B-e-n-c-h L-o-g-a-n."

Pat was excited. "What's happening?"

Doc Savage did not ordinarily talk a great deal. Now that he thought of it, he had talked more tonight than was his custom. He had felt, for some reason or other, more free. It might be because it was his birthday. But the truth was that he had completely overlooked the fact that this was his birthday.

However, Monk and the others needed a general idea of what was happening, in order to start working. It was a bad idea to give Pat the information; she was sure to want to mix up in the thing herself. They always had trouble with her on that point.

Doc said, "Someone is trying to pull a fast one on me. A man named Bill Browder got me interested in a fantastic story about diabetic rats, then in another about a blue dog. Both stories were part of a trick. Browder is probably working for Thomas J. Eleanor, and they want me to catch a man named Bench Logan for them. Everyone seems convinced that the lives of two hundred and fifty people are at stake. I am convinced *that* part is the truth."

Pat gave an exclamation of surprise.

"What a wild story," she said. "Say, Doc, what do you want me to do? What is my part?"

"You are to go home, go to bed, and dream about making fat dowagers grow thin," the bronze man said. "That is, after you get hold of the others, of course."

Pat's laugh was derisive.

"You know me better than that," she said.

She hung up.

Doc Savage gave the dead telephone an intent, and displeased, inspection. This, he saw, was going to be another of those affairs when Pat would insist on taking part in the trouble. Pat loved excitement. She was also capable and was often of great assistance. But Doc disliked the idea of a young woman being exposed to danger, even a young woman who reveled in it.

Patricia Savage normally operated a beauty establishment on Park Avenue, where she charged unearthly prices, and worked miracles at slimming fat women. Pat's methods were hard. She frequently made her clients move to the beauty establishment and get all their meals and sleep there, as well as their exercise. Park Avenue society loved it. Pat was making a fortune off the place—and yearning for something more exciting.

Doc walked out of the phone booth.

He confronted the druggist.

"Is the tap in the back room the only one they had on that telephone?" he asked.

The druggist looked as if he was going to faint.

"I . . . I . . . yes," he gulped.

"How much did they pay you?"

The druggist swallowed several times. "Fuh-fifty dollars," he managed finally. "They . . . that Browder fellow came in this afternoon and wanted to do it. I wouldn't let him. It's against the law, and I didn't like the way it looked. So at first I turned him down."

"What made you change your mind?"

The man hauled in a deep breath.

"Mr. Thomas J. Eleanor, the financier, came in and told me it would be all right," he said. "So I . . . I took their money and let them do it."

"Bill Browder and Thomas J. Eleanor are working together?"

"Yes."

"How long," asked Doc, "has Bill Browder lived in this neighborhood?"

"As far as I know, just today," the druggist replied. "He rented a furnished house down the street yesterday and moved in today."

"And Thomas J. Eleanor?"

"Oh, he has owned that big mansion for a long time," said the druggist. "Ten years, I guess. He's gone a lot. Sometimes you don't see him for years. Then he will turn up." The druggist became more effusive. He seemed to feel that emphasizing his acquaintance with Eleanor would make his act less reprehensible.

"He uses cigars made special in Turkey, Mr. Thomas J. Eleanor does," the man said. "Cost him a dollar each, wholesale. I don't charge him a profit, but he always tips me ten dollars on an order." The druggist leered greedily. "So it's not so unprofitable at that."

"How long has Thomas J. Eleanor been here this time?"

The druggist frowned. "I guess I shouldn't be telling you—"

"How long?" Doc's voice did not rise in tone, but the man jumped and grew pale again.

"Three months," he said.

"Do you know anything about a blue dog?" Doc asked.

"Blue dog? No, can't say I do."

"Or about two hundred and fifty people?"

The druggist just stared.

Doc Savage walked out of the store.

Doc Savage walked rapidly through the night to his parked automobile. He took the key out of his pocket, and used it to tap on the thick bulletproof glass window.

"Get over close to the glass where you can hear me," he said.

The car, due to its peculiar construction—it was gas-tight among other things—was practically soundproof.

The young woman in the car came close to the window.

Doc turned his flashlight on her.

It was the young woman who had accosted Bill Browder and himself and had warned Browder to stop what he was doing.

Doc said, "Drop that gun you are holding. Hold up your hands where I can see them, and be sure the gun is on the floor."

The young woman told him quite specifically where he could go, but did not use any swear words doing it. She was quite angry.

"This car," Doc Savage advised her, "is equipped with a gas device whereby the machine can be flooded, and you will be rendered unconscious. If it becomes necessary to do it that way, you will only inconvenience yourself."

The young woman knew by now that the car was an unusual one. She had not been able to get out of it. The bulletproof glass was nicked in many places where she had pounded it with her gun in an effort to break out.

Furthermore, Doc Savage's matter-of-fact voice had a quality of truth in it that removed all doubts that he might be bluffing.

She dropped her gun on the floor—the same cheap gun with which she had menaced Doc earlier—and held her hands in view.

The bronze man unlocked the machine. The girl immediately made an attempt to scoop up her weapon, but Doc had expected that and beat her to it. He pocketed the gun.

"You have a permit for this weapon?" he asked.

She hesitated, then snapped, "Yes, I have!" It sounded like the truth.

He told her, "We will not throw it away, then. Someone might find it and shoot somebody, and it would get you in trouble. The numbers of the gun are on record."

"Very thoughtful, aren't you?" she snapped.

Doc Savage leaned over the back seat. Bench Logan was lying there—if it was Bench Logan—and breathing deeply. Doc took his pulse. It was about normal. The bronze man felt of Bench Logan's forehead for temperature, and that seemed normal, too.

Doc told the girl, "In case you should get any idea of grabbing your gun out of my pocket, we will just put it in the pocket in the back, here."

He thrust the weapon in the rear door pocket.

"Won't that fellow wake up and get it?" the girl asked.

"It is not likely that he will wake up for some time yet. The gas with which he was overcome is rather potent."

"Oh!"

Doc Savage slid behind the wheel. He started the motor. "You were in the back of the car when I placed the unconscious man in the machine," he said.

"Of course," he girl said briefly. "How else do you think I got into this thing? I couldn't get *out*. What kind of a car is this, anyway?"

Without appearing to hear the query part of the girl's speech, Doc Savage put the car into motion, and drove for a short distance. Then he stopped.

Some of the devices in his pockets seemed to be gouging him, because he squirmed around and put some of them in the dash compartment. He swung around to put another in a rear door pocket. He emitted an exclamation of annoyance.

Anyone knowing the bronze man would have known that he never became upset to the point of showing his emotions with an exclamation of annoyance. The girl, however, was deceived.

She said, "Oh, you spilled something on that fellow in the back! What was it?"

"Merely some liquid," Doc Savage said. "It will not harm him."

The bronze man settled back in the seat and started driving again.

"Now," he said, "you had better tell me who you are, what you are doing, and any other facts you think might be interesting."

She sniffed. She locked her fingers together. "Fat chance you've got of getting anything out of me."

Doc Savage turned onto a highway. The hour was late enough that there was not much traffic.

Doc said, "Bill Browder insisted that he did not know you; that he had no idea who you were."

The young woman's reaction to that was violent. She bolted upright and smacked her knee with a hand.

"Why, the liar!" she exclaimed. "The fibber!"

"He knows you, then?"

"If he doesn't, it's time he started to," the girl said. "We are engaged to be married, Bill and I."

"He insisted he had never seen you before."

"What a whopper for him to tell!"

"Your name is—"

"Nicky Jones," she said. Then she made an angry gesture. "Wait, I wasn't going to tell you anything."

Doc Savage sent the car into the fast-traffic lane.

He remarked, "That was an ingenius bit of herring-dragging you used earlier, when you got away from us. Meaning, of course, the rather plump girl you had waiting in the car. She told me a fairly convincing story."

"She ought to. She used to be an actress."

"She said her name was Fern Reed."

"That is right."

"Bill Browder said he had never heard of Fern Reed."

Nicky Jones stared fixedly at the pavement, which was running toward them like a gray snake.

"Bill seems to have become a stranger to the truth for tonight," she said.

Doc Savage made no comment.

After a while, Nicky demanded, "Who are you, anyway? Right in the beginning, I thought there was something familiar about you. I don't think it's your looks, but it might be. It's more your voice. I bet I've heard your voice before. Where could it have been?"

Doc was silent. He was driving more slowly.

Nicky Jones said, "Yes, there's something familiar about you, but I can't place it. I've heard you, or seen you, but I still believe I've heard you." She pondered for a while. "Say, could it have been on the radio? You made a speech, didn't you? Something about the war situation? I think I begin to remember. It was about two weeks ago. You were on the air—"

Bench Logan heaved up in the back of the car. He had gotten the gun which Doc Savage had placed in the door pocket.

Logan said, "You can clip that speech off right there, young lady. In fact, the next word you say might be your last one!"

He did not sound like a man who was fooling!

Chapter 5
UNWILLING STOWAWAY

Bench Logan remained very still after he spoke. They could feel his tension, his alertness. There had been nothing overexcited in his voice, and there was certainly no hysteria in his manner.

He was a man who was accustomed to trouble.

When Doc and Nicky did not move, Logan said, "That's fine. We understand each other. But in case we don't, I'll explain that I'll shoot the first one of you who bats an eye the wrong way."

There was another silence. Doc Savage drove slowly. The man's gun was a few inches from the back of his neck.

Nicky began, "Say, you, whoever you are—"

"Shut up, little girl!" snapped Bench Logan. "I'd hate to pop a woman, but I might if you push me. As for your pal here, the great Doc Savage, I would shoot him as quick as I would anybody."

Nicky gasped. She stared at the bronze man.

"Doc Savage!" she exclaimed. "That's who you are! For the love of mud, what is a man of your caliber doing in this?"

"Shut up!" ordered Bench Logan.

Doc drove with a steady hand. "Mr. Logan?" he said.

"So you know who I am," grunted Bench Logan. "Well, what do you want?"

"Is this story about the lives of a large number of people being in danger a true story?"

Bench Logan made a snarling sound. "Two hundred and fifty-six of them. It's a safe bet to figure as many as five or six have died by now, so that leaves around two hundred and fifty."

"How do you know there was two hundred and fifty-six of them?"

"There was that many when I left them."

"Then these people are together?"

"Sure." Suddenly Bench Logan put the cold muzzle of the gun against the back of Doc Savage's neck. "Say, what is this—a gag? You know all about it. What you trying to pull?"

"It is possible you misunderstand—"

"Shut up!" snarled Bench Logan. "I don't misunderstand anything. I saw you talking to that Bill Browder. I know Browder is one of Tom Eleanor's pups, and that's enough for me. You're working for Tom Eleanor. What'd Eleanor do—hire you to get me?"

Doc Savage said, "He *tried* to hire me to catch you and turn you over to him."

Bench Logan swore violently and at some length. He mentioned no names, but it was obvious his opinion concerned Thomas J. Eleanor, Doc Savage, and fate in general.

"Excuse the words," he told Nicky Jones when he finished, "but that is the way I feel about it."

Doc began, "Perhaps—"

Bench Logan gouged him in the back of the neck with the gun. "Don't perhaps me," he grated. "I've been away from the United States for ten years, but I've heard about you. The great Doc Savage." He snorted. "I saw a little rat of a gangster turn as white as a snow-shoe rabbit in a café in Rome when your name was mentioned. I saw almost the same thing in Prague, only it was a crooked banker that time."

He was silent a moment. The gun remained against Doc's neck.

"A professional righter of wrongs, they called you," Bench Logan said bitterly. "A guy who does big deeds and doesn't get paid. I says to myself right then: 'This guy Savage is just a big-shot crook; so slick nobody knows it. He's got a racket. He's a two-faced so-and-so.'" He swore again. "You know what I said to myself right then? I said that if this guy Savage ever crosses my trail, I'll pop him out of the way so fast it won't be funny." He tapped Doc with the gun for emphasis. *"And that's what I'm going to do!"*

He shoved two round tablets of whitish color to them, one to Nicky, one to Doc.

"Swallow those and don't waste time about it," he ordered.

Nicky Jones sat quite still for some time. She seemed to be thinking. Doc drove with a steady hand, holding the tablet, but making no effort to swallow it.

Finally Nicky said, "I've got a horror of being poisoned. I'd sooner be shot. Mr. Savage, I'm going to turn around and grab this devil. I've heard that you can keep going for a few seconds after you're shot. Maybe I can get hold of him and keep him from shooting you long enough for you to grab him."

A silence followed that.

Bench Logan broke the quiet with, "Lady, you've got nerve. But you won't need to do it. Those tablets are harmless."

"I'll bet," said Nicky suspiciously.

"Oh, they'll make you unconscious," Bench Logan told her. "But that's all. You see, I lead kind of a rough life. There're times when I want to be unconscious for a long time—in cases where people wanted to make me talk, for instance. So I carry a couple of those tablets. I carry them in my hatband, under a piece of Scotch tape."

Nicky's voice was shaking.

"What . . . what are you going to do with us?" she asked.

"I don't kill people except when I have to in self-defense," said Bench Logan. "So stop worrying. I'm just putting you out of this, is all. When you wake up, you'll be all right, but you won't be where you can make me any more trouble."

Nicky was still suspicious. She snapped, "I won't swallow these things!"

Doc Savage spoke quietly. "It would probably be the best thing to do so, under the circumstances."

Nicky gasped, "But—"

Doc Savage brought his tablet to his lips.

"Turn your head!" barked Bench Logan. "I want to see you swallow that thing."

Doc did so, put the tablet on his tongue, closed his mouth and swallowed.

"All right, open your mouth," Bench Logan ordered. "I want to be sure it went down."

Logan used a flashlight from the bronze man's pocket to make an inspection, and he was satisfied.

"Now you!" he directed Nicky.

She obeyed, but with no enthusiasm. Then she sat there, as if she expected to explode.

"You better park this heap," said Bench Logan.

Doc complied with the order. They sat there. The headlights were on, thrusting out a long fan of gentle light. Cars passed in either direction on the highway, sounding as if they were being blown out of a tube.

Finally Bench Logan swore, "What's wrong with that stuff?"

"I don't feel a thing," said Nicky.

Doc Savage told her, "You will, in a moment."

The bronze man's eyes were beginning to act heavy-lidded. A little at a time, his head slumped, his shoulders loosened, and he tilted over in the seat, against Nicky.

Nicky tried dazedly to push him away but finally gave it up, and they seemed to go to sleep with their heads together.

Bench Logan drove them to a steamship.

The ship was not large; it was obviously old. And if it could be called any color, the color was rust. The vessel did not have the appearance of having been painted, or having anything else done to it in the line of sanitation, for a long time.

Bench Logan consulted no one on the ship. In fact, no one saw him. He took care to see to that.

Due to the war situation, there was a guard near the gangplank. But the *Oscar Fjord*, which was the name of the old kettle of rust, was not a large vessel nor an important one. So there were only two men in the guard, and both of them were breaking the rules by sitting in a shanty, playing cards. The spot was remote, and most of the watching the two guards did was for their commanding officer, or whoever had put them on the job.

Bench Logan climbed up a hawser near the stern, and soon lowered a line over the side. He tied Doc Savage to the end of the line, and hauled the bronze man on board the *Oscar Fjord*. Then Logan clambered back to the dock, tied the girl to the line, scrambled up to the ship and hauled the girl on board.

All of this took the agility of a monkey, but Bench Logan seemed to have energy to spare. He was as tough as a fiddle string.

He stowed the two in a smelly compartment near the stern. He was not even breathing hard when he finished the job.

"Now," he told himself, "that's that."

Bench Logan stood there and contemplated them for a while, then shrugged.

He returned to deck, closing a couple of bulkhead doors behind him. He stood there in the night, gazing at the rusty old bulk of the *Oscar Fjord*, and making sure the two gangplank guards were still playing cards.

The decrepit old steamer seemed quite familiar to him. It was as if he was looking at an old friend, or at least something with which he was well acquainted.

He slid down the rope, hand over hand, to the dock and walked off. He went back to Doc Savage's car, climbed in the machine, turned the switch, stamped on the starter button. He got no results. The starter did not even turn the motor over.

Bench Logan tried repeatedly to start the car.

"Hell!" he said.

He walked down the street. But he traveled only two blocks on foot before he was fortunate enough to hail a passing taxicab. Bench Logan climbed into the cab, and the machine moved away.

Nicky Jones pointed down the darkened street and said to Doc Savage, "There goes Logan. He's leaving in that cab."

Doc Savage did not answer. He climbed into his car, reached under the dash, pressed what could have been mistaken for a rivet head and, after that, started the motor.

Nicky watched the business with the rivet head, and chuckled. "So that's why he couldn't get the car started," she said. "I suppose you have to do that every time before you start it."

Doc did not turn on the headlights. Luminance from street lamps made it unnecessary. The car rolled quietly.

Nicky announced, "He must have been conscious in the back of the car here for a long time. Before you got back and found me in the car, in fact."

Doc said, "He was conscious when I came back, yes."

That was the extent of the bronze man's conversation for some time to come. Nicky, however, rattled on excitedly.

"You found those pills in his hat when you first got him, didn't you?" she said. "And you substituted ordinary shirt buttons for them. They looked like shirt buttons, and when I ate mine, I thought it was darn funny I couldn't chew it. I almost remarked about that. It would have given the thing away, wouldn't it?"

The taxi ahead was obeying speed laws. Doc Savage kept it in view without difficulty. As soon as they encountered traffic, he turned on the headlights; but he left the red police lights dark.

Nicky said, "I caught on to the pills, though. When you passed out, I got it. So I pretended to pass out, too. You know, I'm surprised I was that smart."

Doc approached closer to the taxi ahead. There was sufficient traffic that he could do this safely.

Nicky sighed.

"I had you wrong," she said. "I didn't know who you were in the first place. If I had known, when I confronted you and Bill Browder with my gun tonight, I would have acted differently."

The car climbed up the long ramp approaching a bridge to Manhattan island. A policeman saw Doc's machine, and waved a greeting. And for several minutes, the bronze man kept a close watch on the cab ahead. But apparently Bench Logan had not noticed the policeman wave. At least, he gave no sign.

Nicky leaned back in the seat.

"I'm going to tell you all I know about this," she said.

Doc made no comment.

"It's darn little," Nicky said.

Doc turned north on Broadway, following the cab.

Nicky said, "Bill Browder is mixed up in something bad. I know it. I don't know what it is, but I can tell that it's something serious. And I don't like it."

She was silent a moment. "When you fall in love with a guy, you get so you can read his mind almost. Any girl will tell you that. Or you think you can read his mind. Anyway, I've got the conviction that Bill is headed for trouble."

She grimaced.

"What I should do, I suppose," she added, "is kick the big lug in the pants and tell him to get off my boat. But that's hard to do. I guess I love him. Maybe he isn't worth it, but I love him anyway. I've made some mistakes in my time, too. And that's what Bill is doing now—making a mistake."

She spread her hands wearily, and ended her explanation.

"I just mixed up in the thing to warn Bill; to try to scare him away from whatever he's doing," she said. "And that's every darn thing I know about it. I didn't even know about the two hundred and fifty people everybody keeps talking about."

Doc Savage picked up the transmitter of the short-wave radio apparatus with which the car was equipped. He allowed the tubes time to warm.

"Headquarters," he said.

Patricia's voice answered almost instantly.

"On deck," she said brightly.

"Anyone there?" Doc asked.

"I'm here, but you don't seem to consider me anybody when excitement rolls around," Pat said. "Yes, Renny is sitting here biting his big fingernails. He can't find anybody named Bench Logan or any record of anybody by that name."

Doc said, "Put him on."

Colonel John Renny Renwick had a voice that sounded somewhat like a subway train going through a tunnel. "Hello, Doc. Say, I can't get to first base on anybody named Bench Logan."

"Get a car from the basement garage, one of the machines that has nothing distinguishing about it," Doc Savage said. "Drive south on Broadway. Keep in touch with me by radio, so that you can pick up a cab I am trailing."

"What about this Bench Logan—"

"The man in the cab is Bench Logan."

"Holy cow!" Renny rumbled. "Coming up."

Doc Savage left the radio turned on and drove in silence.

Nicky Jones was staring at him. "You fellows sure have things organized," she remarked.

Doc began keeping a watch for Renny after a few minutes.

Finally Nicky said, "Look, I'm not one to ask favors, but give Bill Browder the breaks, will you? I don't mean let him off. If he's done something, he'll have to take his medicine; and I'll stick by him if he wants me to. But if you can prevent that, I wish you'd do it. Pull him away from the fire before he gets his fingers burned, I mean."

Doc said, "We will do that for anyone who is innocent."

Suddenly Renny's tearing voice came out of the loud-speaker. "All right, Doc," Renny said. "I am behind you now. You just passed me."

"Swing around the block," Doc said, "and get on Broadway ahead of us."

Several minutes later, Renny appeared ahead of them. He was driving a dark, nondescript car.

Doc said, "The cab next you is the one. Pick up the trail. I will pretend to lose out. Notify me where the passenger goes."

Doc Savage drove to headquarters, the establishment which he maintained on the eighty-sixth floor of the mid-city office building. From the garage, he rode upward in a private elevator. The garage was also private and contained an assortment of cars. Nicky Jones was impressed.

Nicky was further impressed by Patricia Savage.

"Goodness, darling," she told Pat, "I didn't know you were *that* Patricia Savage. I've seen your pictures. I've walked past that beautician's place of yours, but never had the nerve to come in."

Doc Savage checked and learned that no reports had yet come in from Monk and Ham, who were investigating Bill Browder. Nor was there anything from Long Tom and Johnny, who were checking up on Thomas J. Eleanor. Their work would probably be more difficult, and would depend on running down and talking to Wall Street financiers who might have some slight information about the rather mysterious Eleanor.

The bronze man entered his laboratory and locked the door behind him. The lab occupied a great floor space, and it was full of complex apparatus for scientific experimenting.

Doc changed clothes. His full-dress suit was, to say the least, conspicuous, and even more so because it was now dilapidated. He changed to a discreet business suit, and put on a bulletproof undergarment that might have been called a vest, although it was made of alloy-metal mesh. It covered his entire body and portions of his legs and arms, and would turn anything up to a slug from a military rifle. It would stop a military slug, too, but the blow would do almost as much damage as the bullet in that case.

He added more gadgets to his equipment.

"Pat," he said, "will you take care of Miss Jones?"

Pat smiled at Nicky Jones.

She told Doc. "You're always giving me somebody to watch, and thinking it will keep me out of the excitement. I don't think that's fair."

Doc said, "This may be—" He did not finish. He had been about to say dangerous. But it was useless. That would just bait Pat on.

"What do you think it is?" Pat asked curiously.

The bronze man hesitated. Might as well tell Pat. She would worm it out of somebody, anyway.

He explained, "The thing is not yet very clear. A man named Bench Logan seems to be the key to the safety of two hundred and fifty—or fifty-six—people. Bench Logan is suspicious of everyone, including us. Thomas J. Eleanor, a more-or-less figure of international mystery, is endeavoring to get hold of Bench Logan and has hired Bill Browder to help him. Browder is Miss Jones' fiancé, and she is worried for fear Bill will get into serious trouble. There is a blue dog in it, too."

He left Pat looking puzzled and full of questions.

Chapter 6
THE SIDETRACK

Colonel John Renny Renwick was a man who had a pair of fists as big as his voice. The rest of him was big, too, but nothing that compared with his fists. He could not get them into quart pails.

Renny looked at Doc Savage. He was looking very sad, which meant that Renny was feeling rather good. He wore his saddest expressions in his happiest moments.

"Nice birthday present for you, this excitement," Renny remarked.

Renny had long ago come to the conclusion that Doc Savage followed his strange career for the same reason that he—Renny—followed it. For the breathlessness of it. The stimulation of excitement.

Doc examined a row of brownstone houses which looked as if they had been built during the days of Napoleon, and probably had been.

"Which one?" he asked.

"Third from the end," Renny said. "Holy cow, you know that fellow was wise that he was being followed. He did some tall ducking and left his cab as soon as he thought he had lost you."

"Do you know what room?"

"Yes," Renny said. "First floor front. You know something? That fellow is scared."

"What makes you think so?"

Renny said, "I've rented the room next to him. That place is a common rooming house, you know. I could hear him pacing the room and doing a lot of swearing and muttering. That guy is scared."

Doc said, "He has reason to know that Thomas J. Eleanor is looking for him."

Renny shook his head.

"I don't mean only scared that way," said the big-fisted man. "I mean—well, he's scared in another way. Inside himself. He's faced with some kind of decision. Terror faces him, no matter which way he decides. That's what I mean. That kind of a thing."

Doc said, "We might pay a visit to this room you rented."

It was a shabby room. They entered by the back door, and attracted no attention. Renny closed the door cautiously, then pressed an ear to the partition.

"Hear him," he said. "He's pounding the floor in there."

This was true. Doc Savage hurriedly rigged a mechanical gadget, a "listener" device utilizing a super-sensitive pick-up microphone, an amplifier and a headset. The amplifier could step up volume to such an extent that a fly would sound as if an airplane was in the room with them.

Bench Logan, however, was not muttering words. He was just muttering.

"Holy cow!" Renny said.

They listened for some time, without gathering any fruit.

Doc Savage gave that up. He let himself quietly into the hall and, at the crack below the door of Bench Logan's room, carefully emptied a bottle containing the anæsthetic gas of the type which he had used on Logan earlier.

He used the gas a very small bit at a time, so that Logan would think he was growing sleepy naturally.

In order to escape the effects himself, the bronze man held his breath and retreated to an open window in Renny's room, at intervals, to get more air.

It was a tedious job, but eventually they heard Bench Logan pile down on his bed and go to sleep.

Five minutes later, Renny asked, "Well, did our phenagling get us anything?"

Doc Savage spread out for inspection what they had found in Bench Logan's room.

There were three suits of business clothing, with shirts, socks, shoes, neckties, all very new, and sales slips showing at least two of the suits had been bought within the last two weeks.

One suit of attire for very cold weather consisted of one pair of bearskin pants, a parka with the hood edged with wolf, a pair of bearskin moccasins. There was nothing new about these. They were, in fact, falling to pieces from age and wear.

There was one short Eskimo knife with the blade made out of a piece of bone. This was sharp.

Six passports: One of them was English, the others French, Italian, German, Yugoslavian and Monrovian. No two of these passports bore the same name, but all of them had the picture of Bench Logan as the bearer.

There was no United States passport. All the other passports bore up-to-date visas—none of them was more than six months old—entitling the passport owner to travel anywhere. This was, considering the state of Europe, unusual.

And there was one diplomatic document from Monrovia, entitling the bearer to special considerations at the border.

These documents were wrapped in an oilskin pouch which was much the worse for wear.

There was one letter. The paper looked as if it had been spotted with drops of water, possibly tears.

The letter was from a noted New York attorney, and read:

My dear Flagle:
    I must advise you that the man you mention, your acquaintance named Bosworth Hurlbert, is still wanted for murder by the authorities.
    I am also sorry to advise you that nothing can be done about "squashing" this murder charge, as you suggest. Murder charges simply are not squashed here in the United States.
    I would further advise you that, if you have any idea of the whereabouts of this man, Bosworth Hurlbert, you turn the matter over to the police.
    My investigation of the matter indicates that Bosworth Hurlbert slew a banker named John Kimball in New York City, five years ago. As I say, the thing for you to do is turn Kimball's murderer over to the police if you know his whereabouts.

Sincerely,
E. E. Kincaid, Attorney

Renny finished reading that. "I wonder who Bosworth Hurlbert is. This letter isn't addressed to this street. It's to a post-office-box number. Bosworth Hurlbert—Bench Logan. Those two names aren't at all alike. But I wonder if Bench Logan could be this Bosworth Hurlbert, who is wanted for murder."

Doc said, "You might check on that."

"I sure will."

Renny ambled back to the Eskimo clothing and picked it up. The tattered condition of the garments intrigued him. He examined the stuff closely.

"Look here," he said. "This stuff has been chewed on, as if the guy who wore it had got kind of hungry and tried to make a meal off his own clothes."

Doc Savage made no comment. He was examining the floor. He beckoned and pointed.

Renny stared at what the bronze man was interested in.

"Doesn't mean anything to me," Renny said. "Just some short hairs. Kind of coarse. And blue."

"Dog hair," Doc Savage said. "And blue."

They were back in their room when Bench Logan awakened. They heard him yawn mightily and turn restlessly on the bed. Thanks to the lack of after effects from the gas, they surmised that he did not know he had been knocked out.

Doc had carefully replaced everything in Logan's room exactly as he had found it.

Sounds ceased coming from Bench Logan's room. The man seemed to be either asleep, or lying on his bed thinking.

Doc whispered, "Renny, you might as well get busy checking up on the Bosworth Hurlbert angle."

"Right," Renny agreed.

"And check that Monrovian passport. Get hold of the Monrovian consulate and have them dig up anything they can regarding Bench Logan."

"Why particularly the Monrovian passport?" Renny asked.*

Doc Savage did not answer that. Renny frowned at him—not because the big-fisted engineer was irritated but because when Doc seemed not to hear an inquiry it usually meant something. It suddenly dawned on Renny that the Monrovian angle must be important.

"Monrovia," he said. "Say, that's the country where they got rid of their dictator about six months ago. There was a revolt, and

---

* Readers familiar with the foreign situation will immediately realize that Monrovia is an entirely fictitious foreign country. Because of the parallel between actual events and certain happenings depicted in this story, the author wishes to point out that it is his policy to deal with fiction only in these stories. Hence, this explanation that Monrovia is a non-existent country and Mungen a non-existent person.

the dictator, named Mungen, committed suicide while besieged in his chancellory."

"That is right," Doc Savage said.

The bronze man did not sound as if he wanted to discuss the matter further. Renny shrugged, put on his hat and left, being careful to make as little noise as possible.

When Renny had gone, Doc Savage seated himself beside the wall and kept the headset of the sound pick-up device over his ears. He could hear Bench Logan breathing. The sound was like a series of deep gasps, but that was the exaggerated effect of the amplifier.

Bench Logan was not asleep, but eventually he did go to sleep.

Doc Savage also slept. He kept the headset over his ears, so that any noise from the other room would awaken him.

Near daylight, Renny returned. He was excited.

"Bench Logan *is* Bosworth Hurlbert, and he's wanted for murder," Renny explained.

The big-fisted engineer had done an industrious job of digging people out of bed, he explained.

"Here's another thing," he said. "Bench Logan was an archenemy of that dictator I mentioned—that lug named Mungen. And Mungen *was* a lug, too. One of the most bloodthirsty devils that have fastened on a nation in centuries, and there've been some bloody ones, too."

"Details," Doc Savage suggested.

"The first record of Bench Logan I was able to dig up," Renny said, "was as a prize fighter, then a vaudeville acrobat. He went to Europe working as an acrobat for a circus and doing strong-man stunts. On a street in Naples, Italy, one day, he saved a little girl who had her foot fast in the stirrup of a runaway horse by grabbing the horse and knocking the horse senseless with a blow of his fist."

Renny paused and glanced toward the adjacent room, where Bench Logan was sleeping.

"He must be quite a guy," he said. "Anyway, the episode of the runaway horse attracted the attention of Thomas J. Eleanor, the international financier, and Eleanor hired Bench Logan as a bodyguard."

"When did Bench Logan enter Eleanor's employ as body-guard?" Doc asked.

"A little more than five years ago."

"Go ahead."

"Well, then there was the murder. It was here in New York. Bench Logan was bodyguarding Thomas J. Eleanor, and some banker named John Kimball went off his top and tried to kill Eleanor. Bench Logan had to kill the banker, Kimball."

"Right there," Renny continued, "Bench Logan did a jackass thing. Thomas J. Eleanor must have paid him to keep his, Eleanor's, name out of it. Because Bench Logan took the imaginary name of Bosworth Hurlbert and covered up his connection with Eleanor, concealing the fact that he was body-guarding Eleanor when he killed this banker in self-defense. Eleanor hired him to keep his name out of it, I haven't a doubt. Bench Logan skipped in a hurry."

Doc Savage had been listening intently. He asked, "Is there any chance that Bench Logan did not think there would be a murder charge when he fled?"

Renny became thoughtful.

"That might be," he said.

"Following this murder, or killing, did Bench Logan remain in Eleanor's employment?"

"Oh, sure! He was working for Eleanor when he got in trouble with this dictator, Mungen, two years later."

"How did that come about?"

Renny grimaced. "You see, I got all this from the Monrovian consul. He jumped out of bed and hurried down to the office and got it out of his files for me. All this stuff about Bench Logan was in his files because they dug it up when Bench tried to kill Mungen, the dictator."

"Logan tried to kill Mungen?"

Renny nodded. "Girl stuff, believe it or not. This Bench Logan was engaged to a showgirl in Bucharest, and the girl fell for Mungen and went to Monrovia. This Mungen, the way I remember his pictures, was no bargain. He was a hog. But the guy must have had something on the ball, because he got the girl."

Doc held up a hand. Sounds were coming from the bedroom, noises which indicated Bench Logan was awakening. But the man did not get up at once.

Doc breathed, "Be careful about noise. But go ahead."

"That Mungen was a devil, and the girl had spirit," Renny said. "Anyway, Mungen had his secret police take care of the girl. She was 'killed' in an automobile accident. I guess that might have fooled some people, but it didn't deceive Bench Logan any. He got a pistol and went for Mungen. Probably he already had the pistol. Anyway, he shot Mungen three times in his bulletproof vest, and once in the leg, and got clean away. You no doubt remember that. It was called an 'attempted political assassination,' and they made quite a fuss. But they didn't catch Bench Logan. I suppose he went back to bodyguarding Thomas J. Eleanor. At least, the records indicate he did."

Doc Savage gestured at the listening apparatus.

"Bench Logan is making a telephone call," he said.

Bench Logan spoke from the telephone in his room. They could hear each word he said, but the other part of the dialogue was not audible.

"Give me his nibs," Bench Logan said, "and hurry up about it. Tell him it's Logan calling. If he's not on here in thirty seconds, I'll hang up."

Renny commented, "He sure gets his feelings in his voice. He sounds like a desperate man who has finally made up his mind."

"Hello," Bench Logan said. "You know who this is. Here's the final. The absolute alternative. Either you have a steamship equipped with planes on its way north to rescue those people in five hours, or I go to the police."

He evidently listened to what the other said for a moment.

"That's all right; I'll face the murder charge," he said. "I've thought it all over. I may get off with a light sentence. All this publicity that will be aroused may work in my favor. Anyway, I'm going to take the chance. There's two hundred and fifty-six people up there, and that's two hundred and fifty-six lives against mine. My life hasn't been any too useful. I guess nobody would hesitate in trading my life for the lives of those people. I've been hesitating because it's my life, and I hate to spend it." He was silent a while. "But *you'll* die with me, you know that!"

The other said something.

Bench Logan swore bitterly.

"I won't argue," he said. "I know you can't get a steamship sailing in five hours, but you can get one started preparing. And you'll have to do it. Either that, or the newspapers will be on the streets with extras telling about the plight of those people."

Again he listened.

Then he laughed violently.

"All right, so I was lying when I told you Doc Savage was working with me," he snarled. "I knew you had found it out. I knew Savage was working for you. But don't start depending too much on Savage. I took care of that. He's on a ship bound to a foreign country, right now, and that ship sailed at midnight. They won't turn around and come back on a radio order, either, because they'll think it's an enemy submarine trying to trick them. Savage is out of the way."

For the last time, Bench Logan listened.

"Five hours," he said, "or I go to the police."

He hung up.

Doc Savage stood with the headset clamped to his ears, and decided that Bench Logan was packing his clothing. Logan seemed to be throwing everything into a suitcase in mad haste.

The bronze man took off the headset.

"Renny," he said in a low voice, "this man is getting ready to leave. He must be afraid that his telephone call will be traced, and they will come here after him."

Renny nodded dubiously.

Doc said, "Follow Logan. Get hold of Monk and Ham by radio, and have them help you. Also, contact Johnny and Long Tom, and have them come here so they can lend a hand if necessary."

Renny took a deep breath. "Holy cow! You want me to go off and leave you? I don't like—"

"Get moving," Doc suggested, "if you want to trail Logan."

The big-fisted engineer put on his hat and left.

Chapter 7
ACTION IN ARK STREET

The man wore a white suit, and he came in a little white wagon. The wagon had a bell—or rather, there was a bell attached to the horse. A tiny and musical bell, it tinkled enough to pleasantly soothe anyone who might be awake and happen to hear it this early in the morning. But not loud enough to awaken anyone.

The milkman got out of the wagon, took a wire basket of white-filled bottles from the back and entered the brownstone-front rooming house where Bench Logan had lived.

He was in the house not more than three minutes, then he came out again. He climbed in his wagon. He drove down the street. The bell tinkled.

The milkman began whipping the horse.

But the horse was old; he knew his pace, and held it. His trot was not fast enough for the milkman.

The man jumped out of the wagon and began running.

Doc Savage was on the roof of the row of buildings. He had kept pace with the milkman. The rooftops of the buildings were the same height throughout the block, separated only by brick walls, three or four feet high.

Doc hooked a folding steel grapple over the edge of the brick wall and flipped out a silk cord which was attached to the grapple. It was the simplest kind of gimmick, but he carried it with him always. He started down.

The front came out of the house where Bench Logan had been! There was, for a split second, no noise. There was just a quick outward jumping of the side of the house. Not a few bricks, nor a few square feet of them. The entire wall.

The wall came outward as if pushed from behind by red hands. The red fingers of the red hands pushed through the wall, breaking it in fragments. And the red fingers were flame, the flame of explosive!

Sound came then. It was sudden, like the rip of a high-powered rifle. Not a roar, but a pop. It did something to eardrums. And the air became a great weight with pressing force.

Doc Savage fell the last dozen feet. The buildings were four-story walk-ups, with areaways and winding steps in front of each. Doc hit a flight of steps. It was not a good spot for landing. He tumbled down to the sidewalk.

The air pressure fled, and suction seemed to follow. Suction that sought to jerk eyes out of sockets and pluck eardrums.

Falling bricks made a great roar.

Doc Savage came to his feet. The stuff the man had planted in the milk bottles had been terrific. A liquid-oxygen explosive of some sort, probably. As destructive as an aerial bomb.

Doc could not hear. His body felt numb. But he got up and began running.

The "milkman" had gone down. This was why he had gotten so impatient with the slow horse. The fellow struggled to his feet.

The horse had stopped dead-still and was just standing there. The animal seemed to be shell-shocked.

The milk wagon had been turned quartering, and upset, and a senseless figure had sprawled out on the pavement. The figure wore only underwear, shoes and a shirt. The genuine milkman, probably.

Doc Savage ran for the fake milkman. He overhauled the fellow, seized him, and bore him to the pavement.

And a car came into the block from the west, a touring car with the top down. A man was standing erect in the back seat with a rifle. He began shooting deliberately!

The "milkman" was soft and smelled faintly of perfume. He discovered Doc Savage's identity and yelled in fright. He tried to fight. The first rifle bullets from the end of the block passed, and the man screamed in terror.

Doc ran with him, sidewise, to the opposite side of the street. There was an entry, three steps down into a basement entrance. He dived into that. The heavy stone steps leading up to the first floor of the house sheltered him.

He tried the door. It was closed by a steel grille. The windows were iron-barred. It was not an unusual construction for basement windows and doorways, but inconvenient.

The bronze man put all his strength against the bars. But all of it was not enough.

The car came down the street. The man with the rifle still stood erect in it. Another man had joined him. This one had a pump-action shotgun.

Another car came into the opposite end of the thoroughfare. A sedan. Men frantically waved their hats out of the windows to identify themselves as friends.

Doc Savage was having no luck with the window bars or door grille. He could hear someone inside the basement—a woman shouting angrily.

He was trapped. He could not show himself. There was at least one military rifle being used, and he did not relish getting shot with that, even with his bulletproof vest.

The touring car came close.

"There he is!" a man howled.

They lost no time. The car veered, bumped the curb, jumped it. An iron railing surrounded the sunken entry. The car rooted this over like a hog going through weeds. It jumped into the pit, crashed the iron window bars, caved them inward! Glass shattered. The woman inside the basement let out a yell.

Doc Savage was clear of the car. He had, of necessity, abandoned the "milkman." The latter was somewhere under the car.

The bronze man worked fast. He heaved up, grabbed hold of the rifle, then the man who held it. Simultaneously, he dropped two smoke bombs. These ripened into palls of dark vapor.

Doc brought the rifleman's head down against the edge of the car door. The man slackened. Another man aimed a revolver, began working the trigger. Doc got down, clear of the bullets. The smoke came up and surrounded him. The shotgun blasted. In the basement, the woman howled.

Bill Browder began screaming orders. Bill Browder was in the sedan which now stood in the street.

"Get out here in the street," he shouted, "where we can tell who's who!"

Doc Savage dived to the car radiator, found that it had done what he had been unable to do—dislodged the window bars. He wedged through the bars. Some glass was out of the window. He dislodged more.

There was a living room, not badly furnished. The woman was not in sight. Doc crossed the living room. There should be a back door.

The woman appeared. She had a round glass percolator bowl full of boiling-hot coffee. She drew back to throw this.

Doc said, "Get out of here quick! The back door!"

She threw the hot coffee anyway. He dodged it. But it hit the wall, splashed back on him. It was like liquid fire coming through his clothing.

He told the woman, "At least, you had better crawl under a bed."

Someone fired a shotgun through the living-room window. The woman turned and ran. She found a back door, opened it. Doc was close behind.

The woman ran down a concrete-floored court, yelling, "Police! Police! Where's a cop?"

Doc Savage took the opposite direction so as to draw attention from the woman.

He covered no more than fifty yards when men poured out into the courtyard behind him. They yelled and fired guns.

Doc dropped containers of tear gas which fell on the concrete courtyard floor and smoked.

He went through a window. The window was not open, and he did not pause to open it; he walked through glass, sash and everything, coat skirts yanked up over his hands and face. The glass opened one of his trouser legs as if a razor had done the work, but he was not cut.

This apartment was empty, unfurnished. He went through it headlong. The front door had a spring lock. He let himself out in the street.

Far away, the woman was yelling, "Police! Police! Where's a

cop!" And now she was adding, "Henry! Henry, for the love of mercy, come home!"

Doc took to the sidewalk and ran. He was in flight. He was making no bones about it. He had expected trouble, but nothing on the scale of this. There were two cars, at least six men in each. A dozen attackers. And they were armed like a panzer squad!

They shot at him. He left a few smoke bombs blooming on the sidewalk as he went. They could not see him, so they missed him with the bullets. And soon he was around a corner.

He turned to the left, because it was urgent that he get out of line of the lead. And left took him toward the river.

The river was naked here, empty of warehouses. The cobbled street sloped down to the concrete river embankment, grim and bare this early in the morning.

There was no shelter, nothing anywhere for cover, except, of course, the houses, from which sleepy heads were thrusting. But to double into any of those would mean danger for the innocent tenants, and probably no permanent safety. Doc kept going. He could hear the moan of automobile engines behind him.

There was, it now dawned on him, at least a third car, and maybe more. The third car had waited at a distance of two or three blocks. But now it bore down! Someone in this third machine fired a tentative shot, and every head that protruded from a window on the block suddenly jerked from view.

Things had moved fast. The woman was still screeching, "Police, police!" and asking Henry to come.

He heard a man bellow, "Great grief, they're attacking the city!"

He went on. The river was before him. Cold. It steamed in the early-morning light as if smoke were coming from its surface. The opposite shore was not visible, nor could he see the spans of the big bridges upstream and downstream.

He swung left. There was, fifty yards away, a small dock—a finger of solid concrete, thrusting out into the river. At the end of this was tied a barge, and the barge had a heaping load of gravel. A small deckhouse, like a match box, made a wart on one end of the barge.

Doc hit the gravel load, sank to his ankles in the soft stuff and waded to the deckhouse.

"Get under cover, quick!" he shouted.

The warning was not necessary, he discovered. There was no watchman in the barge deckhouse; no one aboard except himself.

He raced out of the deckhouse, went flat behind the heaped gravel.

Rifles began making their brittle reports, and jacketed lead cut through the cheesy deckhouse as if it were cardboard. More lead, a tearing volley of it, disturbed the gravel crest, so that the loose stuff rolled down and half covered the bronze man's body where he lay.

"Get grenades ready for him if he goes into the river," a man yelled.

This voice did not belong to Bill Browder, and it was much more bloodthirsty than Bill Browder had sounded.

Doc Savage dug out and hurled an explosive grenade. It was a thing the size of a bantam egg; and when it hatched, it almost took the vicinity apart. Doc had his mouth wide open, ready for the report. The blast kicked loose gravel down the side of the mound.

He looked quickly.

None of the gunmen had been close to the high explosive. Doc had known that. At the end of the dock, there was a hole that would hold a small house, and part of the dock end itself was still in the air. The killers would push no cars out on the dock for cover, or ride out in them as if they were tanks.

Doc knew by now that their cars were armored. That explained their recklessness, their lack of fear of the police.

The bronze man was, as a whole, completely astounded. He had expected no campaign on this scale. Further than that, he was disgusted at his own lack of foresight. It should not have taken a clairvoyant to foresee that the thing was big. The lives of two hundred and fifty people were at stake; that had been called to his attention so repeatedly that it was almost ridiculous. But that should have shown him the affair was big.

He took another look over the gravel, this time using a telescoping periscope that was smaller than a lead pencil. He saw the cars—four of them, now—roll toward the concrete dock and stop.

Doc heaved tear gas again. The stuff surrounded the cars. But the men got out, undisturbed. They wore gas masks.

The voice that did not belong to Bill Browder gave an order.

"Begin pegging hand grenades in the river," it said, "so the concussion will cave him in if he tries to swim for it. The rest of you start working on that gravel barge."

He did not tell them to be careful. Apparently, he didn't care. He added, "Sink the barge!"

He seemed to think Doc was cornered.

Doc prepared a few smoke grenades. The breeze was blowing out over the river. He could, barring a towering case of bad luck, let the smoke sweep across the river and swim with it. The grenades would not damage him greatly on the surface. The gunmen could not see to shoot him.

It was then, when his strategic position was the best it had been since the beginning of the attack, that an interruption came.

It was a car. Black, long, with an unmuffled motor that made the sound of an airplane. Possibly the noise of the motor was the really frightening thing about the car.

The car came close, but not too close, and stopped. A slit of a ventilating window opened, a gun muzzle came through, and the gun let out noise and lead.

Bill Browder shrieked. It was unquestionably Bill Browder's voice which screamed, and there was terror in it, not injured pain. Browder seemed to be in one of the armored automobiles.

"Cops!" a man bellowed.

They sent some well-chosen bullets toward the newly arrived car. Then sent some that were not so well chosen. But this machine also was bulletproofed.

The passing of time might have had something to do with it; police *were* due to arrive. And that bit of resistance broke up the fight.

Bill Browder, in a shaky voice, yelled, "Get away from here, men!"

They got away, like an alley-cat powwow breaking up at the appearance of a bulldog.

The new car pulled up close to the dock.

Thomas J. Eleanor put his head out of the window and shouted, "Are you safe, Mr. Savage?"

It never—goes the saying—rains but what it pours.

Another rescue car appeared. This one was a deep-bronze color and less impressive outwardly than the other armored cars. The moment Doc saw the machine, he became intensely interested.

Thomas J. Eleanor leaped out of his own car and picked his way at a gallop over the blasted end of the dock.

"Oh!" he exclaimed. "You haven't been harmed. I am so glad!"

Doc Savage watched the distant car head for one of the fleeing machines.

"How did you get here?" he asked.

"It's a long story," said Thomas J. Eleanor, excitement making his foreign accent more pronounced. "But I can tell you why I was late helping you. My blasted chauffeur got scared. He refused to drive my car. I had to knock him out, toss him from the machine and drive it myself."

The distant car hit one of the fleeing machines a glancing blow. The fleeing car was knocked half around, so that it veered against a light pole. The light pole snapped off, the ornate glass globe seeming to explode into fragments.

The strain popped open a door of the car that had been hit. A man tumbled out. The machine kept going. The man who had fallen out was partially under it, and the machine ran over him.

The bronze car which had hit the other one slid to a stop in such a position as to protect the man who had been run over, and who was lying on the pavement.

All other cars, except the one driven by Thomas J. Eleanor, got out of sight.

Doc Savage extended his hand to Thomas J. Eleanor.

"Thank you, Mr. Eleanor," said the bronze man, "for saving my life."

Eleanor chuckled.

"As a matter of fact, I did nothing of the kind, and you know it," he said. "As it happened, that bronze machine was—I did not know it, though—amply capable of saving you."

Doc said nothing. He walked toward the bronze machine. Thomas J. Eleanor followed him.

Eleanor said, "Furthermore, I think you could have used those smoke grenades to conceal yourself, and reached safety by swimming in the river."

Doc made no comment.

Patricia Savage got out of the bronze car. She sank to her knees beside the man who had been run over.

"Doc, this man is dying," she said. "He's badly hurt. He's trying to talk."

Doc Savage knelt beside the dying man. The street-light standard which had been knocked over lay beside the man, together with the pole which bore the name of the street. And it was the metal name plate of the street which, when the car ran over the man, had really done the damage. The name on the plate, "Ark Street," was coated with crimson.

Chapter 8
THE MAN IS MAD

The man said, "I'm going to die." He spoke clearly, except for the whistling in his voice and the fact that his voice had no volume.

Because what the man knew about himself was the truth, Doc Savage made no answer.

"You go . . . go—" The man gurgled for a moment. His effort to speak was horrible. "Go north-northwest from Iceland, and—" He closed his eyes.

Doc Savage said, "North-northwest from Iceland—yes. Then what?"

The man mumbled some figures—degrees and minutes.

He was silent again.

"They're there," he said. "Two hundred . . . hun—"

He was quiet again.

He said, "Louise, I didn't mean it. Hello, mom. Hello, pop. Louise, I'm so glad to see you. I wanted to tell you how sorry—"

He did things that a dying man does then, and Pat put her hands over her eyes and turned away.

Doc Savage stood up.

"Dead?" asked Thomas J. Eleanor.

Doc nodded.

"He didn't seem to know me," said Eleanor.

"Did you know *him*?"

Thomas J. Eleanor nodded. "One of my bodyguards."

"Bench Logan is another of your bodyguards?"

"Was—not is," corrected Eleanor.

There were sirens in the distance. Police cars, of course. The whole incredible procession of incidents had taken less than seven or eight minutes; and the police, usually more prompt, seemed to be a little late.

Uneasiness twisted Eleanor's face. "Those sirens—the police, evidently," he said. "I have an enormous dislike of publicity. Is there any reason why we have to stay here?"

"Not necessarily," Doc said.

Pat got behind the wheel of the bronze car. The machine was one of Doc's, an experimental model on which he had tried out

161

new types of armor plating and gasproofing. As a fortress, it fell very little short of an army tank.

They drove away. Eleanor followed in his car.

The river was placid, and the fog still lifted from it like smoke. Darker tendrils of vapor, the smoke from the bombs Doc had used, were blowing across it. Nothing else was peaceful. The neighborhood was coming to life, sticking its collective head out of the window and bellowing demands as to just what had happened.

Doc Savage watched, in the rearview mirror, Eleanor's car following behind them.

"Pat," he said.

Pat chuckled. "Don't start grumbling about my getting mixed up in this," she said. "Renny got Monk and Ham to help him trail Bench Logan. Renny told me you wanted Long Tom and Johnny to show up here and help you, but he said he couldn't contact them. Long Tom and Johnny are investigating this Thomas J. Eleanor, and they must be away from their radios. Well, I couldn't get Long Tom and Johnny to come here and help, so I got worried. I came myself." She made a wry face. "I practically missed the whole thing."

"Where did you leave Nicky Jones?"

"The girl? Oh, I left her at headquarters. She's scared. She'll stay there."

"What makes you so sure of that?"

Pat shrugged. "Oh, she's worried about her boy friend, Bill Browder. And now she's scared something will happen to her. When Bench Logan tried to stow you and her away on that ship that was to sail at midnight—we checked on that ship, incidentally, and found out it sailed, so Logan *was* trying to get rid of you— Nicky had the old fear thrown into her. She'll be at headquarters, all right."

Doc said. "We had better see."

Thomas J. Eleanor sauntered into Doc Savage's skyscraper headquarters as if nothing had happened. Eleanor showed no emotional traces of what had just occurred. He was composed. His dynamic force was unabated. He was so big that he had to turn sidewise somewhat to pass through the door, but he did it with dignity. His bigness was somehow not the blubber of a fat man, but rather the effect of fabulous power carefully stored and guided.

He said, "So this is your establishment, Mr. Savage. I have heard of some such aerie. I am impressed."

Pat went into the library quickly.

"Will you be seated, Mr. Eleanor?" Doc Savage suggested.

The big man chuckled. "Have a seat, eh?" he said. "And give out with some information. Isn't that what you mean?"

"An explanation would not be unwelcome," Doc admitted.

Thomas J. Eleanor nodded as emphatically as he could with his chins.

"All right, I'll tell you everything," he said.

Pat came dashing out of the library.

"She isn't!" Pat gasped.

"Is not what?" Doc asked.

"Isn't here. Nicky Jones. She beat it, the two-faced little liar!" Pat said.

Doc Savage swung to Eleanor. "You might get going with your story."

Pat's hands were against her cheeks. "Oh, Doc, what will I do? How'll I find her?"

Thomas J. Eleanor folded his hands on his stomach. He had lighted a cigar, evidently one of the dollar ones which he bought through the druggist near his suburban home.

"I know this story will intrigue you as much as it did me," said Eleanor.

Pat beat her hands together. "It's my fault!" she wailed. "I was a fool who wanted to get in on some excitement, so I went off and left that girl here. What a sap I was! It's a wonder she didn't wreck the place before she left. She could have. Doc, what will I do?"

Thomas J. Eleanor blew out fragrant blue smoke.

"In the beginning," he said expansively, "I was merely curious. I think my curiosity is what got me involved in it. Curiosity causes a great many people trouble, I have always said."

Pat walked around the room, looking as if she wanted to pull out her hair.

Eleanor said, "It was my bodyguard, Bench Logan, you see. The man was acting as if he had something on his mind. I am a judge of men, and I have had trouble with my employees before. Particularly my bodyguards."

Pat kicked a chair.

"I hire men of hard character, necessarily, as bodyguards," Thomas J. Eleanor pointed out. "Their job is to be tough, and naturally I must employ men capable of being just that." He looked at his fingernails, not embarrassed, but as a gesture to show that it was really, in a way, his fault.

He continued, "I asked Logan about it. I confronted him bluntly. And, of course, he told me nothing. And he did it in such a way that I fired him."

Pat kicked another chair and put her fists on her hips.

Thomas Eleanor said, "As soon as I fired Bench Logan, I made a startling discovery. I found my other bodyguards and all my men were afraid of Bench Logan. And there was an incredible plot between part of my employees and Bench Logan, a plot involving wholesale murder and a tremendous fortune."

Pat stopped displaying her temper and became interested in the story.

"Some of my employees," said Eleanor, "were not mixed in it. But those who were left when Logan left. With one exception."

He smiled the smile of a fat man.

"It is good to find a coward sometimes," he said. "The one employee who did not leave was a coward. He was afraid. He was as yellow as they come, as a good American would say. He broke down and told me the whole thing."

Pat said, "You're using a lot of words to get into this thing."

Eleanor smiled at her. "Once I was young and impetuous, too."

Pat said, "You're not old, now. You're just fat."

Eleanor winced.

Doc said, "The story?" impatiently.

Eleanor spread his hands. "Here is where you become amazed—or disgusted. With me, I mean."

He paused dramatically.

"On an island in the South Pacific," he said, "there is a shipload of people. Two hundred and fifty-six of them, the last anyone knows. They had found something incredible, so incredible that they cannot leave the island alive. One man left the island, and that man is Bench Logan. He knows how to get back. But he does not want to get back. He wants those people to be in his power."

The fat man puffed on his cigar. "Mind you, I admit the story is fabulous," he said. "I did not believe it myself, at first. But I became convinced it was true. And, now—well, you can just see for yourself."

"See what?" Pat asked.

"You saw what an organized effort was made this morning to kill Doc Savage simply because he was interesting himself in the thing," said Eleanor. "Doesn't that prove a great deal is at stake?"

"It proves a lot is at stake," Pat said. "But it doesn't necessarily prove your story is true."

Eleanor looked like a man who was not accustomed to having his word doubted.

"Humph!" he said.

"You said Bench Logan was your bodyguard," Pat said. "Just when did he get on this island?"

Eleanor shrugged. "I gave him a leave of absence for six months last year. It was during a period when I was living incognito in Sun Valley, Idaho, and did not need a bodyguard."

Pat looked at Doc, then at Eleanor.

"Where is this island?" she asked.

"I do not know," Eleanor said. "So help me, I do not. That is what I was trying to find out."

"And why were you so interested?"

Eleanor smiled. "Believe it or not, I am a humanitarian at heart. There are those who say differently. I want to save the lives of those two hundred and fifty-six people."

"You weren't by chance interested in the fantastic thing they have found—which is the reason they can't leave?"

Eleanor leaned forward. "I will tell you the truth. Yes. Yes, if there is a profit in it for me, I am definitely interested. I am interested in anything that shows a profit." His lips twisted ruefully. "I am a machine for making money, they say."

"What is the thing?"

"I do not know."

"Then why are you so intrigued by it?"

The fat man spread his hands. "Obviously, since so many men are involved in it, and so violently, there must be a great profit at stake for someone."

Pat said, "Just how was Doc involved in this? We would like to know that."

"I contacted Bench Logan and demanded that he give me the location of the island and these people," said Eleanor. "I'll be frank. I threatened him. He told me . . . er . . . to go jump in the lake, was the way he put it. He said Doc Savage was working with him; and with help like that, he wasn't afraid of me. He was lying, I know now. But at the time, I believed him. So I took measures to contact Mr. Savage. Unusual measures, perhaps."

"You had Bill Browder call Doc out to the district and tell him the story about the blue dog?"

"Yes. The blue-dog story was by way of sounding out Doc Savage to see whether he knew anything."

"Bill Browder is working for you, then?"

"Oh, no. He's one of the enemy. You see, I unfortunately discovered that last night, after Mr. Savage was out there."

Pat asked, "How'd you find it out?"

"Through a drugstore owner who purchases cigars for me. It seems Mr. Savage was there and caught Bill Browder eavesdropping on a telephone. Browder had hired the druggist to let him do this."

Pat frowned suddenly. "You didn't know anything about tapping the wire in that drugstore, eh?"

Thomas J. Eleanor grimaced. "I should have. As a matter of fact, Bill Browder had brought me to the drugstore and had been so clever in a conversation that I unwittingly gave the druggist the impression it was all right with me to tap the wires. It sounds silly for me to tell you that, I know. But it is true. Browder had me go to the druggist and O.K. what I presumed was the 'tapping' of my supply of cigars for himself. Browder told me he wanted to buy some of the cigars. I thought he was silly to pay a dollar apiece for cigars, but it was his money."

Doc Savage had been silent throughout. Now, he spoke.

He asked, "What about the spot north and east from Iceland mentioned by the dying man?"

"It was north and west of Iceland," said Thomas J. Eleanor.

"You did notice it, then."

"Ah, so you gave the wrong direction to ascertain if I had. Yes, I noticed. It means nothing to me. The dying man mentioned latitude and longitude figures, did he not?"

"Yes."

"A spot north-northwest of Iceland means nothing to me," insisted Thomas J. Eleanor.

The telephone lines into the headquarters did not connect to regulation bells, but to high-frequency buzzers which had different notes that were not unmusical. One of them sang out a long, rather imperative note. Pat picked up the instrument.

"Renny," she said, turning.

Doc took the telephone and said, "Yes?"

Renny's deep voice had a grim uneasiness.

"We bit into a sour apple," he said.

"What do you mean?" Doc asked.

"We need a little help." The big-fisted engineer was silent a moment. "You know this guy Bench Logan? Well, he's not playing alone. He's got five or six guys with him."

Renny was silent a moment. He sounded unnatural.

"We have them spotted," he said. "They are not aware they are being watched. I am in a yacht-building boatyard at College Point—in the big building as you come into the yard from the street. The place is abandoned. Just walk right in. We'll be waiting for you and show you where Bench Logan has holed up. And, say—come right out, will you? I think something is developing."

Doc Savage stared at the telephone.

"I will be there shortly," he said.

"Good!" Renny said. He hung up.

Doc replaced the receiver, and again his flake-gold eyes fixed on the instrument. He made, after a moment, the low trilling sound which was his unconscious habit in moments of mental stress.

Renny was in trouble. Someone had held a weapon on him, forced him to make that call.

Because situations of the kind had developed before, Doc and the others had worked out a simple code to verify the genuineness of telephone conversations. The code did not depend on inserting a key word in a false conversation. Sometimes that was impossible. Rather, in every genuine conversation, they inserted a key word. Leaving out the word was a warning. Renny had left it out.

Renny, then, was in imminent danger. Possibly Monk and Ham, as well.

Doc Savage's face had no expression.

"Pat," he said. "About Nicky Jones—"

Pat winced. "Yes?"

"You recall that she had a friend." Doc glanced at Thomas J. Eleanor. "A very fat girl named Fern Reed, the one who led me off on a false trail the first time."

"Yes, I remember that," Pat said.

"Get hold of the newspaper offices," Doc Savage told Pat, "and ask them to report to you, immediately, any humorous news story which may crop up about a car with an odor. The odor will be a completely different one. Nobody will be familiar with it. It will be a striking scent. Also contact the milk companies and have them broadcast a request for their drivers to report an unusual-smelling car. Offer a small reward. Better do the same with the taxicab companies. It is still early enough in the morning for you to catch the day-shift drivers before they go on duty."

Pat was astounded.

"A car that smells funny," she said.

Doc explained, "I was fortunate enough to manage to break a vial of chemical on Fern Reed's car. It will have a peculiar odor."

Thomas J. Eleanor burst out in a gust of laughter.

"That's sure a goofy thing!" Then he sobered suddenly. "But it's just the kind of a thing that would work."

There was a noise at the door, and Long Tom and Johnny came in.

Major Thomas J. Long Tom Roberts was a thin and unhealthy-looking fellow with a subway complexion and the general aspect of being an early client for an undertaker. His looks, though, were deceptive. He was not only quite healthy; he had the physical qualities of a wild cat. He was, in the profession of electricity, considered somewhat incredible.

"So you're Thomas J. Eleanor," he told the fat man. "We have the same first name and initial. I wish there was some other similarity between us."

"Meaning my fat?" asked Eleanor.

"Meaning your money," said Long Tom unkindly.

William Harper Johnny Littlejohn was as thin as Long Tom, and nearly twice as long. He was astoundingly thin. He wore, dangling from a lapel, a monocle which was never in his eye.

"I'll be superamalgamated," Johnny remarked to Eleanor. "The Homoousian hypostasis under perscrutination."

Eleanor smiled and said, "So you have been investigating me. You found my deeds have been satisfactorily dark, I hope."

Johnny was surprised. Strangers usually did not understand his words.

"Mansuetude indicates aphonics," he said.

"Contumeliousity is not a propendency," said Eleanor.

Johnny swallowed.

Pat said, "Great sails on the sea! We've finally run into somebody who can choke Johnny on his own words."

Doc Savage moved to the door. He addressed Eleanor.

"Mr. Eleanor, will you be kind enough to remain here with my associates and give them what aid you can?" he said. "It will be necessary for me to absent myself for a while."

Thomas J. Eleanor bowed.

"Of course," he said. "I will be delighted."

Doc Savage left the building.

As he wheeled his car out into the traffic, a newsboy was shouting an early edition.

"Reward offered for insane killer loose in city!" the newsboy called. "Reward for Bench Logan! Another battle in Europe. Early editions."

Chapter 9
PERILS NORTH

The scientific training which Doc Savage had undergone from childhood had given him a remarkable control of his nerves and of his emotions. Because of this, all but close associates were inclined to claim that he had no nerves or emotions, and few human qualities. This was an error. He could, for instance, become as astonished as the next man.

He was astonished, now. He sat there in the car and nearly rammed a cab in his path. He stopped the machine.

"War in Europe," called the newsboy. "Big reward for madman!"

Doc said, "Boy, paper."

The advertisement was half a page on Page 2.

$20,000 REWARD FOR A MADMAN

This sum will be paid for the apprehension, or information leading to the apprehension, of the man known as Bench Logan, alias Bosworth Hurlbert, accused murderer.

This man is known to have insanity in the family, both his parents having died in an institution.

Communicate with this newspaper.

Doc Savage drove two blocks and parked. The bronze man was frowning. He entered a cigar-store telephone booth and called the newspaper.

"Who inserted that advertisement offering a reward for Bench Logan?" he asked.

"The chairman of a group interested in public welfare," came the answer.

"What name?"

"I am sorry. The advertiser wishes that to remain anonymous. But I can assure you the money will be paid if and when you can—"

Doc Savage said, "Give me someone in authority around there. Connect me with Carl Mowbern, the business manager."

Carl Mowbern happened to be an individual with whom Doc

Savage was acquainted. He was not yet at the office. Doc called Mowbern's home. The man sounded sleepy.

"Oh, that ad?" Mowbern said. "They telephoned me last night before we published it—this morning, rather. You see, it is possibly libelous, labeling the man Bench Logan as crazy—"

"Who had it published?" Doc put in.

"Thomas J. Eleanor," said the business manager.

"Thank you," Doc said.

The bronze man ran to his car, sent the machine toward College Point, the spot from which Renny's telephone call had come—or, at least, from where Renny had said he'd been calling. It was not a long drive—express highway most of the distance.

He slowed his speed as he came near the address which Renny had given, the yacht-building boatyard at College Point. There were a number of these, but Renny could mean only one that was isolated from the others—the only one which was currently abandoned.

Half a dozen blocks from the boatyard, Doc parked his car.

Ten minutes later, a raging fire broke out in an old shack across the street from the boatyard. It was a raging fire in respect to the amount of smoke it created; otherwise, it was not much of a blaze. The College Point fire department soon extinguished it and stopped the smoke which was pouring across the boatyard.

The smoke and the firemen had created enough diversion for Doc Savage to get into the boatyard.

When he found a serviceable cabin cruiser tied to the ramshackle old dock at the back of the yard, he went no farther. He climbed aboard and concealed himself in the locker alongside the engine, the only hiding place of sufficient size.

A few minutes later, men climbed on the boat in a hurry.

Bench Logan said, "Let's get out of here. I don't like that fire."

"It was just an accident, maybe," a man suggested. "One of those things that happen."

Bench Logan swore. "All right, so maybe it was. We get out, anyway. Savage is going to be suspicious when he sees that fire—if he didn't show up while it was burning."

The engine alongside Doc Savage burst into life. It gave off heat, and the boat rushed through the water.

There was at least six inches of odorous bilge in the bottom of the boat, and the odor of it was not pleasant. The boat ran at high speed for perhaps thirty minutes, then lost way and bumped against a dock. They made lines fast.

"No, the trap for Savage blew up," Bench Logan told someone irritably.

They left the boat. Doc lay quiet long enough to be fairly certain no guard had been left on the craft. Then he threw back the engine-compartment hatch, climbed out of the cramped place.

The dock was about as ramshackle as it could be. Beyond it was a sloping bank with brush. In the other direction, there was an expanse of marsh grass and, far in the distance, higher ground with houses. One of the inlets on Long Island Sound close to the city.

Moving with care, keeping out of sight of the bank, Doc slid over the side of the boat. The water was cold. He submerged, swam rapidly, came up close to the bank. A moment later he was in the weeds.

He kept clear of a path which climbed the bank. The brush was profuse; ample concealment. He came to a mound of discarded clam shells and tin cans, skirted them and inspected a shack.

The place was obviously a miserable fisherman's shanty. Men sat on a shed porch, or walked around nervously.

Doc crawled to the rear wall. Tar paper had been tacked over cracks. He very carefully tore a bit of it loose.

Renny was tied to a chair inside, as were Monk and Ham.

Bench Logan stood spraddle-legged in the middle of the floor, glaring at the morning newspaper which he held in his hands. Copies of other newspapers lay on an old table.

Doc caught a small sound nearby and turned his head. He discovered that two animals had come close in the brush and were watching him. One animal was a pig, the other a species of large monkey or small ape.

The pig and the chimp were obviously friendly. Doc made a gesture with one hand, a gesture he knew would insure quiet. The animals were well trained.

The chimp was the pet of Brigadier General Theodore Marley Ham Brooks. The pig—it had enormous ears and the legs of a rabbit—belonged to Lieutenant Colonel Andrew Blodgett Monk Mayfair. The animals had evidently escaped when their owners were caught.

A burst of rage exploded from the shack. Doc put his eye to the crack.

Bench Logan stamped on the newspaper.

"Now I can't go to the police!" he yelled. "Damn that fiend!"

One of the men with Logan shook his head. "Bench, if you ask me, you couldn't have done it, anyway."

"You mean because of that old murder charge?" Logan asked.

"Sure! What else?"

Bench Logan compressed his lips. "Listen, I had decided to take that chance. It was the electric chair for me—or life for all those people. I—Well, hell! What else was there for me to do?"

The man came over and put a hand on Bench Logan's shoulder. "Bench, you're a great guy. You're three hundred percent for our money. And we're for you."

Logan bit his lips. "Thanks, Pete. But I'm licked on that giving myself up."

"You sure?"

Logan cursed violently. "Of course, I'm sure. You see this advertisement calling me a madman? You know what the police would say if I gave myself up?"

The other frowned. "They might doubt your story."

"Might! Hell, they *would*!" Logan groaned. "That part about my parents dying in an institution would cinch it."

"Were they in an insane asylum?"

"Sure! But it wasn't anything they had that I could inherit."

"Maybe you could prove that."

"I'd have a devil of a time doing it. My mother and father went nuts worrying about my kid brother. At least, they were right on the verge of it when the kid brother got killed in a holdup. That cinched it. But nobody knows that about my kid brother. I've kept it quiet. You see, he had a wife and kid at the time, and I didn't want them to know."

A man—there were six men here in addition to Bench Logan, it appeared—came into the shack, walked over and tested the ropes holding Renny, Monk and Ham.

Monk tried to kick the fellow. Monk was a wide, stocky man with a coat of reddish hair that looked like rusted shingle nails. Monk's general aspect was that of an agreeable ape; in fact, he resembled Ham's pet chimp.

Ham had acquired the chimp, and named him Chemistry, for that reason. To irritate Monk.

Ham and Renny only scowled as the man jerked at their ropes. Ham was an extremely dapper gentleman, even in his present difficulty. He always looked well dressed.

"Bench, what are we going to do?" asked the man who was talking to Logan.

Bench Logan shook his head. "This whole story is so fantastic that the police will not believe me—not with this insanity thing planted in their minds," he said. "They would not even investigate it."

The other smiled grimly. "Well, we're not licked."

Logan looked around at them. "You're a swell bunch of guys," he said sincerely. "There's no dough in this for you. I've told you that. But I ask you for help, and you pitch right in like there was a hundred bucks a day in it for you." He grinned ruefully. "I happen to know most of you make that much dough when you work, too."

The other man laughed. "Not often," he said. "This soldier-of-fortune racket ain't what it used to be."

There was a silence.

Doc Savage studied Logan's associates. They were, like Logan, capable men, and hard. They were in good physical condition, lean-faced, showing no sign of owning such handicaps as nerves. Stamped with the mark of adventurers, each of them.

"Bench, what about Doc Savage?" the man asked.

Bench Logan spread his hands in a gesture of indecision.

"That's why I wanted to get hold of Savage in this," he said. "First, I place him as against me. But I think it over some more, and I'm not so sure."

Renny rumbled, "You fool! The reason Doc Savage is in this is to save those people. You say that's your reason, too."

Logan rubbed his jaw.

"You've said that before," he muttered. "You almost got me believing you."

"Look, guy," Renny said, "don't be a sucker."

Logan frowned. "You think I am?"

Renny said, "You've got the most high-powered help you could have right at hand, *if* you're sincere. I mean Doc and our organization. I don't know what is behind all this, but my guess is that Doc would be more help than the police. He can move fast."

Bench Logan hesitated.

"How about planes?" he asked. "We would need a heck of a big plane, one that could land on leads in the ice, on water. More than one plane, probably, although one big ship could do it, making several trips."

Renny said, "We've got planes."

"First, we'd have to take in food," Logan said. "They're starving by now. There was almost no food when I got away. Then we could bring them out a few at a time." He fell silent.

The man who had talked to Logan said, "He may have something there, Bench. I've always heard Savage was straight."

Logan grimaced. "If he is, I've made a prize jackass out of myself."

Renny asked, "What makes you think Doc is a crook, anyway?"

Logan hesitated. "I— Well, it doesn't seem logical that he would go to all this trouble that he's supposed to go through to help people, without a profit. It ain't reasonable. It has been my experience that when you run into something like that, there is a joker somewhere."

Renny said, "Doc doesn't need money."

"Don't kid me," Bench Logan said. "Everybody needs money."

"What I mean," Renny said, "is that Doc has a source of money—all he needs."

"Where?"

Renny shrugged. "Sorry, but I can't say."*

Doc Savage got to his feet, walked around the shack, and entered. He paid no attention to the startled stares and the guns which appeared.

"Logan," he said, "I think we have identical aims in this matter."

Whatever Logan might have said to that, whatever his reaction might have been, remained a mystery because, from in the brush outside, a rifle smashed once; and Pete, the man who had been talking to Bench Logan, opened his mouth and his eyes to their extreme widest and fell on the floor. A lake of red grew under Pete immediately.

Like hot steel dropping into the utter silence that followed, Doc Savage spoke.

"You fellows have been surrounded," he said. "They saw me come in, and they are attacking. They are after me as much as they are after you. We had better work together."

He was, naturally, not believed.

Bench Logan seemed to trust the bronze man. But before Bench could speak, a man whipped up a pistol. Doc leaped for the fellow, got the gun. But by that time there was uproar, and lead coming through the thin planking of the shack like big bees.

---

* The source of Doc Savage's funds is, as far as the public is concerned, a secret. It comes from a remote Central American valley inhabited by descendants of the ancient Mayan civilization. It is furnished Doc Savage, in the form of gold, by the natives as an expression of gratitude for services they received from Doc during the course of an adventure related in the initial Doc Savage novel, "The Man of Bronze."

Doc sprang to Renny, hauling out a pocketknife. He cut the big-fisted engineer's bonds. Then he freed Monk and Ham.

Monk, Ham and Renny knew about fights. They got on the floor instantly.

They did another thing; they protected themselves against tear gas. Each of them tore the lining of the outside breast pocket out of his coat. The pockets were actually elastic, rubberlike material that was transparent and merely basted in place. Like toy balloons, the elastic pockets would stretch. They pulled them over their heads, and the elastic snapped tight below chin level.

The things were not comfortable. But they were transparent, and they would keep gas out of the eyes.

The enemy rushed the shack.

Doc took a board off the wall with a shoulder, and went outside. He flattened in the brush instantly and did not again get to his feet.

Rain water had dug a ditch. He rolled into that. Renny and Ham were almost on top of him. Monk popped another board off the wall, to make a hole of his own, and came through.

Doc said, "This way!"

His primary idea was to get his men to safety. Then he would return and do what he could in the brawl.

The attack on the cabin was sudden, violent and short. It consisted of a flurry of tear-gas bombs, then a wave of men armed with guns, protected by bulletproof vests.

Bench Logan and his men were like sitting birds. They had nothing but great rage, intense desire to fight. It did not help them.

The attack ended abruptly.

The assailants gathered up those who were still alive and left.

It was like that. No waiting. No fooling around. Doc was surprised.

The bronze man wheeled back. "Wait here," he said. "That quick retreat may be a trap."

Monk and Renny both bellowed. Monk said, "Trap or no trap, it's about time I got my hands on somebody." They followed Doc.

Ham Brooks was too perturbed over a rip in the leg of his striped morning pants to speak. How Ham had gotten into morning pants in the middle of such excitement was a mystery, but it was typical of him. He bounded after them.

Ham dashed into the shack when they reached it. There was courage in the act, as it developed when a smoking fuse came flying out of the door like a thin gray snake.

Ham appeared in the door with two objects in his hands.

"They left a suitcase full of dynamite to destroy the evidence," he remarked, exhibiting the suitcase.

The other object was an innocent-looking black cane. Ham's sword cane, which had been taken from him.

Doc Savage said, "Ham, you and the others see if you can get any evidence here."

The bronze man went on, following the raiding party. He ran, but kept his eyes alert for trouble. The dynamite might not be the only gesture the attackers had made. Nor was it.

He stopped suddenly, eyes on a black thread across the path. He followed it, found it a stout black silk bait-casting line attached to the pin of a grenade that was rigged to explode instantly.

He threw the grenade off in the brush, where it let go with violence! Then he went on.

They were piling in cars. They were out of breath and sweating, and some of them were staggering from the weight of their bulletproof vests. One man had gotten into the tear gas and was being led by the rest. The gang had carried the prisoners.

Bench Logan was still fighting. They clubbed him repeatedly, but it seemed to do no good. Snarling, Logan got a man by the throat.

The victim put a revolver against Logan's temple.

A man, the one in charge, leaped forward and struck up the gun.

"You fool!" he snarled. "Bench Logan is the only man who has the actual latitude and longitude figures."

The man lowered the gun. "But I thought—"

"Sure, the boss has the figures, but he's not sure they are correct. He left the place in a hell of a hurry, and he's not sure about its location. Bench Logan is sure. He's a navigator, and he had a sextant when he was picked up by the steamer *Oscar Fjord*."

The man put his gun in his pocket. He helped wrestle Bench Logan into the car. Then he turned to the spokesman.

"Say, you say we're going up there with bombs and knock off all those people?"

"Sure!"

"That's a hell of a thing."

The other scowled. "You squeamish?"

Shrugging, the first man said, "I did the same thing in Spain and Ethiopia for less money. No, I'm not squeamish. But I do wonder what in hell is behind it."

"The thing behind our part of it is the money we get paid. I don't think it's too smart to wonder about the rest."

"I ain't smart. I wonder."

The straw boss chuckled.

"So do I," he said. "We're to take off in planes with bombs and find these two hundred and fifty people in the arctic. If we can't find them, we're to make Bench Logan tell us where they are. Then we're to bomb and machine gun them until not a one is left alive."

He was silent a moment. Then he grimaced, shuddered, said, "All right. Let's get at our work."

They climbed in the cars and left in a hurry.

Chapter 10
RACE

Doc Savage lowered his small telescope. He was a lip reader, and he had deciphered most of what the two men had said.

There was nothing he could do about it at the moment. No earthly thing. There was open ground all around the cars, and the men were armed. They would have seen him. His bulletproof undergarment might have helped, but they would soon have cut his legs from under him.

He noted the direction taken by the cars—a bit of information which would probably have no value.

He went back to the shack.

"Any evidence?" he asked.

"Two of them," Ham said wearily. "But, unfortunately, both are dead."

Monk scowled at Ham and demanded, "Listen, was that supposed to be humor, you shyster?"

Ham frowned. "What are you trying to do—get yourself skinned alive, you mistake of nature?"

Renny rumbled, "Cut it out, you two!"

Doc Savage's gaze sharpened. Monk and Ham were in the habit of conducting a kind of perpetual quarrel that ran various scales of violence, practical jokes and plain insults. Always in good fun, and in secret glee, although a stranger would think they were on the verge of homicide.

But this time it was a little different. Renny, for instance, was trying to keep them apart.

Monk glowered, and the hand in which Ham clenched his sword cane trembled slightly.

Doc Savage said, "Renny is there anything to be done here?"

"Nothing that I can see," Renny rumbled.

"There is a boat at the dock," the bronze man explained. "We can return to the city in that. Or is your car handy?"

Renny glanced quickly at Monk and Ham. "The car isn't handy," he said.

Monk, staring at Ham, said, "I'll say it isn't!"

"Lay off me!" Ham grated.

They moved toward the inlet, Monk and Ham obviously on bitter terms.

Doc Savage dropped behind with Renny, and asked, "What happened?"

Renny grinned without humor. "You know the way Ham likes his clothes. Changes three or four times a day. Morning suit, afternoon suit, dinner jacket—a regular routine."

"Yes."

"Well, you know how Monk always ribs him about it."

"Yes."

"Bench Logan and his men caught us," Renny said, "because Ham stopped to put on his morning suit. Monk and Ham were having one of their usual quarrels, and Ham got reckless and went back to the car for the suitcase containing his morning suit. I think he was doing it as a gag, to rib Monk. But Bench Logan's man was watching the car, and the first thing you know, they had us. So Monk came out and told Ham that he was responsible. Ham doesn't like it."

Doc Savage was patiently silent. When something like this happened, he invariably said nothing in criticism, no matter what piece of foolishness had caused the trouble.

His aides were efficient. Monk was an eminent chemist and Ham was a great lawyer, although the two of them together frequently seemed more like a clown act.

Renny said, "They ran our car in the bay."

The cabin cruiser ran toward the city with a rag of foam in its teeth.

When they were passing under Queensborough Bridge, a police launch drew alongside. The officer in charge knew Doc Savage, because the patrol boat covered a beat past the big hangar and boathouse which Doc maintained, disguised as an abandoned warehouse, on the Hudson River water front.

"That boat you're using," said the police-launch skipper, "is a stolen one. It was taken from City Island this morning."

Doc suggested, "Run down to the midtown piers with us, and we will turn the boat over to you to take back to the owner."

Renny got out a handkerchief and wiped his forehead.

"It's lucky we have special police commissions," he said.

Monk Mayfair remarked, "Bench Logan must have stolen this boat. You know, that guy is a strange combination of mighty tough egg and soft heart."

They took a taxicab to headquarters, after putting the boat in the hands of the harbor police.

Monk and Ham and Renny met Thomas J. Eleanor for the first time.

Monk was impressed by the fat man's size, and Ham was impressed by the tailoring quality of Eleanor's business suit.

"I've heard a great deal about you," Ham told him, shaking hands.

"Well, I have certainly heard of you, too," said Thomas J. Eleanor. "I am becoming astounded by your associate, Mr. Savage."

Pat Savage looked at Doc and moved an eyebrow around in a way that meant a signal. She moved into the laboratory. Doc followed.

"I found the car with a peculiar odor," she said. "I did not dream it would work this fast. A newsboy noticed it when he was making his deliveries. I had the delivery and circulation departments of the newspapers check on their newsboys, as part of my hunt."

Doc asked, "Have you said anything to anyone about finding the car?"

"No. I haven't even told Johnny and Long Tom. They have been talking to Mr. Eleanor."

"They learn anything?"

"Eleanor is in an uproar about a half-page advertisement in the newspapers—that one offering a reward for the capture of Bench Logan and stating that Logan is crazy."

"Did Eleanor insert those advertisements?"

"He says he did not."

"The newspapers say that he did," Doc replied.

"So he found out, when he telephoned them." Pat grimaced. "You should have heard Eleanor blow up when he found that out. He threatened the poor newspapers with all kinds of libel suits."

"What are the newspapers going to do about that?"

"They say they took reasonable precautions by telephoning Mr. Eleanor's home to get corroboration of the advertising copy. They say a voice which said it belonged to Thomas J. Eleanor, and from Eleanor's home, assured them everything was all right and to go ahead and insert the advertisements."

"How does Eleanor explain that?"

"One of his servants on the telephone—a crooked one."

Doc Savage went into the reception room.

"You fellows," he told his men, "had better be getting our big plane ready. Load it with plenty of concentrated food, enough for emergency rations for two hundred and fifty people. And put aboard ample fighting equipment."

Thomas J. Eleanor heaved upright. He looked eager. "You have found the location of those people?" he asked.

Doc Savage shook his head slowly. "Mr. Eleanor, have you the least idea of the whereabouts of this tropical island on which you were told these people were marooned?"

Eleanor hesitated. "Not . . . well, not very accurately. Not within four or five hundred miles."

Renny rumbled, "Holy cow! If we know within four or five hundred miles of where an island is, we can find it."

"Get the plane ready," Doc Savage said.

He beckoned to Pat, and she followed him out into the hall. Big-fisted Renny trailed along behind.

"Hey, Doc," Renny said. "What's this tropical stuff? I thought we were heading for the arctic. Which is it? It'll make a lot of difference in the equipment we take."

"The artic," Doc said.

Patricia Savage touched Doc's arm, then ordered the cab in which they were riding to continue to the end of the block and stop.

"Yonder," said Pat, "is the number of the house where the paper-delivery boy reported a car with a funny odor."

Doc said, "That is the car, standing in front of the garage at the rear of the house."

Pat smiled. She was in good spirits, highly pleased by the increasing excitement and mystery of the affair in which they were involved.

They approached the house from two directions. Pat drew a shawl over her head, hooked a basket over one arm, stooped her shoulders and walked like an old woman to the door. She knocked.

Simultaneously, Doc came to the house from the rear. He put an ear against the back door. There was the sound of Pat's knocking, but nothing else. Only silence.

He worked on the lock of the door for a few moments, then entered.

He made, as soon as he was inside, the low, exotic trilling sound which was his absent-minded habit. He walked through the house slowly, eyes busy.

Pat came in quickly when he opened the front door.

Pat exclaimed, "Say, isn't anybody—" Her eyes flew wide. "What's happened in here?"

Chairs were upset. Rugs were askew, lamps broken, a radio kicked over.

Doc Savage picked up a coat with one sleeve torn half off. A woman's coat. He said, "Nicky Jones was wearing this, was she not?"

"Yes," Pat said. "That means Nicky came here after she skipped. And someone raided the place and grabbed her."

The bronze man gave the house a rapid search. He found that the place was occupied by the fat girl—whose name was really Fern Reed—and that she had been living alone for a week, her parents being in Ohio on a visit to relatives.

"They must have kidnaped the fat girl, too," Pat said.

The plane was vast and shining, graceful even sitting on the Hudson River surface. It was the color of the natural alloy with which it was covered. Paint on a ship of such size would add hundreds of pounds of weight and give nothing but color, so paint had been eliminated in the interest of efficiency.

Long Tom Roberts, Monk Mayfair, Ham Brooks, Renny Renwick and Johnny Littlejohn were loading the last supplies aboard.

Thomas J. Eleanor made an indignant jaw for Doc Savage's benefit.

"Really, now," said Eleanor, "the idea that I go with you is preposterous."

"You seem to be involved in this," Doc explained patiently.

"Only through my curiosity," snapped Eleanor. "I told you about that—how I became curious and interested in saving the lives of those people."

"Your interest in their lives has ebbed, then?"

"Of course not!"

"I see."

"No, you don't see, either," said Eleanor. "Maybe I did not make it clear, but I had no intention of rescuing these people *myself.* As soon as I found out where they were, I was going to hire the rescuing job done.''

Doc Savage seemed satisfied. "I see," he said. "Then we will not press you to go along."

Eleanor relaxed. He extended his hand. "I hope you are successful," he said.

Eventually, the fat man took his departure.

Monk Mayfair watched him go and remarked, "You know, you can just *feel* that guy is like a powerhouse connected to big business. I never really understood what they meant by 'dynamic' until I met him."

Long Tom ambled over.

"Doc," said the pale electrical wizard, "we dug up some stuff on Eleanor. This is the first time I've had a chance to give it to you. It doesn't seem important, anyway. Just history."

"We might hear it," Doc suggested.

Long Tom nodded. "Well, the fellow is hard to get much on. When the newspapers call him a mysterious international figure, they sure call the turn. He's supposed to be mixed up in the European munition business, and you know that is a throat-cutting game over there. He is supposed to have been asked to leave several countries. And in Monrovia, they will shoot him on sight. Or maybe they won't now that the dictator, Mungen, is dead."

Doc Savage showed marked interest.

"Mungen and Thomas J. Eleanor had a connection?" he asked. "What was it?"

Long Tom grinned. "The kind of connection that a lighted match and gun powder would have. Several years ago, Thomas Eleanor called the dictator, Mungen, the Mad Dog of Europe. That didn't make a hit with Mungen. One thing must have led to another—I do not know the exact incidents that led up to it—and Mungen ordered Thomas J. Eleanor arrested and shot on sight if he ever put a foot in Monrovia. There was a hullaballoo about it."

Doc remarked, "It was my impression that Thomas J. Eleanor always avoids publicity."

"He does. But Mungen didn't. You remember Mungen—a great hulk of a devil with a gold snake for a tongue. He never shirked publicity. In fact, he was the biggest limelight hog of the dictator crop."

"Mungen went out of his way, then, to draw notice to his hate for Thomas J. Eleanor?"

"Yes. But Mungen wasn't bashful about letting people know he hated them."

"I see."

"Mungen hated plenty of them, too."

Doc nodded.

Long Tom grinned. "But more of them hated Mungen. You remember what the population did to his body after he was killed—cut it up in pieces and fed it to the alligator in the Monrovian National Zoo, according to one story."

Long Tom was silent a moment.

"The most hated man in this century—that Mungen," he said.

Thomas J. Eleanor returned as they were on the verge of taking the air. The fat man came charging down the long cavernlike hangar-warehouse, waving his arms and bellowing.

"Wait!" Eleanor howled. "I'm going along!"

He reached them and stopped. He was white-faced, panting. His foreign accent was more pronounced.

"Those fiends!" he snarled. "You know what they did? They stole my plane! My big, new plane—the private one I use for transatlantic crossings."

Monk Mayfair stared at him. "You have a private plane for transatlantic crossings?"

"Of course," said Eleanor, as if it was nothing more extraordinary than dollar cigars. "And they stole it."

"Who did?"

Eleanor put back his head and swore some very expressive oaths in a foreign language.

"I seem to have had only two loyal servants in my employ," he said. "They gave me the information. One of them has been shot, trying to stop the theft of the plane."

Monk said, "I asked you who—"

"And I heard you," Eleanor snapped. "I keep the plane in a private hangar on the Sound. This raiding party appeared about an hour ago. It was led, as nearly as I can judge from descriptions, by Bill Browder. Browder has a large gang of thugs working with him. He also had prisoners."

Thomas J. Eleanor paused dramatically, a habit he had in such moments.

"The prisoners," he said, "seem to have been Bench Logan, the girl Nicky Jones, her fat girl friend and some other men. All prisoners were taken along."

"It must be a big plane," Monk said.

Thomas J. Eleanor glanced at Doc Savage's ship. "Somewhat larger than this," he said. "In fact, it is a late-model European bomber which I . . . er . . . received as a slight gift of esteem from a certain government."

Doc Savage entered the conversation, asking, "And now you wish to go with us?"

"I certainly do," said Thomas J. Eleanor.

"Why?"

The fat man banged a hand into a fist. "I'm mad!"

Somehow that one word was an ample explanation, the way he said it.

Big-fisted Renny rumbled, "So they've got a plane as fast as ours. That makes it a race, doesn't it?"

Pat shuddered.

"A race with two hundred and fifty lives for the stake," she said.

Chapter 11
ICE TRAP!

They refueled in Nova Scotia, flying that far with minimum fuel load for what added speed this would give.

Long Tom, the electrical expert, rode the radio continually. He called every airport on the Atlantic coast north of New York, and inland, and what Canadian fields he could contact.

While a fuel barge was pumping high-test aviation gas into their tanks in a Nova Scotia port, Long Tom summarized his results.

"Nobody," he said, "has seen hide or hair of the plane."

Thomas J. Eleanor approached them. He had made a discovery.

"This is Nova Scotia," he said. "You're flying north. I thought we were headed for the South Seas."

Doc Savage said nothing.

"Have you the least idea where you're going?" Eleanor demanded.

"You recall the latitude and longitude figures mumbled by the man who was dying in Ark Street?" Doc asked.

Eleanor blinked. "You're seeing if there is anything there?"

"Yes."

The fat man frowned. "Where am I going to get some clothes fit for a thing like this? The North, I mean."

"We will make a stop in Greenland," Doc told him. "And another in Iceland, if the military authorities will permit it."

Doc Savage took the plane off the bay, set a course by the gyro compass, then turned the flying of the ship over to the robot-pilot apparatus. He went back to the radio room.

"Long Tom," he said, "establish a radio contact with the steamer *Oscar Fjord*."

"That is the vessel Bench Logan tried to stow you and Miss Jones away on," Long Tom remarked.

"Yes. Describe Bench Logan to the *Oscar Fjord*. Give them his name, but also describe him and the blue dog. Ask them if they can get us any information concerning both."

Long Tom nodded and went to work on the radio.

Thomas J. Eleanor had moved to their side in time to hear part of the speech. He walked gingerly, as if he was afraid the cabin floor of the plane might not hold his weight.

Eleanor said, "Did you know about the dog?"

"What about it?"

"The animal has been literally a trade-mark of Bench Logan's," Eleanor explained. "The blue dog is always with Logan. The beast is merely a freak coloration in a mongrel police dog. From its size, I suspect it is a cross between a black Dane and a shepherd. Logan and the dog have never been far apart for years."

Doc said, "Then you knew Bench Logan was near your estate when you saw the blue dog."

"That is right," Eleanor acknowledged.

"And so you used the story of the blue dog to have me—or rather, to have Bill Browder get me there. You wanted to find out if I were really working with Bench Logan."

"Yes."

"Is that all?"

"Yes."

"I thought," said Doc Savage, "that you might have some important information about the dog."

"Oh, no, it's not important." The fat man grinned slightly. "That dog is vicious and cunning. It has gotten Bench Logan into plenty of trouble. Once it bit the dictator of Monrovia, Mungen. The cur got hold of Mungen's . . . er . . . major anatomy, shall we say, and it took four of his guard to pry the beast loose."

Doc Savage asked idly, "You knew Mungen?"

The fat man laughed. Even his laughter was dynamic, forceful, like pistols exploding.

"Don't tell me you haven't checked up on me," he said. "I feel sure you are cautious enough to have done so. You know that Mungen and I were acquainted. I was No. 1 on Mungen's list of what he called Enemies of a Stalwart Europe. I am rather proud of the distinction. To be a rich man does not make me great. To be first enemy of Mungen, the dictator, does make me great."

He sat down carefully, wedging himself in one of the seats, and smoked one of his dollar cigars with much satisfaction.

Two hours later, Long Tom Roberts handed Doc Savage a sheet of paper on which was typing. "Doc, here is what the skipper of the steamer, *Oscar Fjord*, was able to give us."

The typing read:

Man you describe did not give us name of Bench Logan. Told us he was Hans Svenson, Canadian aviator forced down while ferrying plane across North Atlantic. We picked him up adrift in crude homemade sealskin canoe with vicious blue dog. Put him ashore in New York. He said matter of lost plane he was flying was military secret and asked us say nothing about it. We didn't.

Long Tom said, "It looks as if Bench Logan was picked up off the coast of Greenland. The skipper doesn't give the position where he was picked up, but the radio operator told me orally that it was off Greenland."

Doc said, "Go back and ask the radioman of the *Oscar Fjord* what condition Bench Logan was in when they rescued him."

The electrical expert departed, spent some time with the radio.

He reported, "Bad, the operator says. Very bad. The man was practically dead."

"From exposure?"

"And hardship." Long Tom frowned. "Here's another thing: The operator said they all figured Logan was a goner. There was a doctor on the *Oscar Fjord* at the time, he gave up hope of saving Logan's life. But the operator says Logan pulled through by main courage. The operator put it in these words: 'Logan acted as if the devil had given him a thing to do and he couldn't take time out to die before he did it.'"

"Was Logan delirious on the steamer?"

Long Tom nodded. "I thought of that. Yes, he was. He mumbled stuff about two hundred and fifty people dying. On the *Oscar Fjord*, they misunderstood that. They thought he was a naval pilot who had bombed a ship and killed two hundred and fifty people, and it was preying on his mind."

"What made them connect a ship with the two hundred and fifty people?"

"Logan kept mentioning a ship when he was delirious. He mumbled about the ship in connection with the two hundred and fifty people."

"The name of the ship—did you get that?"

"It was something like the *Christine Gerry*, they thought."

Doc Savage made, unexpectedly, his trilling note. He was startled.

"The *Grin Gueterre*," he said.

"Huh?"

Doc Savage looked thoughtfully at the sea that seemed to stand still beneath the plane, so high were they flying.

He said, "Long Tom, get hold of the Monrovian consul. It may be possible for you to contact the Monrovian government directly by short wave. The *Grin Gueterre*, or the *Green Guard*, as the name would translate, was a Monrovian vessel. Find out when it sailed and what happened to it."

That took Long Tom nearly two hours.

He reported, "The *Grin Gueterre* sailed four months and three days ago from a Portuguese port," he said. "The ship has disappeared. Not a thing has been heard from it since. It was believed a submarine victim, because of the war trouble over there."

"Four months and three days ago?"

"Yes."

"That was two days after Mungen, the dictator, killed himself," Doc said.

The midnight sun was hanging in its interminable spot above the horizon when Long Tom thrust his head out of the radio cubicle again. He yelled, "Doc, you better listen to this!"

The bronze man hurried forward. Long Tom handed him a headset, explaining, "The signal is mighty weak."

Doc listened. It was radiotelephone; a voice. Bill Browder's voice, unquestionably. It was saying, "Our plane wrecked. Please send help. Position north-northwest of Iceland. Don't know how far. Several hundred miles. Edge of ice pack. Please send help."

Doc said, "Get a radio bearing on the voice. Then wait a few minutes and get a cross-bearing."

"It may be a trap," Long Tom suggested.

"Get the bearings," Doc said.

* * *

Later, they took the two bearings, and Doc worked with the protractors, finally making a cross on the chart.

He indicated the spot. "Get there as fast as you can," he told Monk, who had taken over the controls.

Monk nodded.

Monk and Ham seemed to be on better terms, although their bad feeling had not entirely abated. Normally, they would have enlivened the trip by insulting each other repeatedly, but they had been almost polite.

They had brought along their pets, Chemistry and Habeas Corpus. The two animals seemed to be sharing the sour feelings of their masters. Usually they fought continually. But they had been ignoring each other.

There was a bay. It was a bay in pack ice. Thin haze lay over the place, so that they had to fly low.

They came in fast, riding the radio-compass bearing like a hound approaching a scent.

Patricia Savage cried out excitedly. "There—a wrecked plane!" She pointed.

The ship was not on the bay; it was almost a mile deeper in the pack ice.

Doc Savage, noting the direction of the winds as indicated by the waves in the bay, decided the plane had been making a circle in order to land on the bay against the wind, when something had gone wrong.

He told Monk, "Circle several times."

He used binoculars. The others did likewise. The wrecked plane was not badly damaged. It had skated over a level floe, digging up a great groove of snow, which had wiped out its undercarriage and buckled a wing against an ice pinnacle.

A man appeared beside the plane. He waved.

"Bill Browder," Doc decided.

They saw no one else.

"Land on the bay," Doc directed.

Thomas J. Eleanor wiped his forehead. "This may be a trap. I advise caution." He had put on an extra parka which Renny, the biggest member of their party, had brought along. It fitted him tightly, but would serve.

Monk put the plane down on the bay. The water was rough, and the plane hammered violently for a while. Then it was almost motionless, its multiple motors pulling it up to the ice.

Renny put a grappling iron on a floe, made the end of the attached line snug about a streamlined cleat. He yanked back the slide in the top of the pilot's compartment and stood erect. He stared around.

"No chance of anybody sneaking up on us here," he said. "You can see over the ice for half a mile."

Doc Savage pulled on a parka and changed his footgear to shoes with ice calks. He slung a portable radio "transceiver" over his back.

"Keep in continual touch with me," he said. "If there is more than one man alive at the plane, assistance may be necessary."

He climbed out on the hull snout, then to a wingtip. Monk gunned the motors and tramped on the rudder, and the wing swung slowly over the ice. Doc dropped on to the floes.

He moved rapidly, although the going was treacherous. The plane motors muttered contentedly behind him.

Soon the pack ice became more solid. It was piled up in blocks, ridges, pinnacles. There was the frequent, ripping, gunshot reports typical of pack ice near the rim.

He climbed a pressure ridge and after that it was like being in the Dakota badlands, only this was ice. He ran when he could. His steel calks left long ripping scratches down the slopes; ice particles showered his ankles.

Bill Browder was a hundred yards from the wrecked plane. Browder, trying to claw his way up an ice ridge, having helpless going of it, saw the bronze man. He released his grip and slid backward a dozen yards.

He stared at Doc. Then he held out his wrists, which were slashed.

"Twenty minutes ago," he said vacantly, "I was trying to commit suicide."

Doc grasped one of the man's wrists, then the other, and looked at them.

"They are not bad," he said.

Bill Browder seemed about to break into tears. "I had nothing to cut them with except a torn piece of the skin metal from the plane," he said.

"Anyone else in the plane?"

Browder shuddered. "Three," he said. He put his face in his arms. "They are dead. The crash."

Doc Savage went to the plane. It was a big ship, but of American manufacture. He went over it closely enough to learn that it was an airlines craft and had been recently in use for that purpose. The stewardess' locker was even stocked with the usual kit. The ship had probably been stolen.

He recognized the three men. They had taken part in the raid on the shack on the banks of Long Island Sound—the attack in which they had made off with Bench Logan and his men.

There was no life in them.

Bill Browder was sobbing when Doc returned to him. As always when a strong man cries, this was rather terrible.

"Poor Nicky," he moaned finally.

Doc went to a knee beside him. The man was trembling.

"What happened to her?" he asked.

Bill Browder shook so violently that speech failed him, as hysteria, nerves and the biting cold combined to cause a violent chill. Doc gave him tablets of quick-acting sedative and waited.

Finally, "They took . . . took Nicky with them. And Fern Reed," Browder said. "Fern Reed was the fat girl." Wetness filled his eyes again. "They're going to k-kill them . . . with the others."

"With the people on the steamer *Grin Gueterre*?" Doc asked.

Browder nodded. "I didn't know you knew about that ship." He licked his lips. "Tell me this—why are they so anxious to kill everyone who was on the *Grin Gueterre*?"

Doc Savage's metallic features were expressionless. "You know why, do you not?"

Browder shook his head. "No. It has puzzled me from the first."

Incredulity was in the bronze man's flake-gold eyes for a moment.

"Then why are you involved in it?"

Bill Browder looked ill. "A hundred dollars a day," he said.

"Paid by whom?"

"I don't know. Not by Thomas J. Eleanor, though. I thought at first that it was coming from him, but it isn't. They were just using Eleanor because—well, I think this whole thing started among Eleanor's bodyguards. He had five of them. Bench Logan was one, and there were four others."

The sedative was taking effect, allowing Browder's teeth to stop rattling, his voice to become more calm.

Doc said, "Give me your summary of the whole situation, Browder."

The man was silent, gathering his thoughts.

"Something is at stake," he said. "To get it, all those people on the *Grin Gueterre* will have to be killed. You see, the ship got into the arctic, was caught in the pack ice, crushed, and the passengers marooned. Bench Logan was aboard. He got away." He stopped.

"Logan got away, and was picked up by the *Oscar Fjord*?"

"Yes." Browder dampened his lips. His words drove short bursts of steam off his lips as he said, "That's how it was. Then Bench Logan got to New York and interested the rest of Thomas J. Eleanor's bodyguards in going back and killing the passengers and getting whatever there is to get."

"Bench Logan is not working with them, now," Doc pointed out.

Browder nodded. "I know that. They quarreled. Logan developed a human streak and wanted to save the people instead of killing them. So the other bodyguards assembled more cronies as tough as themselves and went after Logan. Logan got together his own tough pals, and they've been going around and around ever since."

Browder lowered his face for a moment, then looked up. There was a proud expression on his face.

"I balked at the wholesale killing, too," he said. "That's why they left me here. They thought I would die."

"This plane was stolen?"

"From an airline," Browder said. "They have another ship, a tremendous thing. They stole that one from Thomas J. Eleanor." He looked at the twisted plane lying on the ice. "I caused that wreck," he said.

Doc Savage eyed him thoughtfully. "You caused it?"

"Yes, I ripped the oil lines loose on the motors. I thought they would land on the bay. But I miscalculated. They didn't make it to the bay." His lips compressed. "So they left me to die. The other plane picked them up."

"The other plane has gone on to where those people are marooned?"

"Yes."

"Do you know where that is?"

"Yes."

"Come on," Doc Savage said.

Chapter 12
HOPE BLACKS OUT

Thomas J. Eleanor met them at the plane.

"What happened?" he demanded.

Doc entered the plane. The others were sitting in the seats.

"They wrecked one plane and abandoned Bill Browder," he said. "They have gone on to commit their wholesale murder. There is no time to lose."

He moved forward to the controls.

"Put on your parachutes, everybody," he ordered. "There is no telling what will happen."

Monk compressed his lips. He looked at Eleanor, who was close behind Doc.

"You . . . you better fly this thing, Doc," Monk said. "I'm not sure I can handle it on this rough water."

Monk was an excellent aviator, but Doc made no comment. He got behind the controls. Thomas J. Eleanor took the other control-compartment seat.

"The tension is getting everybody jittery," he said.

Doc let the plane drift back away from the rim of ice, gunned the motors, ran downwind for a mile, then came about again. It was rough. Twice, the wingtips of the plane knifed into the surface. But he straightened the craft. Once it had speed, keeping it level was more simple.

He heaved it off the surface, and the ice pack slashed past with hungry white fangs.

"Get Bill Browder up here," he said. "He has to point out the location of the marooned group."

Browder came forward. He was white, but his hand was steady. He seemed to want to say something. But finally he jabbed a pencil at the chart.

"There," he said.

It was close—no more than twenty miles.

"All right," the bronze man told him.

Browder retreated. Thomas J. Eleanor squirmed uncomfortably on his seat-pack parachute. He was so very big that the seat did not fit him.

Ten minutes later—no more than that—the bronze man discerned the castaways.

They had put out a distress signal of some kind. He dropped the ship lower, discovered that they had built snow huts so that they spelled out for help, S O S. Tops of the snow structures had been darkened in some fashion.

Half a mile from the cluster of structures was an ice lead that was open, full of surging green water.

The plane was there.

Thomas J. Eleanor pointed, said, "There is the ship they stole from me, the devils!"

Doc Savage reached up, grasped Thomas J. Eleanor around the shoulders, and pitched backward. The plane—the bronze man had designed it for a military-type craft with a big hatch for pilot escape—lurched somewhat. Doc and Eleanor went out into space!

Eleanor screamed, and it was a squawl of plain terror. He had been brave enough previously. But to be suddenly seized and tossed out into space broke his nerve for a moment.

Doc Savage kept a grip on Eleanor. They fell, the air beginning to scream around them. Doc got hold of the rip-cord ring of the fat man's 'chute, and thrust it in his hand.

"Pull!" he said.

Eleanor pulled. Silk popped out, and the man was yanked out of Doc's grip.

Doc cracked his own 'chute. The difference in their weight was sufficient that Eleanor passed him, hit the ice first. But by only a few seconds.

The fat man showed knowledge of parachute behavior. The wind in the big mushroom hauled him over the ice, up ice pinnacles and down the other side, but he got hold of the shrouds and spilled the air. He was safe when Doc reached him.

Eleanor stared at Doc. He seemed completely wordless.

"When did you get wise?" he asked.

"Not," Doc Savage said, "until a moment ago."

"What tipped you off?"

"No one particular thing. I noticed, of course, that everyone was pale and strange when I returned with Bill Browder. But I did not grasp it; I was too worried over the fate of these people on the ice."

Eleanor said, "They were hiding in the ice floes around the bay. They got us by surprise. They were in the back of the plane, waiting for you to take off. I think they wanted to attack you in the air, where there was no chance of your escaping. But you fooled them—unwittingly—when you put on a parachute." The fat man scowled. "That Bill Browder must have been bait in their trap."

Doc pointed upward.

"Then why did Browder jump, too?" he asked.

Eleanor stared at the blooming white disk of silk which was lowering a dark figure. It was Browder. He landed nearly two hundred yards from them, and was groveling on the ice when they reached him.

"My ankle!" he gasped. His eyes rolled up at the plane. "They were in the back of the plane—the washroom or whatever is in the back of the ship," he said. "They must have come aboard while you were rescuing me, Mr. Savage."

"When did you first realize that?" Doc asked.

"When you jumped. They all rushed out then." Browder groaned. "They'll kill your friends."

Doc said, "That is not likely." He sounded confident.

Bill Browder tried to get up. He bit his lips until his teeth sank in, and a ribbon of blood crawled down over his chin.

"Sprained." He gripped his ankle and groaned. Then he lurched to his feet by sheer nerve force. "What are we going to do—"

His eyes twisted upward.

Fear made Thomas J. Eleanor put both hands to his cheeks, like a woman.

"Watch out!" he screamed. He made a running dive for the nearest ice crevice.

The plane was coming down at them like a dive bomber.

Doc landed beside Eleanor in the ice crack. Eleanor bellowed, "Scatter! If we're together, they may drop a bomb!"

"They have not had time to find bombs in the equipment," Doc said. "And it is doubtful if they carried anything but hand grenades aboard."

The plane pulled out of its dive. A few bullets chipped ice, but none were very close. The ship climbed, turning first north, then south, as if the pilot was puzzled as to just what to do.

Suddenly a figure toppled out of the craft.

"See!" Eleanor yelled. "They're throwing your friends overboard!"

A parachute bloomed over the dark, falling form.

It was Monk. He spilled one side of his 'chute so as to land not far from them. The homely chemist disengaged the fabric harness, gave his trousers a hitch. He was wearing nothing but khaki pants and a gaudy sweater.

"I can't understand it," he declared. "Darnedest thing I ever ran into."

Eleanor grabbed him by the arm. The fat man was shaking.

"Oh, this is— What'll we do?" Eleanor gasped. "What'll *they* do? Are they going to kill—"

"Brother, you sure blow up fast," Monk told him. "You were as cool as cucumbers all along, and I said to myself, 'Monk, that guy is made of iron.' And here you are, more scared than an old maid in a barber college."

The fat man only gasped and shook.

Monk turned. "Doc, they have a proposition. They want to trade."

The bronze man was silent.

Monk added, "They kicked me out to tell you that, if you would promise to clear out and forget the whole thing, they would let us do that. But we are not to interfere with what they intend to do to those people on the ice, yonder."

Eleanor stiffened.

Doc asked, "You mean that they are offering to trade our lives for the lives of two hundred and fifty people?"

Monk shrugged. "I don't know *what* the trade is. It's got me bamboozled. But it's a sure thing that if we clear out, they'll polish off those people. They've got bombs and poison gas to do the job with."

"Poison gas!" The bronze man was grim. "That means they have been preparing to do this job for some time. You do not just step out and buy poison gas the way you buy a gun."

Monk's temper suddenly got the best of him. He waved his arms. "But what're they wanting to trade for? How do they think we can save that gang?"

Doc was silent again.

Words burst out of Eleanor.

"Accept!" he shouted. "Don't delay! It's a chance to save our lives!"

Monk glanced upward, then looked in the direction of the other plane. He also glanced toward the camp. Both plane and camp were concealed behind the ice pinnacles.

"I was to take off my shirt and wave it around my head if we accepted," he said. "They will land our plane down the shore a short distance, and leave it, with Pat and the others safe aboard."

Eleanor clawed at his clothing.

Monk stared at him. "What are you doing?"

"Taking off my shirt," Eleanor gasped. "I'm going to signal them."

Monk looked at Doc. Then the homely chemist stepped close to the fabulous Thomas J. Eleanor.

"Friend, I always like to hit a rich man," Monk said. "Keep that shirt on, or you'll think a mule got to you."

Eleanor gaped at him. "You fool! You are not suggesting we sacrifice *our* lives!"

Monk gave his pants another hitch. He was turning blue from the cold. He looked at Doc Savage.

"Doc, shall I tell this guy what I think you're thinking?" he asked.

The bronze man nodded almost imperceptibly.

Monk shivered, flapped his arms.

He said, "For some time now, we have made a business of righting wrongs and punishing evildoers. It sounds kind of silly when you say it in so many words, but we haven't found it that way. In fact, we're proud of what we've done; we're proud of Doc Savage and glad we have had the privilege of working with him. We've liked taking chances, and we've taken plenty of them. We've always known what we were doing. We haven't gone into anything blindfolded. Puzzled, maybe, but never without knowing that there would be risks. We have accepted those risks as part of the game."

Monk glanced up at the grimly circling plane.

"Always in our minds, I think, has been the knowledge that we would have to accept death sometime," he continued. "And I think we will do just that without hesitating. I know that's the way I feel, and I know the others see eye to eye with me. You take Ham, up there; Ham has insulted and browbeaten me, told my best girl the awfulest lies, and we've had our spats. But I wouldn't be afraid to have Ham speak for me, even if the word was death. I know I can speak for Ham the same way. And for the others, as I say. And so I'm saying for them—we ride straight ahead! There are two hundred and fifty people yonder on the ice. We may save them; we may not. But we will try. The trouble Pat, Long Tom, Renny and Johnny and Ham are in, up there in the plane, and the trouble Doc and I are in down here, is all part of the bargain. We won't welsh. So—and maybe I should have just said this and nothing else—to hell with any trade for our lives."

Doc Savage had remained silent through the speech, which was one of the longest Monk had ever made.

The bronze man extended a hand. There was a hint of dampness in his eyes.

"I am glad you made that speech," he said.

Monk snorted. "It's what you'd have said, isn't it? Maybe you'd have used less words."

Doc nodded.

Thomas J. Eleanor lowered his head, his arms.

"What a pack of fools you are!" he said. "But . . . but there is something in what— Well, I'm ashamed of myself."

Chapter 13
FEAR ON THE FLOES

Monk Mayfair watched Doc Savage strip off his parka and say, "Better put this on, Monk." Monk took the parka, but muttered, "Oh, I'm not cold."

Saying he was not cold was the largest lie Monk had told recently. He felt he was getting so cold that, shivering as he was, he would soon shatter into pieces like a chunk of ice. He put on the parka.

As a matter of fact, Monk knew the weather was quite mild. Not below freezing more than a few degrees. The wind, however, was like a million animals with sharp teeth.

Doc said, "Monk, you had better go warn those people on the ice." The bronze man stooped, removed his shoes—sheep-lined pacs of the arctic type—which had the ice calks. "Here, wear these. We will swap shoes."

Monk said, "Oh, I can make it all right."

But after he had gone a hundred feet over the ice, he came back and changed shoes with Doc. The calked pacs were tight on Monk's feet. He had a hunch Doc would be able to step out of his own fleece-lined flying boots without unzipping them, if he wished.

Monk pointed. "I think that camp on the ice is in this direction. That right?"

The bronze man nodded.

Monk set out. The calked footgear helped a lot. He galloped along at the best speed he could manage.

He glanced back. Doc Savage and Thomas J. Eleanor were standing on the ice, watching him.

"The big baby!" Monk said, meaning Eleanor.

Monk had—the impression had been growing on him the last

few minutes—the feeling that Doc Savage was working out some deliberate plan aimed at securing safety.

Monk shuddered. The situation looked hopeless to him.

The plane suddenly ended its circling and came down in a whistling dive. There was a sound as if several big, invisible dogs were galloping around Monk.

The homely chemist took a run, a dive and did his best to disappear into a snowdrift. He was intensely grateful for the parka, which was white and would help hide him against the snow.

Bullets continued to make the sound of big dogs, but they were not close, now. From a diving plane armed only with rifles, a single man dressed in white on a snow background was an almost impossible target.

The plane pulled up, its motors an angry roaring which jumped against the ice and back.

Monk leaped out of the snow and sprinted. He covered some distance before the plane came back again.

He sparred like a chicken trying to escape a hawk, until the line of huts came into view.

He felt an enormous pity for the people who met him.

There was on their faces the mark of incredible suffering. Of hunger, privation, of fear and cold, courage and hopelessness. They did not have arctic clothing, except that they had improvised it after a fashion of rags and untanned sealskins, here and there a bearskin.

He came upon them unexpectedly. Four men, hatchet-faced from privation, stood up in a snowdrift.

One said, "You had better get down, my friend. Those are real bullets from that plane, even though they are badly aimed."

Monk slid feet-foremost into the snow, so that the flakes covered his dark khaki trouser legs.

"Warn the others!" he exclaimed. "The guys in those planes are going to bomb and machine-gun them to death."

The man with the wan face nodded.

"They know that," he said.

Monk was startled. "They do!"

The other nodded.

"We have been fearing something of this kind for months," he said.

Monk stared at him. The fellow seemed to be on the last stretch of starvation.

"How many of you are left?" Monk asked.

The man smiled. There was a trace of pride. "Two hundred and fifty-three of us, still. It is a miracle, my friend. A miracle—and a herd of seal which came."

"Did you save much from the ship?"

"From the *Grin Gueterre*?" The man shrugged. "So pitifully little that it is not worth mentioning. You should guess that."

Monk was puzzled. "Why should I have guessed it?"

"Did you not know we were first driven off the *Grin Gueterre*? Driven ashore to die?"

"I didn't know that," Monk told him. "I just supposed the ship smashed up on the rocks, and you got on to the ice where you were marooned. I supposed Bench Logan got away and reached New York, and then——" He stopped.

"And then what?" prompted the other.

"And then I got kind of puzzled," Monk admitted. "Bench Logan wanted to get help to you, but he could not come out openly and ask for it because he was wanted by the police on a murder charge. As sure as Bench Logan had come out with such a fantastic story, he would have been investigated and arrested for murder. Moreover, they got out a story that Bench Logan was insane, in order to discredit the story if he did tell it."

"*They?*" the man said.

"Yeah, they," Monk replied vaguely.

"You do not sound as if you know who *they* are."

"I don't."

"It isn't *they*. It is one individual."

Monk said, "Right now would be a good time——" and stopped. He looked up. "No, it wouldn't."

The second plane had taken the air. It climbed in a purposefully straight line, heading for the castaway camp on the ice. In moments, the ship was overhead, and high.

Monk was watching the craft, but he did not see the two bombs until they had detached and were almost on the ice pack. He barely had time to fall flat.

The ice jerked under him, jarred by the devastating rip of modern high-concussion bombs! Shattered ice, smoke and snow climbed upward. They could hear and feel the uneasy cracking of the great pack under them.

It dawned on Monk that the bombs had missed the nearest snow hut by nearly two hundred feet. Yet, the blast had been sufficient to topple down several snow walls.

The plane swung in a circle, went back to the ice bay from which it had taken off and landed.

"Just shaking their fists," Monk decided. "They could have come a lot closer than that with those bombs. They're just showing us what they can do."

The four emaciated men were staring at Monk.

"Who are you?" asked the spokesman. "Perhaps it would ease our minds if you told us."

Monk started. "Oh, I overlooked that."

He told them who he was, who Doc Savage was, and sketched briefly the course of events. He finished, "I have a hunch Doc knows what is behind it all, but I'll sure say *I* don't. Those guys seem to think that all of you people have to be killed, but I can't see why."

They looked at him queerly.

"Would you care to look over our camp?" one asked. "Perhaps you can suggest a defense."

Monk nodded. They walked among the huts. The workmanship of these, considering that they had ice and only a few bits of wreckage with which to work, was good. But they were not bomb shelters.

Condition of the castaways moved Monk to pity, almost to tears. And he was a grizzled fellow who did not cry easily. Everywhere was evidence of the most gruesome suffering. Bodies that were emaciated to skeleton thinness. In one hut, where they were cooking a kind of communal meal over a pitiful flame of blubber, he got the grisly impression that the principal ingredient of a stew was a pair of shoes. He had heard arctic explorers speak humorously of eating their shoes; it was the first time he had run into the real thing. It was not pleasant.

He said, "It is incredible to me that you did not save more stuff in the shipwreck."

The spokesman said. "We were off the ship before it was wrecked. We were put off."

Monk frowned. "You mean you didn't have to desert the ship because it was wrecked."

"No."

"Then why?"

"We were prisoners on the steamer *Grin Gueterre* for weeks before we were put ashore here. Or rather, marooned on the ice to die. And then, as the ship was attempting to leave after it marooned us, it struck an iceberg and sank."

"What about the crew who was on it then?"

The man's lips became thin. "They got away safely in a power launch, after hanging around and sinking every lifeboat and making sure no wreckage drifted to the ice pack where we could get it.''

Monk scowled. "They got away, eh?"

The man pointed at the plane in the air, at the spot where the other plane had landed.

"Those," he said, "are the men who marooned us!"

Monk hitched at his pants, the way he habitually did when he was mad.

"Look, we better scatter these people over the floes," he said. "That way, they won't make targets. Those fellows may get a few, but it won't be easy. All bunched up in these huts, it'll be like shooting sitting birds."

The other winced. "I am sorry."

"What do you mean—sorry? Why not do it?"

The man beckoned. "Come to these other huts," he said.

Monk followed the man and was shown one hut after another. Horror grew inside Monk. And hopelessness.

These people, he realized, could not go out and scatter over the ice pack. They did not have enough clothing. They would freeze to death.

"You see," the man said, "we four are more warmly dressed than any of the others. They have contributed their clothing, all of these people, to dress a few hunters who venture out in quest of the few seal and walrus that are to be found."

Futility crowded Monk's voice as he snarled, "This is a devilish thing! What is behind it, anyway?"

Without a word, the man entered a hut. He was gone only a moment and had a picture in his hand when he reappeared. It was a poster, a photograph, with a legend below it.

He handed the poster to Monk.

"Does that explain things?" he asked.

Monk stared at the thing in unbelieving astonishment.

"Great grief!" he muttered finally. "Do you mean to tell me that these people here are the only ones who know this?"

"We are the only ones who know it and would tell the world," the man said. "That is why we have to die."

Monk glowered at the poster. "And I thought there was a treasure behind this thing!"

"There is," the man said. "Quite a sinister treasure, don't you think?"

Chapter 14
WHITE STRINGS TO DEATH

The great international financier, Thomas J. Eleanor, beat his arms against his sides for warmth.

"The situation seems to be stalemated," he said. "What can we do? What can they do? And *why* don't they do what they came up here for—kill those people? I don't understand that."

Doc Savage had climbed an ice pinnacle. Twice, a rifle had cracked at him from a distance, but the bullets had gone wide. He had been able to look around.

Now he slid down the sharp slope of ice.

"Mr. Eleanor," he said, "will you stay here? Position yourself on a high spot and keep a lookout. If you hear or see anything suspicious, if they should send out a party to hunt us down, give an alarm. Browder, you stay with Eleanor."

Eleanor said, "They are not likely to send out a hunting party for you. I think they have a great respect for your fighting ability, Mr. Savage. Meeting you at even terms on the pack ice is not something they are likely to try, except as a last resort."

Doc made no comment on that.

He did say, "In case you wish to give an alarm, do it with a very long shout. A long shout will carry, whereas a short yell might be mistaken for grinding noises of the ice pack or the barking of a seal."

Eleanor muttered, "I'd rather go with you."

Bill Browder said, "I can watch. My ankle is jammed, but I can watch."

"It is necessary for someone to keep a lookout so that I will not get into a trap. And Browder may need help."

Eleanor scowled.

"All right, I'll watch," he said. "I'll stay with Browder."

Doc Savage then went away. He walked upright, and seemed to take no precautions to conceal himself; yet he was suddenly out of sight of Eleanor.

Eleanor stared at where the bronze man had been, rubbed his jaw indecisively and finally took a position on a high point of ice, where he remained, as he had been bidden.

Doc Savage traveled rapidly, acting like a man with definite ideas and specific things to do.

First, he got a distant survey of the little bay in the edge of the ice pack where the planes were landing. Both planes were now on the water. Their crews had gathered on the ice, apparently for a war conference.

Some distance from them, a hundred yards but no more, stood another group. Doc could identify them. These were Long Tom, Ham, Pat, Renny, Bench Logan, Nicky Jones, the fat girl Fern Reed, and Bench Logan's friends.

These prisoners were alive, and possibly battered, but at least under their own motive power. They were being watched by men with rifles.

One of the planes—Doc Savage's ship—had been pegged to the ice, like a chicken tied to a stake. The other ship was ready for the air, because its motors were turning over. The motors on the first ship, however, had been shut off; and canvas weather covers for heater units were being fitted over the motors.

It seemed obvious that they planned to use only the big plane they had stolen from Thomas J. Eleanor for whatever their plans contemplated. The craft was probably loaded with bombs and weapons.

Doc proceeded with his plans.

The bronze man went to the parachutes which he, Eleanor and Monk had used. He gathered up all three of them, then went to work with his pocketknife.

First, he cut loose some of the shrouds, but not all of them. Then he ripped up one of the parachutes in squares about the size of bed sheets.

These preparations over with, he carried the parachutes, the shrouds and the sections the size of bed sheets and walked northward.

He had difficult going because he wore Monk's shoes, and they not only did not fit him but the soles did not offer much grip on the ice.

He came to what he had noticed earlier. He had seen it first from the air, when coming down by parachute, and later he had checked its existence from an ice pinnacle while making his survey. It was a stretch of pack ice level enough for a plane to land.

The ice, in fact, was as level as a floor and carpeted with firm snow. It was a lead, a great crack which had opened in the floe, then frozen. It was shaped somewhat like an hourglass, or a figure 8, with a narrow spot.

Drawing near the stretch of level ice, Doc Savage apparently took time off from the serious business at hand to chase a seal. He stalked the seal with great care.

By wrapping the white parachute fabric around himself to get the coloration of the snow, he managed to approach close to the seal. He sprang upon the startled animal and, avoiding its teeth, overcame it.

He tied the seal's jaws together in such a way that it could not bite through the silk cord.

Then he picketed the seal to the edge of the hole in the ice where it had been loitering.

Doc examined the hole in the ice. It was not as large as he wished, so he laboriously enlarged it with the sharp hooks of the collapsible grappling iron which he always carried.

The seal floundered around at the end of a parachute cord, which Doc had anchored by tying it to a small bundle of parachute fabric, wetted and frozen into a depression in the ice.

All of this took time. Though the temperature was below freezing, the freezing of the seal anchor was by no means instantaneous.

Doc Savage showed no impatience. He wetted the sheet-size pieces of parachute fabric which he had torn. He let these freeze in the form of long, thin stakes, which he fashioned by rolling the wet sheets.

He carried these white stakes—they were somewhat over eight feet in length—with him. He also took along water in a bundle which he made out of parachute fabric.

At the narrow part of the figure 8, or hourglass-shaped patch of smooth snow, he erected the stakes he had made by freezing.

He put them in a line across the narrow neck of the hourglass. He used as few of them as he could.

Then he rigged the parachute cords the way he wanted them. The cords were almost as strong as piano wire. He spent a long time on his contraption, arranging it to his liking.

The picketed seal made indignant muffled noises at him as he passed it in leaving.

Thomas Eleanor looked indignant, and Browder relieved, when Doc Savage returned.

"We thought something had happened to you," Eleanor snapped.

Browder said, "Your man, Monk, came back. He says those people in the camp are incapable of defending themselves. He says, furthermore, that they won't talk to him; they won't tell him anything."

Doc Savage's flake-gold eyes showed interest. "Monk said *what*?"

"That these castaways won't cooperate. They are suspicious of him."

Eleanor snapped, "That's fine thanks we get when we come all the way up here to rescue them."

Doc Savage frowned.

"We are without food," he said, "but I have found a seal. I think, if you will help me, Mr. Eleanor, that I can seize the seal. I believe we should do that. Food may become very necessary."

The fat man nodded. "I'm hungry, now," he said. "And freezing to death, too. Don't they get heat out of seal blubber some way?"

"Come on," Doc told him.

The bronze man conducted Thomas Eleanor to a spot from which they could see the seal. Due to the poor light, the loose snow blowing along the surface of the ice, and the general haziness, there was no indication whatever that the seal was already a captive.

"Here is the plan to catch that seal," Doc Savage said. "You wait here, and I will go around to the other side. Then you show yourself. You will distract the seal's attention, and I will creep up on it. I have a piece of white parachute silk which I can wrap around myself, so the seal will be less likely to see me."

Eleanor said, "All right. Wave your arms when you are ready to have the seal distracted."

It did not take many minutes for Doc Savage to work his way around to the opposite side of the seal. He waved his arms. The fat Eleanor immediately showed himself.

Since the seal was already staked out, it was not difficult to approach it.

Doc Savage made a headlong dive and grabbed the seal. The seal naturally struggled. In the struggle, Doc lost his footing and slid into the seal's hole! He went through the ice into the sea below.

Thomas J. Eleanor stood stockstill and stared. Obviously, he was astounded at the turn of events. It seemed impossible that Doc Savage, so capable, could have met with an accident.

Eleanor dashed forward, and stood beside the seal hole, waiting for the bronze man to reappear. But Doc did not come up.

The fat man looked completely blank.

Then he began to smile. He tried not to smile at first, but

finally—as he became positive Doc Savage had drowned in a fantastic accident—he did not hold back the grin. He gave way to it.

He burst into laughter.

Then he began to run toward the distant planes. But the going was tough, so bad that he looked at the level stretch of ice and changed his mind.

Eleanor climbed to an ice pressure ridge, produced a match and a small flare; the flare proved to be inside one of his big cigars. He simply stripped off the tobacco wrapper, and there it was. He lighted it. He waved this signal, which gave off smoke and a distinctive red light in the hazy half-darkness of the midnight sun.

Soon, one of the planes took the air. It was the ship which Eleanor had complained about being stolen from him.

The craft circled overhead.

Eleanor made imperative gestures with his arms. The signals he gave were orders. As soon as those in the plane understood the commands, they obeyed them.

The plane prepared to land.

In order to land with any degree of safety, the ship had to come down against the wind and pass through the narrow part of the hourglass with its hull already on the snow. The craft was an amphibian, with wheels, and the snow was not so deep but that it could land successfully.

It made this type of landing, and hit the parachute cords which Doc Savage had stretched across the neck of the hourglass. The cords, being white, were invisible in the haze and thinly blowing snow.

Results were astounding. In a fraction of a second, the big port motor was enwrapped in a flying devil of silk. All three parachutes, or what remained of them, were tangled about the engine and the landing gear.

The ship was thrown sharply to the left, hit the rough ice, took a fantastic jump, a great hop, came down on its nose. And the earth seemed to blow to bits!

The load of bombs had exploded.

Eleanor lay where he had fallen on the ice, staring in horror at fragments flying around in the air and falling back into the blue-green water which boiled up through the broken ice. Then he got up and ran away, making low noises that were just sounds.

Chapter 15
WHO WAS MUNGEN?

Doc Savage was not far from the plane that survived when the explosion came.

Rough ice at this point extended close to the water, and it was his hope to enter the water—which was possible, if not comfortable—and swim to the plane, then take it over during the excitement.

But, when he endeavored to use the tiny gadget which supplied enough oxygen for a few minutes under water—the "lung" which he had used after he went through the seal hole—he found the thing frozen. It would not work. There was no time to thaw it out.

The "lung" contrivance also doubled as a gas mask, which was why Doc happened to carry it as one of his regular pieces of equipment. But it was useless, now.

So he took a chance. He kept as low as he could, ran forward and charged the man with the rifle who was guarding Bench Logan and the other prisoners.

The rifleman saw him while he was still a few yards distant. But the fellow's wits were so embroiled, what with the ripping echoes of the explosion booming across the ice and the visible evidences of terrific destruction of the doomed plane, that he was too slow. Doc Savage got to him.

Doc hit him, grabbed his rifle and tossed it to Renny, who was nearest. Renny, so smoothly that they might have rehearsed the thing for weeks in advance, swung the rifle and shot a man in the leg, shot another in the shoulder, drove the rifle out of a third's hands, then discovered the gun was empty. So he went into action with a club.

What really saved the situation was that Doc had realized, before he tried his reckless tactics, that none of the prisoners were tied because of the cold.

At least, he thought they were not tied because of the cold, at the time. Later, he discovered it was no such humanitarian reason. It was simply that there had been nothing in the planes with which to tie them effectively. So they had been allowed to stand free.

The others were in action, now. Ham went down with a man who had a pistol, and they grunted, strained and scuffed up snow. Johnny tied himself up with two others like a bundle of sticks.

Long Tom tried to box bare-fisted with a man. The man hit Long Tom between the eyes. Long Tom sat down on the ice and remained sitting there. He said afterward that it was fifteen minutes before he understood just what had hit him.

Doc Savage rushed another man. But Pat and Nicky Jones got there ahead of him. Pat put a finger in the man's eye, Nicky kicked him in the shins so that he upset. And Fern Reed, the fat girl, fell on the man, thereby injuring him more seriously than any of the others.

There was no one left.

It took them a bit more than five hours to distribute the emergency rations among the marooned unfortunates. They had trouble in some instances because of hunger craze. And there were more than a dozen cases of outright insanity—curable, Doc Savage believed—brought on by the hardships.

They loaded the worst cases in the plane; and, with Renny at the controls, the ship took off for the nearest American base in Greenland. It would bring back emergency food, which had been ordered by radio.

Monk watched the plane become nothing in the distance. He crossed his fingers.

"I hope Renny has no accidents," he said. "I wouldn't hanker to stay here."

It was the first time Doc Savage had had an opportunity to speak privately to Monk.

"Monk, that was clever of you not to give the situation away," he said. "I mean, when you told Eleanor and Browder that these people were suspicious and would not talk to you."

Monk grinned. "They had talked to me, of course. I knew the whole story. But I got to thinking about you, and it dawned on me you must have known the story for some time. You know what tipped me off that you did know?"

"What?"

"I got to remembering back," Monk said, "and I couldn't recall your ever having turned your back on Thomas J. Eleanor."

Pretty Nicky Jones approached them. "Mr. Savage, I want to thank you for what you did," she said. "Thanks aren't much, unless you feel them the way Bill Browder and I feel them."

"You and Bill have made up?"

"Bill just got mixed up in it because there was so much money to be made," Nicky said. "When he found out there was to be killing, he backed out. Bill is all right. He won't be so money-hungry in the future. He's going to take a job operating a filling station after we're married."

Doc asked her, "Why were you and Fern brought along?"

"Oh, I found out the truth about Eleanor," Nicky said. "And I ran and told Fern. We were talking about it when Eleanor's men showed up and overheard us. They had to either kill us or take us along. So they brought us. They were going to murder us up here, where we would never be found."

Monk said, "They went to a lot of trouble."

"I think they thought that if I disappeared, you fellows might think I was guilty and waste time looking around New York for me," Nicky explained.

"That's probably the reason," Monk told her.

"Where is Bench Logan?" Nicky asked.

No one answered.

Pat spoke up, saying, "Why, I saw him right after the fight ended. He was heading off into the pack ice."

"What did he say?" Monk asked sharply.

"Said he was going to rescue Mr. Eleanor," Pat explained. "Said he did not want any harm to come to Mr. Eleanor. I thought that was very thoughtful of him."

Monk stared at her unbelievingly. "Holy cow—as Renny would say! You're serious."

"Why not?" Pat asked. "It seemed nice of Logan to want to save Eleanor—"

"Don't you know the story behind this?" Monk demanded.

Pat frowned.

"No," she said. "And I think it's time somebody told me, too."

Monk took a deep breath. "You remember Mungen, the dictator of Monrovia?"

"That fiendish fellow who committed suicide when his people rebelled?"

"He didn't commit suicide, Pat," Monk told her. "The guy who got killed was just a guy who looked like Mungen. Mungen arranged that. Mungen got away."

"Got away?"

Monk nodded. "This Mungen had stolen millions and millions of dollars while he was dictator, and he built up another identity. It was as this other identity, in masquerade, that he fled. He got on the steamer *Grin Gueterre*, with his bodyguards—plenty of them.

"Bench Logan was one of the bodyguards, but he didn't know

he was working for Mungen. He had never known it before. Logan hated Mungen, because of something that Mungen had done to a girl Logan loved.

"Logan found out that his boss was the notorious Mungen. This happened while the steamer *Grin Gueterre* was in the Atlantic. Bench Logan wirelessed the Monrovian authorities about it, and they sent a warship to get Mungen. The warship chased the steamer up here into the arctic, and lost it."

Monk grimaced. "By then, everyone on the steamer knew who Mungen was. So he had to get rid of them all to protect the identity he had built up as someone else—and to protect the wealth he had amassed in the name of that identity. So he marooned everyone. Then he accidentally wrecked the ship getting away, but he reached safety with most of his bodyguards." Monk spread his hands. "You know the rest: How Bench Logan got to New York, what he tried to do, what he had to do because he couldn't go to the police with a murder charge hanging over him."

Pat stared fixedly.

"So *he* was Mungen," she said.

Monk fumbled in a pocket and produced the poster which he had been shown when he first visited the refugees on the ice. He showed this to Pat. "Notice the likeness," he said.

Pat examined the picture. She nodded. "Take off the trick mustache and whiskers, make the hair darker— Yes, Thomas J. Eleanor is Mungen!"

The homely chemist snorted.

"Whether Eleanor is or *was* Mungen, will depend on how Bench Logan has gotten along with his rescuing, I bet," he said.

Pat put a hand to her lips. "Logan went out to find Eleanor—or Mungen—and kill him?"

Monk, whose sensibilities on a point like this were about as calloused as the heel of his foot, only grinned.

Later, when Bench Logan came back, battered and showing signs of having been in a terrific fight, Monk greeted him casually.

"How did the rescue go?" asked Monk.

"Satisfactorily," said Bench Logan.

And that was all he ever did say about it.

THE REMARKABLE #1 BESTSELLER
NOW IN PAPERBACK

JOHN
LE CARRÉ

THE LITTLE
DRUMMER GIRL

Here is the terrifying adventure of Charlie, a young actress forced to play the ultimate role in the secret pursuit of a dangerous and elusive terrorist leader. This is John le Carré's richest and most thrilling novel yet, plunging us into entirely new labyrinths of intrigue, into the dark heart of modern-day terrorism.

"A TRIUMPH." —*Time*

"AN IRRESISTIBLE BOOK . . . CHARLIE IS THE ULTIMATE DOUBLE AGENT." —*The New York Times*

Buy THE LITTLE DRUMMER GIRL, on sale April 1, 1984, wherever Bantam paperbacks are sold, or use the handy coupon below for ordering:

To the world at large, Doc Savage is a strange, mysterious figure of glistening bronze skin and golden eyes. To his fans he is the greatest adventure hero of all time, whose fantastic exploits are unequaled for hair-raising thrills, breathtaking escapes, blood-curdling excitement!

☐ 23364   **PIRATE ISLE #115 &**   **$2.75**
           THE SPEAKING STONE #116

☐ 23851   **THE GOLDEN MAN #117 &**   **$2.95**
           PERIL IN THE NORTH #118

SPECIAL
MONEY SAVING
OFFER

Now you can have an up-to-date listing of Bantam's hundreds of titles plus take advantage of our unique and exciting bonus book offer. A special offer which gives you the opportunity to purchase a Bantam book for only 50¢. Here's how!

By ordering any five books at the regular price per order, you can also choose any other single book listed (up to a $4.95 value) for just 50¢. Some restrictions do apply, but for further details why not send for Bantam's listing of titles today!

Just send us your name and address plus 50¢ to defray the postage and handling costs.